SLADE

SLADE
Copyright © 2022 by Robb Grindstaff

FIRST EDITION SOFTCOVER
ISBN: 1622532813
ISBN-13: 978-1-62253-281-0

Editor: Jessica West
Cover Artist: Kabir Shah
Interior Designer: Lane Diamond

EVOLVED PUBLISHING™

www.EvolvedPub.com
Evolved Publishing LLC
Butler, Wisconsin, USA

Printed (main text) in Book Antiqua font.

BOOKS BY ROBB GRINDSTAFF

Carry Me Away**
Hannah's Voice**
Slade
Turning Trixie

June Bug Gothic: Tales from the South [Anthology]

**Upon completing *Slade*, please continue to the special bonus content we've included at the end of this book. There, you'll enjoy a special sneak preview of each of Robb Grindstaff's first two books: *Hannah's Voice* and *Carry Me Away*.

DEDICATION

For Linda, my wife, best friend, and my family for thirty-eight years, who encourages and supports me in my writing, prods when I need prodding, and provides honest and insightful input as my first reader. She also cooks me Cajun, Creole, Italian, Mexican, Indian, and home-cooked soul food to give me the nutrition and energy to sit in a chair and type for hours at a time. She also has to remind me on occasion that I should pay attention to real people, not just the make-believe characters who live in my head.

SLADE

A Novel (of sorts) by
ROBB GRINDSTAFF

THE SLADE INTERVIEWS

**"When my final chapter is written, it will be half a story about half a man who lived half a life and died twice."
~ Slade Bennington**

The following is a collection of my interviews with Slade Bennington over the course of several months, along with snippets from other sources, such as his books, news articles, and additional interviews with those who knew him best.

There are some discrepancies between different people's recollections, as there always will be. Slade was the best at telling his own story, often without ever revealing anything solid enough to grasp, like trying to grab a handful of fog.

Due to an unusual request – demand, really – I freely admit that my memory may have introduced errors into these transcripts. Slade insisted that I not bring any recording devices and that I not take any notes as we talked, often for hours. "Stretch your brain," he said. "Exercise your memory. Soak it all in, then go home and start typing what you remember. Replay our conversations in your mind and take dictation then. But here, now, be in the here and now. Be with me and talk with me. That's more important than getting every quote precise. You want the truth, not the words. The words aren't important, man."

While there are contradictions even among Slade's inner circle, there was one constant refrain – from family members, close personal friends, business associates, and even from some who had only brief interactions with him.

They would smile, often with an ethereal glow, and say that Slade was the greatest man they ever knew.

A small handful of others, most of whom refused to be interviewed on the record, referred to him as a manipulative con artist, a sociopath. Svengali or Rasputin.

I started these interviews highly skeptical of the reverence and awe he inspired in what seemed a cult-like following of a highly unlikely celebrity, a cult he dismissed with a wave of his hand. He felt sorry for them and wanted nothing to do with the adulation they offered. By the time our final interview concluded, I wasn't sure what to make of him.

Days before this manuscript was due to the publisher, I received a brief letter from Slade – an old-fashioned, handwritten note, not an email or text.

I received it the day after he died.

I draw no conclusions here about Slade Bennington, the man or the myth. Readers will have to make up their own minds.

Robb Grindstaff

INTERVIEW #1

"If you live the life you want, you will love the life you live. The more you love your life, the easier it is to accept your eventual death."
~ Slade Bennington

Interviewer: Tell me about the accident. What do you remember from that night?

Slade: I died, man. I died in that moment nearly thirty years ago. But nothing in life is an accident.

Interviewer: You're sitting here conversing with me now. You're very much alive.

Slade: More alive than ever. More alive than before that night. Before, I wasn't living the life I was meant to live. I was selfish and doing things that brought me pleasure, but with no purpose. I knew that too. I knew I wasn't living. Something was missing, some intention to life. But I was young, you know, and I figured I'd settle down and live the way I knew I should once I'd sowed my wild oats. Sowing wild oats. That's a cliché, isn't it? My agent is always pointing out when I use clichés. Apparently, I like them.

When I was nineteen, I thought I could start being a responsible adult when I was twenty-one. At twenty-one, I thought twenty-five sounded like a good age to mature. Then thirty sounded like the right age to become a grown-up.

But at twenty-nine, life ended. I knew my life was ending. When something like that happens, you know you're dead. And you see.

Interviewer: Your life flashed before your eyes?

Slade: Now *that's* a cliché. Life didn't so much flash before my eyes, but I could suddenly see it all clearly. The life I was intended to live, the life I'd avoided, procrastinated, put off until I was older. And now I would never be older. I'd missed that opportunity. We're all given one chance at life, and we don't think it's going to end suddenly like that.

And when it ends, you see how it was meant to be. It's like getting to the station just as your train pulls out, and it's the last one. You missed it. There's nothing you can do. Nothing to be done.

And so I died.

Interviewer: Are you saying the doctors revived you in the hospital?

Slade: I'm saying the old me died. I was reborn the moment of the crash. The doctors, bless them, did the best they could with what they had to work with. I was fully aware the whole time. Fourteen days in a coma and I heard every word and saw every person who walked into my room. Hovered over the operating table and watched whenever they performed surgeries.

Once I was conscious, the doctor sat beside my bed to update me on my situation. I interrupted and recited to him everything he was going to say. I already knew. I'd heard it all before. And I smiled and patted his hand and told him everything was going to be fine. He started crying. Uncontrollable sobbing. It's hard to witness a grown man weep like that.

The new me was conceived even before they got me to the hospital. The surgeries, the months in the hospital, and recovery were all equivalent to childbirth. The new me being born.

Interviewer: Do you ever ask why?

Slade: These things just happen. One person dies. Someone else survives. Another is reborn.

Interviewer: God's plan or random chance?

Slade: Is there a difference?

INTERVIEW #2

"Brothers and sisters are extensions of yourself, your DNA,
your mind, your heart and soul. They always know you best.
No one ever puts up a false front with siblings.
Make everyone you meet a brother or sister."
~ Slade Bennington

Interviewer: Tell me about Matt, your brother.

Slade: Ah, what an absolute joy he is. Having an older brother is special. But he wasn't always a joy, you know.

I'm laying in bed one day, and Matt walks in. Asks if I want to go for a ride, see some friends. I hadn't left the house in six months other than to doctors' offices and hospitals. Seventeen surgeries in six months. Getting out sounded great.

"Sure," I said.

And Matt said, "Okay, let's go. Meet you at the car." Then he left. Just flat walked out.

I didn't even say anything. I didn't know what to say. I lay in bed and listened as the screen door slammed. A few minutes later, his car started. It sat there idling for a few minutes, then he drove away. I thought he was trying to be funny and he'd be back in a couple minutes. But he didn't come back. Not until after midnight.

"Where have you been?" I think I was yelling at him. "Why did you leave me here?" He shook his head and went to his room. Didn't say a word.

A few days later, he walks in and says the same thing. "Want to go for a ride?"

I said, "Yeah, but don't just drive off and leave me here this time."

"Fine, then. Get out of that bed and get your ass in the car. You got five minutes." And he went out to start the car.

I got mad and fumed for a minute, but I really wanted out of the house. So I rolled out of bed. And it was a standard bed, you know, a couple feet off the ground. Hardwood floors. That really hurt when I landed. But I got my arms under me and dragged myself out of the bedroom, down the hall, out the front door to the porch. My mom's house, only three steps down from the porch to the driveway where Matt sat in his car. A red Camaro Z28 that he was way too proud of.

Those three steps looked like eternity. It was a struggle, but I made it down the stairs and into the car without his help. He didn't offer, and I wasn't going to ask.

"Glad you decided to join me. Buckle up."

I pulled the seat belt across. First time I'd tried to buckle up since the crash. That's when I realized the seat belt wasn't really going to work for me anymore.

"How can I buckle in when I don't have a lap?"

"Use the shoulder strap then. Can't have you messing up your pretty face on my windshield."

The shoulder strap hit me across the throat. The lap belt lay uselessly on the seat where my legs used to be.

A few days later, Matt lifts me out of bed and moves me to the couch. He goes out to the shed and loads up some tools. Hauls them into my room. I hear him banging and sawing for nearly an hour. Then he carries me back to my room. He'd amputated the legs off the bed so it sat only a couple inches off the ground. I'd be able to crawl off the mattress to the floor without busting my ass.

That was so thoughtful of him that I didn't have the heart to ask why he didn't just get rid of the bed frame and put the mattress on the floor. That would've been a whole lot simpler.

INTERVIEW #3

**"Mom's whole life was slick tires on an icy road,
and she never could keep it between the ditches."
~ Matt Bennington**

Interviewer: *What was it like growing up with Slade?*

Matt: He won't admit it still, but he was always the troublemaker and I was the responsible older brother. Ha! Yet somehow he managed to influence me more than I could influence him.

He'd say, "Let's spray paint bad words on the neighbor's garage," and I'd say, "No way, man, we'll get in trouble." Then about two in the morning, I'd be gathering cans of spray paint from our shed and helping him out the window.

And it wasn't like we could get away with anything. Two boys running around more or less unsupervised, if anything happened on our street, neighbors came knocking on our door. Or the cops.

Mom would deny it and defend us, give us an alibi, say she was up at two a.m. helping us with our homework or something like that. Then she'd whoop our butts with a belt or a spatula. We'd be good for about two weeks and then do something else.

Interviewer: *Ever get into any serious trouble?*

Matt: Slade spent six months in juvie after letting the air out of a cop's tires. While the cop was sitting in the car. He got suspended from school a couple of times for fighting. Held back to repeat seventh grade because he skipped so much school.

In eighth grade, he got busted for stealing some of Mom's birth control pills and trying to sell them at school. Told everyone they were Ecstasy. When they found out it wasn't really Ecstasy, they dropped the drug charges, but he got suspended again for three days.

That's about the time Mom got pregnant with Jolene, so that kid was totally Slade's responsibility.

Interviewer: Sounds like he was a real delinquent.

Matt: Oh, not really. I'm just raggin' on him. He was a good kid, good heart, but we didn't have no real parental supervision, ya know. And he was just out to have fun. Harmless fun. Never did things to hurt people or rob anyone. Just pranks and mischief. I tried to be the parent, but I was just a kid too, so eventually the mischief would overcome my more mature sensibilities. Somehow, I never got caught.

Like when Slade let the air out of the cop's tires – the cop was parked on the corner of our street while I watched out the window. When Slade gave me the signal, I called 911 to report a prowler a few houses down so we could watch the cop try to drive away with three flat tires.

As the cop started to pull away from the curb, he spotted Slade, jumped out of his car, and nabbed him. I should have waited until Slade was clear away before I called 911, but I jumped the gun and Slade went to lockup. They assumed Slade was the prowler that got called in, so in a way, I ratted him out. Not intentionally, of course, just too quick on the buttons.

And he never ratted me out as his accomplice.

Interviewer: What about in high school? More of the same?

Matt: Not so much. Slade got quieter. Kind of studious. Actually went to class and did his homework. Started getting good grades, wasn't getting into any trouble. He tried to stay out of Mom's way while I tended to get in Mom's face, especially after Jolene came along.

And when Slade wasn't getting into trouble anymore, neither was I. But I was never the student Slade was.

But one day Mom smacked Slade around a bit too much. I intervened to keep her from beating him. Slade never raised a hand to her, not even to defend himself. He'd just stand there and take it.

Afterward, he comes to me with his duffel bag in his hand and says he's leaving. I ask where he's planning to go, and he had no idea. I told him you can't go live in the street. And don't leave me here with Mom and Jolene by myself. He started crying and hugging me and told me he had to get out or he was going to go crazy. So I said, "Let's come up with a plan and do it right then."

He unpacked his bag.

A couple months later, I was turning eighteen. I was a senior. Slade was almost seventeen and still a sophomore since he got held back that one year. I'm about fourteen months older, and we were always one year apart in school until then. Our plan was that when I turned eighteen, I'd get an apartment in my name, but Slade would move in there and I'd stay at home with Mom and Jolene. He had a bicycle to get to school, and he'd have to get a part-time job, and he had to stay in school. Those were my rules if he was going to move out.

He agreed, and he did all that. Pretty soon, he had saved enough money to buy a junker. I paid most of the rent out of my jobs, but he had to pay some rent and the utilities. He didn't one time and got the electric turned off on him in January. He didn't miss any more utility bills after spending a few nights in a dark apartment with no heat. But he stayed there rather than coming home. Didn't tell me about it until later.

I don't know if he was that responsible or just that stubborn. Maybe his natural stubbornness evolved into taking responsibility. But he grew up real fast at that point.

Interviewer: You were going to school and working?
Matt: Usually had two or three jobs. Had a paper route for a long time. Got up at oh-dark-thirty to deliver the *Star-Telegram.* Worked at McDonald's for three or four hours after school for a while. Then I did pizza delivery at night and on weekends. Made some good cash when I partnered with a pot dealer. His customers would call him and place an order, then he'd call Pizza Hut for a pizza and specifically request me as the delivery driver. I'd get the pizza, swing by the dealer and pick up the baggie, slip it inside the pizza box and then deliver the pizza. The customer would pay me for the pizza and the pot, plus a nice tip. At the end of the night, I'd swing by the dealer and pay him for the pot. He'd pay me and give me a nice tip too. So I was raking it in for a while.

Until I delivered the pizza with the baggie to the wrong house. No one ever called the police, but they called the Pizza Hut manager. He fired me, of course. I told him I had no idea how it got there, but then I realized that meant I was blaming the cook. I owned up and asked him not to bust me, so he said just get your stuff and get out.

The guy that got the wrong order – the large pepperoni with a side of cheesy bread sticks and Hindu Kush – never called the cops either. He kept the pizza and the pot. Not like I was going back to his house and ask for it back. He paid for it. He looked a little confused when I told him the total price, but he paid it and shorted me on the tip.

So I swung by the dealer and told him I was out of business.

I was delivering for Domino's the next week, so we were back up again. I was a little more careful after that.

Interviewer: What did your mother think about Slade moving out when he was sixteen and still in school?

Matt: She acted like she didn't care and that it was a good idea. One less mouth for her to feed, not like she was feeding him anyway. She had moved out on her own when she was fourteen, and I was born she was fifteen, so she was probably more concerned with why I was eighteen and still living at home. But since I took care of Jolene, she tolerated me.

Interviewer: You were taking care of Jolene during this time too?

Matt: Yeah, that wasn't good of me to be running pot. But, ya know, I was still a kid and thought I was being responsible by bringing in good money. Mom wasn't working most of the time. She'd get fired every few months when she'd go on a binge and not show up to work for a week. She was getting some welfare or disability or something most of the time. I'd try to get that money from her for food and to pay the bills, but mostly it went to Southern Comfort.

She used to go out to the bar most nights, so I had to make sure I was home before then or she'd leave Jolene home alone. I finally convinced Mom she had to stay home with the kid so I could work. She could go to the bar on the nights I didn't work, or after I got home at nine or ten. So she kept a few bottles at home to get started.

Sometimes I'd come home from work and Mom was passed out on the couch, Jolene was sitting there hungry, dirty, crying. It was better when Slade was still at home 'cause he'd take care of her while I was at work. But I had to be home to take care of her after Slade moved out, so eventually I had to give up the gig at Mickey D's.

When Jolene started kindergarten, I couldn't get her to school and pick her up and get to my jobs on time. I had graduated high school and was working a good job and didn't want to screw that up. They put me on second shift, so I couldn't be home to make sure Jolene got fed supper and put to bed. So I asked Slade to come get Jolene for a few months.

Interviewer: He was still in school then?

Matt: Yeah, he was a senior. It was a lot to put on him, but I thought it would just be for a little while, and it worked better with his schedule to get her to school and pick her up.

Then it turned into a permanent arrangement.

Interviewer: How did your mother react to her daughter going to Slade's?

Matt: Depended on the day. At first, she put up a fuss, but she didn't protest too much. Gave her more freedom to go out, and she could bring a guy home without a kid there.

She got used to it and seemed to like being free of the responsibility. Then some nights she'd get really drunk and cry about how much she missed her baby. She'd sober up for a few days and want her back home. We'd let Jolene come visit when Mom was clean, of course, but we never let her move back in.

After a while, everyone was good with the new arrangement. Slade and Jolene were inseparable. Slade became a very responsible father-figure, believe it or not. More responsible in a lot of ways than I was.

Interviewer: How so?

Matt: He didn't just make sure she got to school every day. He did homework with her. Met with her teachers. He joined the frickin' PTA. Took her to after-school activities. He made sure he set up his work schedule so he could be there for her. Never left her home alone. He was a much better parent than Mom, that's for sure.

After one time when Jolene got up in the middle of the night for a drink of water and caught Slade hitting a bong, he stopped doing that. I think maybe it reminded him of when we'd see Mom all shitfaced. Slade told me there would never be any drugs allowed in the apartment under any circumstances. He got all serious about it, and that was a good thing.

I'd always been the more responsible one, but he surpassed me in that regard. He didn't stop smoking pot, just never at home or anywhere near Jolene.

Interviewer: Tell me about the night of the accident. Or life event, whatever you prefer to call it.

Matt: Yeah, Slade always calls it an event. Says there are no accidents. Well, he didn't drive his car off the road on purpose, so to me, that's an accident.

Interviewer: Was he drinking or anything?

Matt: No. He didn't drink, smoke pot, nothing at that time. He'd stopped everything. Turned into a very boring little brother. He might have been tired from working all day. Jolene had gotten herself knocked up and asked Slade to drive her to the clinic to take care of things.

That caused a huge fight between them. He didn't think that was right. Said she should tell her boyfriend. But they'd just broken up. He was a giant jerk-off. I'd told her before that he was bad news. I told Slade to make her stop seeing this guy. Slade said that would just make it worse.

So she catches this asshat with another girl – in Slade's apartment, in Jolene's bed. At a time the guy knew Slade would be at work and Jolene would be coming home. Like he did it just to rub her face in it. She kicked him out and broke up with him. She also punched his nose hard enough to draw blood.

Then she finds out she's pregnant a few weeks later.

While Slade and Jolene are arguing over him driving her to the clinic, Slade calls me up and tries to enlist my help.

I told him, "No way. She's too young for a baby, and you don't want that douchebag to have to be part of her life and the baby's life for the next eighteen years. Take her to the damn clinic and get over yourself. Your moral standards don't affect you, but they'll affect her the rest of her life."

So Slade took her.

Interviewer: *And they never made it.*

Matt: No, never got there. Hit an icy patch on the road going around the bend over by Benbrook Lake. Slade's tires were bald. He'd finally saved enough money to buy new ones but was spending it on an abortion instead.

Interviewer: *How did you feel about convincing Slade to take her to the clinic and them getting in an accident? Guilt or remorse over that?*

Matt: Oh, tons. It was all my fault. If I'd gone along with Slade's opinion, they'd both be fine and I'd have a niece or nephew. Or if I'd said, "Let me come get her and I'll take her," maybe I wouldn't have had the accident. I had good tires. But I was at work and thought that was more important.

But that kind of thinking will mess with your head. And it did. Slade was the one that finally talked me down off that trap door. He said it wasn't an accident. It was meant to be. It was an event. No one's fault. You can't change fate. All that sort of stuff. I don't dive as deep into all that as Slade does, but it makes sense. You can't let guilt over something you had no control over destroy your life. It is what it is. Learn and move on.

When Slade's daughters were little, they'd run around the house singing "Let It Go" until you wanted to shove an icepick in your ears, but it's pretty sound advice.

Interviewer: Then your mother died too.

Matt: Yeah. I didn't feel any guilt over that one. In fact, there was some relief. Then I felt guilt over feeling relieved. But Slade said that was natural too. He said this was all on Mom, but not to be too hard on her either 'cause she couldn't control it any more than he could control a car on icy roads with slick tires.

Mom's whole life was slick tires on an icy road, and she never could keep it between the ditches.

INTERVIEW #4

**"There are so many clichés about love,
and they are all true."
~ Slade Bennington**

Interviewer: I'd like to hear about you and Schuyler, how you met, how your relationship started. It was all quite controversial at the time.

Slade: Oh, it was rather scandalous, wasn't it? Heh. Never thought I'd see my ugly mug on the cover of Hollywood gossip rags.

Interviewer: You two met on the movie set. What was that like?

Slade: It was surreal on every level. My first book had come out – I've had six books published now. Did I mention that already? Anyway, the first book had published and suddenly the world turned upside down again. Then I get this call from some guy who says he's a Hollywood producer and they want to turn my story into a movie. I thought it was a scam, so I hung up on him. Three times. Fortunately, he tracked down my agent.

It all took three years to come together. Do you have any idea how complicated it is to get a movie made? I didn't. They paid me for the script rights to my book and paid me to be on set as a technical adviser. Randall Kleifisch directed. Randall Freakin' Kleifisch. He'd made alien movies and monster movies and a few of those teen slasher movies. Seemed like a good fit to me. But he said this was going to be a serious film and he wanted the movie to be as accurate as possible. He wanted me to meet the script writers, the actors, everyone. Sometimes I'd give an opinion, but mostly I tried to absorb everything that was going on and wrap my head around it all.

When they told me Annie was going to play Jolene—

Interviewer: And Annie is Schuyler.

Slade: Oh, yes. Schuyler Jones. Annamarie Jones is her real name. She's always gone by Annie with family and friends. Schuyler was her stage name from the age of six. If you look at the credits from her first season of *The Family Crest*, you'll see they misspelled her name as S-K-Y-L-A-R. They fixed it for the second season.

Interviewer: Why did she spell it the way she did?
Slade: Her mother's maiden name. She decided – at age six – that she wanted her mother's maiden name as her stage name. Her decision.

Anyway, Schuyler Jones was going to play my sister Jolene, but I objected. Jolene was older than that – a teenager. Schuyler was this child actor from a TV sitcom. Only I guess I hadn't watched many movies since I'd gotten out of the hospital. Child actors grow up. She was stuck in my mind as a precocious nine-year-old, but apparently she was sixteen now and had turned into a serious young actress. And Randall Kleifisch was trying to be a serious director. Who knew?

Interviewer: How old were you at the time?
Slade: Thirty-five. Yeah, I know, old enough to be really creepy to a teenage girl, and I had no romantic inclinations, or any other kind of inclinations, towards her whatsoever. She was still a kid no matter what she looked like. And I looked like what I looked like, so I had no illusions of romance with anyone in my future.

She was also way too tall for Jolene, taller than Tom Fallon. But Randall said that wouldn't be a problem. Camera angles and such. And nobody knew how tall Jolene was in real life, so it didn't matter.

When filming started, Annie and I never crossed paths. She was busy, and I spent most of my time sitting in my motorized chair next to Randall. If she wasn't on the set, she was in class with a tutor. I hardly ever saw her the first few weeks. Then it was time to film her first major scene, and she did really great. It was strange to watch when Randall yelled "Action," and this quiet, introspective kid transformed into a brash, loud-mouthed, rebellious teenager – very much like my sister. As soon as he said cut, she was back to exuding this quiet confidence that was way beyond her years. But I didn't say anything to her, and she didn't come talk to me like some of the other actors did.

Tom Fallon was always talking to me, asking how I would say this line or how I would react in this situation. I was still trying to absorb Fallon playing me. He was the number one box office actor at the time. I heard McConaughey turned down the role because he didn't want to sit for the required makeup for hours every day.

The day we were going to do Annie's biggest scene, a couple of months into shooting, I glanced up to see her standing beside me – like she wanted to speak but didn't know what to say or was afraid she'd be interrupting me. We finally said hello, and I motioned for her to take a seat next to me.

Even sitting down, she was taller than me. Not even sure if she'd reached her full height yet. Her eyes had a depth to them, like she was sixty years old, not sixteen. Like she'd lived a full life. Those eyes had seen things, man. They knew things.

She asked me a few questions about Jolene, but not the standard "what was she like, how did her voice sound, how would she say this line" type of questions I'd come to expect from the actors. She asked deep questions that didn't really seem to have anything to do with how to portray her in the movie. She asked if Jolene believed in God. What were her favorite bands and favorite songs? Chocolate or strawberry? Tell me about her first boyfriend. How did I have a sister thirteen years younger than me? Annie just asked questions and – and by the way, she didn't take any notes. She looked intently into my eyes – okay, my eye – and waited for me to answer.

When I'd answer a question, she'd sit quietly and keep looking at me. Not many people could look at me that way. She'd sit there and wait for me to say more, encouraging me to keep talking about my sister. Those long, awkward pauses where you keep talking to fill the void. When I did, this tiny little smile, almost imperceptible, would curl the corners of her lips. I realized what she'd done, manipulating me into filling the silences, but I kept talking anyway. It felt good to talk about Jolene.

She sat there and listened and prodded with these random questions for two hours. Then she squeezed my hand and said, "Thank you so much. Jolene sounds like a wonderful sister. I hope I can do her justice."

Randall walked up and asked if she would be ready for her scene in an hour. She said she was ready right now. Then she asked Randall – no, she didn't actually ask. It was a statement, a gentle demand, not a question. "I want to reshoot my previous scene. I can do it better."

Randall said no, she did great, it was a great scene, and it was already done. We weren't going back to reshoot a scene that was already in the can. Annie pushed a little bit, then dropped it. Obviously, we weren't going to spend the time and money to redo a scene that was already complete.

So, Schuyler Jones has her big scene. After about an hour of getting everything set up, walking through the steps, where she has to stand, where she walks to, where the cameras will be, what lights are to be where, on and on, Randall says, "Let's do this."

It's the scene where Annie begs and manipulates Fallon – or rather, where Jolene begged and manipulated me – into driving her to the clinic to terminate her pregnancy after she found out her boyfriend had been cheating on her. She hadn't told him she was pregnant yet. She was only about eight or ten weeks along, I think.

Randall does his director thing, Fallon has a few lines, Annie enters through a door and starts talking. The whole scene is only about six minutes, but that's a pretty long scene. Fallon has a few more lines here and there, but it's mostly Annie, and I swear, her face morphed into my sister's face. Her voice sounded like Jolene, which I'm not sure how since she'd never heard Jolene speak. I felt like I was watching my sister possess Annie's body, or Annie channeled my sister's ghost, or something paranormal like that. It was spooky, I tell ya.

The scene ended. Keep in mind they would usually shoot a scene several times to get it just right. The whole set, cast and crew, goes dead quiet and waits for Randall to give some direction and instructions to do it over. But Randall just sits there, staring at the ceiling. Everyone stayed quiet and held their positions to give him space to think. But ya know, after a couple of minutes or so, it starts to get real uncomfortable. Did he love it? Hate it? Did he have a stroke and he's dying while we're all waiting because we don't want to interrupt him?

Finally, it was probably close to five minutes but seemed like hours, he looks around at everyone, glances at me, then to Annie, and he says, "This is a print. And let's set up Scene 11 for a reshoot."

Randall had tears streaming down his face. He knew. And at that moment, I knew too. A star had been born in that scene, and his movie – my movie – was going to be huge. It was unmistakable, and everyone on set felt the exact same thing. It was like an electric current running through the place.

Interviewer: Is this when your relationship with Schuyler started? She was sixteen and you were thirty-five?

Slade: Oh, no, no, no. Nothing like that. Well, we started a relationship, but it was purely platonic. There were a lot of disgusting rumors about our relationship, none of which were true. She and I would chat for hours on set when she wasn't needed. About her English class, social studies, or some political issue that was on her mind. Or life in general. I found her fascinating. And somehow, she took to talking to me. What teenage girl would want to be in the same room with someone who looks like me? Most adults had to force themselves to act naturally in my presence. She was... she was just herself. There was no one else for her to be unless she was reciting lines in front of a camera.

She had her seventeenth birthday during filming, and they threw a big party for her. Combination birthday and high school graduation, even though she'd never actually attended a high school. I met her parents then – wonderful, wonderful people. Very easy to see where she got her intelligence and grace.

Don't get me wrong. I was quite enamored with her even then. But, as you pointed out, she was a teenager. There was absolutely no reason for a beautiful young woman – girl – to be attracted to me. I was intrigued that she wasn't repulsed. But it never occurred to me that anything more would grow from this.

Interviewer: How and when did this change?

Slade: We stayed in touch over the course of the next year. Email, phone calls, postcards, letters. A couple of visits. She had moved to Paris for a few months to attend university. She gave me some ideas for my next book, and she was my first test reader. Her rather pointed critique was better than any input my editor had ever provided, even if some of it stung a little bit.

One night, she calls me at two a.m. I was sound asleep, which is a bit unusual for me. She was squealing and crying, and it took a few minutes for me to wake up enough to grasp why she was calling, for her to calm down enough to tell me. She'd just received word about her Oscar nomination.

We spoke for about an hour, and right before hanging up, she invited me to attend the Academy Awards as her guest, along with her parents. We would have a block of seats down front, along with Randall, Tom Fallon, and a slew of others.

The film had gotten a total of seven noms. Besides Annie for best supporting actress, there was Randall for best director, best drama, best screen adaptation, and a few others, I can't even remember what all. I do remember that Tom didn't get nominated for best actor, but I couldn't even be mildly irritated over that because I was so excited for Annie. She'd brought my sister back to life for a few minutes, and over the course of the last eighteen months, she had become one of my best friends. Maybe my only friend besides my brother.

Interviewer: Ah, yes, the famous awards ceremony.

Slade: Infamous, more likely. I was just happy to be there, and they let me park my chair at the end of the row where I wouldn't be blocking anyone's exit. Annie sat next to me, her parents next, Randall and his husband Ethan on the other side of them. And about twenty more people from our film. Tom didn't come, said he was in Mexico filming, but I know he could have come if he'd wanted to. He seemed a little peeved, or maybe embarrassed. Awards sure mean a lot to these Hollywood folks. I have trouble understanding the psychological underpinnings of why that is.

And do you have any idea how hard it is to get a tuxedo with shorts instead of pants?

I'm sitting in the audience, surrounded by hundreds of famous, beautiful people who are so insecure. They crave constant attention, are overwhelmed when they get it and depressed when they don't. They all see therapists, drink, take drugs, have sex with as many people as possible – it's like they want to be loved by everyone but aren't capable of accepting love and aren't capable of loving anyone but themselves, and they hate themselves for being that way. At first, I thought these Hollywood types were shallow, but that's not really the case. They can be quite deep. So deep, they're on the verge of drowning in themselves. They are caught in the riptide of self.

Put a couple thousand of those folks in one room together to give each other awards, and you can smell the antidepressants in the air.

But I'm sitting next to the most rock-solid, secure, confident eighteen-year-old you've ever met in your life. Her parents were excited to be there, but they could also see through the veneer that surrounded them. I could see it in their eyes. Raising a kid like Annie, who'd been in TV shows and movies since she was barely old enough to talk, they were no longer in awe of celebrities, but they were supportive of their daughter's career. You could tell they didn't quite fit in. They were respectful observers of a foreign and somewhat inferior culture.

Interviewer: When they announced the winner, that was quite the scene.

Slade: Oh, yeah. When they announced Schuyler Jones as Best Supporting Actress, she didn't make a sound. She stood and hugged her parents. They were crying. Randall leaned across her folks and hugged her. As she started to exit the row to go get her statue, she leaned in for a hug from me. I held my arms up to hug her back. That's when she planted a big kiss on me. Completely unexpected. Not a peck on the cheek, but that famous big wet kiss right on the lips.

Well, right where my lips used to be. Lips seem to be the hardest thing for plastic surgeons to reconstruct.

She headed to the stage and thanked everyone for the honor, thanked Randall and her parents and the producers and Tom Fallon, who couldn't be here tonight, and on and on. She thanked her agent and manager and God and Jesus Christ.

Have you noticed people will thank God and Jesus, but they never thank the Holy Spirit? Is he the forgotten person of the Trinity? Never gets any recognition. He just gets ghosted.

Then she thanked me and said the biggest honor was the opportunity to play Jolene and meeting me. She said I'd changed her life.

I didn't know I'd changed her life. I didn't know how I'd changed it. I had no idea what she was talking about.

Interviewer: And that kiss was broadcast up close on national television. I have to admit you looked surprised and bit uncomfortable. As surprised as her parents.

Slade: Yeah, I don't think they were none too happy. But they never said anything.

Interviewer: What about you?

Slade: That was my first kiss.

Interviewer: Your first kiss ever?

Slade: First kiss since my rebirth. The dead me had kissed a lot of women. And a couple of guys. I mean, who would want to kiss this face? Annie did. The famous, beautiful, teenage Oscar-winning actress passionately kissed me on national television. It grossed out an audience in the millions. Thousands of beautiful people and she kissed the ugliest man in the room.

Afterwards, all the milling about, people talking and drinking and signing autographs, photographers everywhere, Annie never left my side. I knew she'd gotten carried away in the emotions of the moment, but I got this definite vibe that maybe she had some kind of romantic thoughts toward me. I kept shaking it off. We were just friends. I was twice her age. She was twice my height. She'd kissed me and that reawakened a part of me, buried somewhere deep, that maybe someone could still love me. But I kept pushing that thought away. No way she would be feeling the same thing I was feeling, thinking what I was thinking. If I'd expressed any of the thoughts crossing my mind right then, well, I knew I was misreading the nonexistent signals and it would drive her away. She was my best friend. An unlikely best friend, but best friend, nonetheless.

We stayed in constant touch. She announced she was taking time off from acting to go to college, and she finished her four-year degree in less than three years, splitting her time between universities in Paris and Rome. She flew back to the states twice a year to see her parents, and she'd come visit me on those trips. Her parents live in Chicago. I was in Fort Worth most of the time, so it wasn't like I was close.

I was still living with Matt, in the house we bought together, and the first time she came to visit, you should've seen his face. He stuttered and stammered, maybe drooled a little bit. Fussed over her like royalty, asking if she wanted some hot tea. We never drank hot tea. I doubt we even had any. She asked for a Diet Coke.

All the neighbors gawked out their windows or went out to check their mail several times a day, hoping to catch a glimpse of her. Matt finally pulled out the shotgun to chase off the paparazzi. Being in Texas, they probably assumed he'd actually use it.

We'd sit up and talk all night long, then she'd catch a taxi back to the airport. Said she'd sleep on the plane.

Interviewer: What would you talk about?
Slade: Everything. Life. Death. Politics. The best color curtains to go with the sofa Matt and I had bought. Her schooling and how that was going. She was starting to wonder what she wanted to do with her life. We talked about God and religion. She was deeply religious, a devout Christian. Which was strange because both her parents are agnostic at best. She said she'd discovered Jesus Christ when she was five. On her own. Her parents tolerated her "little fantasy," as they called it, thinking she would grow out of it, but they didn't discourage or belittle her faith either. She had read the entire Bible twice by the time she was nine years old. Her parents finally just acquiesced and accepted this part of her, but they don't understand it to this day.

I asked if she was going to resume her acting career after college, but she wasn't sure. She'd been on the screen and the set her whole life.

Commercials as a toddler. TV sitcom from age six to twelve. Movies starting at nine. Broadway at fifteen. By the time she was eighteen, she'd won an Emmy, a Tony, and an Oscar. Where do you go from there? She turned down starring roles to go to school in Europe.

She said acting was her childhood, and maybe it was time to put away childish things.

Interviewer: So often you hear about parents mismanaging, or even stealing, money from a child's acting career. I've read that Schuyler – Annie – had a very different experience.

Slade: It was so much the opposite, it's unimaginable. Goes to show what kind of people her parents are. Her father is a professor, teaches literature. Her mother's a romance novelist, quite successful. They lived off their income. All of Annie's earnings from the time she did her first commercial were kept in a trust in her name and invested wisely. And successfully.

Now, I'd earned a few bucks from my books and I was financially set. My first book sold six million copies in hardback. At thirty dollars a pop. The publisher keeps the lion's share of that, my agent takes 15 percent of what's left, and that still left me with more money than I'll ever be able to spend in my lifetime.

Compared to Annie, I was poverty stricken. When we married, I insisted on a prenup to keep her funds separate, but she refused. 'Til death do us part, what's mine is yours, two shall become one flesh. Those are her clichés.

When I saw the financial reports, I was floored. I had no idea. What exactly does someone do with $400 million?

That's why she could afford to turn down a $10 million movie role. Plus, they wanted her to do a nude scene, and she rejected that out of hand.

Interviewer: Is it true she speaks five languages?

Slade: She's up to six now. Fluent too. Not like my Spanish. I can order a *cervesa* and say *gracias*, and I can cuss in three languages. That's about the extent of my language skills. She speaks better Cantonese than I do English. You can hand her a Hebrew version of the Bible, and she can read it out loud in English, translating in real time.

Interviewer: So, your relationship didn't immediately turn romantic after that Academy kiss. When did that evolve?

Slade: Not until much later. The kiss was what caught the nation's attention, and probably caused a few people to lose their supper. Then, when we did announce our engagement, people assumed, incorrectly, that we'd been a couple all along.

But we'd remained just friends. She graduated college, took another year for her master's degree, another for her PhD. We saw each other once or twice a year between the awards night and when she finished her schooling. We spoke on the phone and stayed in contact, but it was all very platonic.

Every now and then, I'd get this sense that she, quite inexplicably, had some deeper feelings for me, but I'd take one look in the mirror and disabuse myself of that notion. We loved each other, no doubt. I knew she loved me as a friend, a confidant, an adviser, a listening ear. And she had such a way to get me to open up and talk about things I had never voiced, in this life or my previous life. I'd never had that person. Not even Matt or Jolene, certainly not my mother. I never would have written that second book without her pulling it out of me.

She came to visit me the first Christmas after she'd become Dr. Jones. Twenty-two years old and a PhD. Hard to fathom, isn't it? And she was still a kid who had no idea what she wanted to be when she grew up. She asked if I could take her on the rollercoasters at Six Flags. She had to ride by herself though. I wasn't tall enough.

Interviewer: What's her degree in?

Slade: Comparative religions. Her doctoral dissertation was a fact-based look at the argument's pros and cons about Jesus actually being the Son of God and literally coming back from the dead after three days. Not based just on the Bible or tradition or faith, but also on outside historical analysis, archaeology, and other sources.

Interviewer: What was her conclusion?

Slade: Her dissertation allows the reader to decide. She had decided for herself many years ago. But at the very least, it makes the most ardent atheist stop and think, realize there is the possibility, regardless of how remote one might think it.

Interviewer: And what does someone do with a PhD in comparative religions? Teach it to other students?

Slade: At first, she didn't want to teach. She wanted to write. She wanted to write books that taught. Books that were important. Books that enlighten. Not like the crap I write.

At the same time, she wanted a traditional home and family. She always said she was born in the wrong decade, that she could have been a 1950s housewife and been perfectly happy. Minus all that racism and sexism stuff, of course.

Interviewer: So that Christmas she came to visit...

Slade: Ah yes, thanks for getting me back on track. I'd bought her a gift, which we never did for each other. I mean, it's not like I could buy her anything she couldn't afford on her own, and she certainly didn't need to buy me any socks.

But I'd bought her a dress. A 1950s housewife-style dress. Literally. It was auctioned off by a studio for a charity fundraiser. Barbara Billingsley wore it on *Leave it to Beaver*. I had no idea if it would fit her. Annie's much taller.

She loved it. That earned me my second kiss, and this time without an audience.

When she pulled away, she immediately apologized, which of course, I refused to accept. I didn't understand. I couldn't understand. I didn't want to accept that she might have any feelings for me, romantic feelings, despite the feelings I had for her that I'd never let be known to her or anyone else.

That's when she told me she loved me and wanted to be with me but didn't think I would ever accept her. Which really confused me. Ha!

So, I finally told her how I felt about her. She asked why I'd kept it a secret – that she'd loved me for years and thought I didn't feel the same about her.

Interviewer: What did you say to her?

Slade: I said, "I'm half the man I used to be and I have the face of a burnt toad. Why would I ever think you'd love me?"

She said, "You're more of a man than any I've ever met. I feel like half a person, but with you I am whole."

And we kissed again. By the end of the day, we were discussing wedding plans. Mainly how to break the news to her parents as well as to the rest of the world.

Interviewer: It had been four years between kisses?

Slade: More than four. Almost five.

She also stated quite emphatically that she was done with acting. She'd been called the most brilliant up-and-coming actress in Hollywood, and she walked away. Studios kept upping their offers. I mean, can you imagine someone offering you a job for one year and they'll pay you $30 million, and you just go, "Um, naw, I'll pass."

Every producer wanted to be the one to bring her back to the screen. Spielberg. Scorsese. Redford. Tyler Perry called her, and they talked for two hours. He was the only one who came close to getting her to reconsider. She wouldn't even take Julia Roberts's call.

INTERVIEW #5

**"Children are a blessing. Parents are a curse.
We must break the spell."
~ Slade Bennington**

Interviewer: You and Schuyler – Annie – have been married how long now?
Slade: Sixteen years next month. My anchor. My muse.

Interviewer: And you have three children, right?
Slade: Yes, three girls. Jolene is the oldest, fifteen. Already taller than her mother, if you can believe that. Evangeline is thirteen. Amanda is six, and nearly as tall as me. But that's a low bar.

Interviewer: You named your first child after your sister.
Slade: Well, either after my sister or after Annie's Oscar character. But my sister was named for the Dolly Parton song, so I guess Jo was named for that song as well. I suppose Dolly named the song for someone, so indirectly, that's who Jo is named after, whoever that was. Apparently some young girl who was a fan, and Dolly just liked the name.

Interviewer: Big gap between the middle and the youngest. An accident?
Slade: Not at all. First of all, there ain't no accidents in life. Not even my accident was an accident. Everything happens for a reason.

But in Amanda's case, Annie and I had settled on having two children. A few years went by after Evangeline was born, and I thought the baby-making factory was closed. Then one morning over coffee, Annie asked if we could have another. I've never refused Annie anything.

It's so funny how every child is born with their personality intact. Yes, parents and friends and events can shape a person's life, but I believe each person is born with their full personality embedded. How else can you explain siblings that are so different, raised in the same home by the same parents? And you can see the difference so early. Even in utero.

Jo kicked and thrashed about in the womb so much, she would knock Annie to her knees sometimes. I could hold my hand on her belly, and Jo would swim over to my touch and press out so hard you could see the outline of her foot.

She came out kicking and screaming too. And never really stopped. She's the spitting image of my sister personality-wise, so the name fits her perfectly. Rebellious. Stubborn. Hard-headed. A wild streak. And the most tender, loving heart you can imagine. So fragile inside that the shell outside grows harder. Her and her mother clashed frequently, and I had to be the peacemaker.

That's starting to settle down now – they still clash, but they're also best friends. I love to hear them in the other room chattering away. Warms my heart.

Evvy – Evangeline – completely different story. So quiet and still during pregnancy that Annie was terrified. After her first pregnancy experience, she just knew there was something wrong with the baby. I would reassure her, her mother would reassure her, the doctor would reassure her, but there was no consoling her. She wept for months. I would hold her and tell her everything would be fine, but in my heart, I was worried too. I tried to be strong for Annie. My fear was that Annie's intuition was right – that something was wrong.

Evvy was perfectly healthy. A quiet, relaxed baby, born with that same quiet confidence as her mother. From day one.

There is never a reason for fear, and Evvy has no fear. She is the quiet balance to Jo. And the two of them are so close. Inseparable. What's amazing is that Jo, the oldest, goes to Evvy for advice. Evvy is wise beyond her years and always has been. Jo is smart enough to recognize that.

Interviewer: *And Amanda, the late arrival?*
Slade: Mandy is the clown. Since she was an infant, her greatest joy has been to make others laugh and smile. She is always smiling. At three years old, she would play pranks on her older sisters. My concern for Mandy is that all the laughter is hiding some deeper sadness. She has night terrors. Sleepwalks. She never seems to remember any of it and wakes up giggling in the morning.

I have been blessed beyond belief. I often wonder what I ever did to deserve such riches as these three brilliant, beautiful, amazing humans-in-training. My goal as a father is to not screw them up too bad.

My second goal is to prepare the world for the day they leave the nest. I want the world to be a better place for them. And the world needs to be ready for the whirlwinds about to be unleashed on it.

INTERVIEW #6

"I have no idea why I had to fall in love with the most infuriating man on the planet. But I did. And still am."
~ Dr. Annamarie Bennington, PhD, aka Schuyler Jones

Interviewer: Do you go by Dr. Jones or Dr. Bennington?
Annie: I took my husband's name, so it's Bennington. But you can call me Annie. Doctor seems a little formal and pretentious. As many times as you've been over to visit Slade, you're a family friend now. Can I get you something to drink? Sweet tea, water? Diet Coke or coffee maybe?

Interviewer: Actually, a cup of coffee does sound good.
Annie: I'll put a pot on. Be right back.

Interviewer: No, don't go to any trouble. Water is fine.
Annie: Nonsense. It only takes a moment.

***

Interviewer: Thank you for the coffee, and for agreeing to meet with me. I understand you haven't done any interviews in, what, fifteen, sixteen years?
Annie: On the contrary, I've done dozens of interviews. Maybe hundreds. Academic journals, book reviews, magazine articles, seminars and conferences, universities.

Interviewer: I should have been more specific. A more personal interview – about your life, your family, your acting career.
Annie: My life is private and personal. Not fodder for gossip magazines and celebrity stuff. That life is behind me.

Interviewer: But you've agreed to talk to me today, and I'm not here to discuss your latest theological treatise.

Annie: I'm here to talk to you about Slade, his work and his life. Not my own.

Interviewer: Your life and his are rather intertwined, wouldn't you agree?
Annie: Of course. They are the same. What's your first question?

Interviewer: Slade warned me you were direct and down to business. I appreciate that. I'd like to start at the beginning to get a full picture. When you first met, how you fell in love, what was it like during those earliest days of your relationship? That sort of thing. What would you like me to know about that phase?
Annie: Everyone always asks me some version of those questions. I appreciate the more delicate manner in which you framed them. They usually want to know if I was underage when our relationship started. They want to know how a woman can fall in love with someone who looks like Slade. It defies society's norms and expectations. What kind of brainwashed control does he have over me? They want to know why I would give up a promising career in film to become a mother and housewife. They want to know why I would turn my back on fame and fortune to marry a double-amputee burn victim, raise children, can vegetables, and write theology books. And many seem rather disturbingly obsessed with our sex life.

Interviewer: How do you answer those questions?
Annie: I don't. Do you have another question?

Interviewer: Let's leave out the sordid, prying parts of the question, as that's not really where I wanted to go. You met a man, fell in love, gave up your acting career, and married him. Sixteen years and three children later, and by all outward appearances, you have a successful marriage and a happy home. You are wealthy by any material measure, yet you live quite modestly. You could have snapped your fingers at a maid to fetch me a cup of coffee, but you're a full-time homemaker: cleaning, cooking, raising kids —
Annie: Homeschooling the kids as well.

Interviewer: I'm more impressed every minute.
Annie: You should be. They don't offer PhDs in being a wife and mother, and it's by far the most complex and challenging role anyone will ever fulfill. There are no rulebooks, no training courses, no aptitude tests. Anyone can do it. No one can do it.

Interviewer: And while being a full-time homemaker, you've written five academic books, including a graduate-level textbook, and numerous scholarly articles. You've been a guest lecturer at Harvard Divinity School.

Annie: Don't leave out my most difficult job. I'm Slade Bennington's editor. It's an odious chore, but someone has to do it.

Interviewer: I can only imagine. But please, let's go back to when you first met. What drew you to him? What about him caused you to fall in love?

Annie: I knew he'd never run around on me.

Interviewer: So his loyalty and faithfulness... [at this point in the interview, the first hint of a smile traced across Annie's face and I realized she'd made a joke]. Oh, never mind. Yeah.

Annie: You know the saying, "Beauty is only skin deep." One of Slade's favorite things to say is, "Ugly is only skin deep too."

When I was much younger, I had a friend, I think we were ten or eleven. She lived in the same Burbank apartment building where my parents set up a second home when I was working on *The Family Crest*. My friend, Sylvie, was deaf. She could hear a little with a hearing aid, and she could read lips pretty well. She could speak, but she sounded different because she'd learned to talk without hearing her own voice.

When we first met and started playing together, I had trouble understanding her. She didn't pronounce some sounds properly. Words felt distorted, mumbled. Like someone with a heavy foreign accent who might be speaking perfect English, but it's hard to make out what they're saying. I would have to ask her to repeat herself a few times until I could catch it. Sometimes she'd get frustrated and write it down in her notebook for me to read.

But after a couple of weeks, her voice became clearer to me. I had to ask her to repeat herself less and less. Her voice hadn't changed. I'd become accustomed to it. Within a month, I didn't even notice that her voice sounded unusual anymore. If another friend joined us and couldn't understand Sylvie, I would get irritated. Why couldn't she understand Sylvie? She sounded perfectly normal to me.

It was the same with Slade. Yes, his appearance was a bit jarring at first. But I knew his story, what had happened. I'd seen pictures of him from before. I had trouble reconciling how different he looked, how disfigured, how he could even want to go on living like that.

I also recognized how immature it was of me to even think such a thing. I'd read his book. Three times. It moved me to my core. So, I eventually worked up the nerve to talk to him. He intimidated me immensely.

Interviewer: You don't seem like you would have ever been intimidated by anyone.

Annie: When I was fourteen, Quentin Tarantino called me. That didn't intimidate me. Nothing and no one intimidated me until I saw Slade the first time. Took me weeks to work up the nerve to talk to him.

And when I did, I saw this beautiful soul. A brilliant mind. A gentle, caring heart for others. Someone who knew more about life than anyone I'd ever met. A man who had faced death and loss, trauma that would have destroyed most people. A man whose final steps were to carry his dying sister to the road for help while his legs were literally on fire.

After talking for a few minutes, his outer shell melted away in my sight. Like Sylvie's voice sounded normal to me, Slade had the most beautiful face I'd ever seen.

ARTICLES #1

"Counselors will be made available to all students."
~ School officials

29 years earlier
Fort Worth Star-Telegram, January 24
Crash, explosion kills two near Benbrook Lake

A single-car accident resulted in two fatalities Monday night when the driver apparently lost control, and the vehicle rolled down an embankment near Benbrook Lake and burst into flames. No other vehicles were involved. Police have not released the names of the deceased, awaiting notification of next of kin.

***

Fort Worth Star-Telegram, January 25
Police identify dead, injured in Benbrook car fire

Fort Worth Police Department spokesperson Captain Frederica Elan stated that the fatal car crash and explosion Monday night took the life of Jolene Bennington, 16, of Fort Worth. She was pronounced dead at the scene.

Police said the apparent driver of the car was her brother, Slade Bennington, 29, also of Fort Worth. Slade Bennington is in grave condition at Harris Methodist Hospital. No other details as to the cause of the crash or Mr. Bennington's injuries were released.

Initial police reports erroneously stated that both occupants of the vehicle had died in the crash.

Jolene Bennington was a sophomore at Amon Carter Riverside High School, and the daughter of Reba Cobb-White of Fort Worth.

School officials said that counselors will be available at the high school to meet with students grieving the loss of their classmate.

INTERVIEW #7

**"You begin to die the moment you're born.
You begin to live the moment you choose."
~ Slade Bennington**

Slade: There you have it. The police and the *Star-by-God-Telegram* are proof that I died.

They made another mistake too, which they never corrected as far as I know. Jolene didn't die at the scene. She was still alive and talking when they put her in the ambulance. I knew she wasn't going to make it all the way to the hospital, but I knew I wasn't going to either. Until I did.

Interviewer: How did your mother take the news? You've barely mentioned your parents. Tell me about them.

Slade: Not much to tell. Never knew my real father. Had a couple of stepfathers, neither worth mentioning. But Mom was really the second fatality in this story. She wasn't in great shape before the crash, and she never recovered. Alcohol, drugs, a series of horrible relationships. She never found her life, you know. I swore I'd never fall into that same trap, and yet there I was, following in her unstable footsteps.

I was surprised the newspaper even mentioned Mom. She was never really a mother to Jolene. I'd left home when I was sixteen, and when I was eighteen, I took Jolene in. She was five. I went to Mom's one day and took my sister. Told Mom she was coming to live with me now, and Mom just said okay. She knew.

I raised Jolene as best I could for the next eleven years. And then this. Mom tried to blame me for taking her away and killing her, but truth is, Jolene would have died years earlier if I hadn't taken her, and Mom knew that too.

Matt, he was the oldest of us three, a year older than me, and he always stayed with Mom. Never left home. Worked two, sometimes three jobs to support her, so he was never home to watch over Jolene.

He did his best to protect Mom, to keep her from killing herself one way or another. He called me one day and said, "Come get your sister. She can't stay here." So I did. I took in Jolene. Matt stayed and babysat Mom.

Before I even got out of the hospital, Mom drank herself to death one night. Drink and pills. Not sure if it was intentional or if it just got away from her. She usually passed out before it got that far. Or maybe her liver finally surrendered. She never came to see me in the hospital. I don't think she could have taken it. I didn't want her coming.

When I got discharged, Matt moved me into Mom's home with him. Matt's home then. I didn't have Jolene to take care of anymore. Matt didn't have Mom. So Matt became my caretaker. He's always been the caretaker. But a tough-love caretaker. He wouldn't take any crap off Mom or me. Still doesn't. But he took better care of me than I took with Jolene.

After I got the advance on my first book, we sold Mom's place and bought something a little nicer, all fixed up for my chariot – wide hallways and doors, low countertops and light switches, that sort of thing.

When Annie and I got married, we bought this little place in the country, and Matt still lives in that first home we bought together, along with Chelsea.

Interviewer: Who is Chelsea?

Slade: Matt's girlfriend. Or partner. Partner sounds like a business arrangement, but girlfriend sounds rather juvenile for a couple pushing sixty. The chick he's been living in sin with for twenty-plus years.

Interviewer: Something I spoke with Annie about as well is that despite your success and financial situation, you live very modestly, simply. Some would say austere.

Slade: Do you think we'd be happier if we spent more money?

INTERVIEW #8

"We have never ridiculed Annie for her beliefs."
~ Celeste Schuyler-Jones, aka Celeste Rousseau

"And she has never condemned us for ours."
~ Dr. Richard Jones

Interviewer: What was life like raising Annie as "Schuyler Jones, Child Star?"

Celeste (Annie's mother): She was an absolute joy of a daughter, but it was a strain to try to give her a normal childhood.

Richard (Annie's father): A strain is putting it lightly. I don't think we succeeded in providing a normal life for her. But we tried to keep her grounded in normality.

Interviewer: When and how did she first get into show business?

Celeste: My book publisher was working on the cover art for my debut novel, which was about a single mother finding love while working for an ad agency in Chicago. They were looking at various models for the cover, including a small girl to represent the daughter in the book. Annie was two years old, about the same as the character in the book, and I jokingly said, "Well, I've got the cutest kid in the world. We could use her."

The book editor laughed but said, "Send me a pic." I did, and they went for it. Had to fly to New York with a toddler for an all-day photo shoot. The plane trip was horrible, and I thought this was going to be a disaster. She was irritable, crying, her ears hurt, temper tantrum on the plane because she didn't want to sit still and stay buckled up.

But at the studio, pull out a camera and she became a total ham for attention. Did everything they asked her to do, and her face would light up.

One moment... Here it is. That's her, right here on this cover. See?

Interviewer: Did you write the character based on Annie?

Celeste: Oh no. I'd written the book before Annie was born. Just took that long to find an agent and get published.

The photographer asked if I'd let Annie model for him for other works. He was a pretty well-known New York photographer for ad agencies, catalogs, clothing lines, that sort of thing, and he always needed children. I hesitated because of how awful the plane trip was. Told him I'd have to think about it.

Richard: We talked about it afterward, and decided there were photographers, modeling agencies, ad agencies, all that sort of thing here in Chicago. No need to fly to New York for those kinds of jobs. We talked to a few people in the business, and next thing we know, Annie is doing photo shoots for kids' clothing ads and websites.

Celeste: Then one of the brands did a video shoot for their website. So now, Annie was doing video. The woman in charge of that video production got a job a few months later with a production company in California, a nice career step for her. She called about three weeks later and asked if we'd be interested in having Annie in a TV commercial.

Richard: At first, we said no. Not interested in flying to LA to do something like that. The pay was pretty awesome, and they covered all expenses, but that's a lot to handle. We both worked, and as Cel mentioned, flying with a toddler isn't much fun.

Celeste: But my work was as a writer. I had times when I could be very busy, and times when I could be very flexible. I thought it would be a lot of fun for Annie, earn some money that we'd put into her college fund, that sort of thing. Thought it would only happen once.

Richard: So Cel talked me into it. That happened a lot. Still does. She's very good at that.

Interviewer: And from there?

Celeste: It never let up after that first commercial. The next commercial, she was three years old and had her first speaking line. That commercial for children's cold syrup where the little girl hates taking medicine, spits it out all over the mother's face, until she tastes the fruit-flavor and suddenly becomes a happy child who loves taking her meds and her cold goes away. That commercial really set her career in motion. It was so cute.

Interviewer: I remember that commercial. I didn't realize that was her.

Richard: We had to get her an agent-manager at that point, we were getting so many calls.

Celeste: We'd fly from Chicago to LA once or twice a month. Sometimes just me and Annie, sometimes Richard would go with us. Each trip would last anywhere from two days to a week.

Richard: After a year of that, we were ready to call it done. Interesting experience, met some really nice people, but that's too much to put on a family, let alone a three- or four-year-old.

Celeste: So we stopped. That only lasted a year though.

Interviewer: What brought you back to show business?

Celeste: Annie was five when her agent called. Said they were casting for a new family situation comedy on NBC. They were looking for a child about Annie's age and description. Would we be interested in flying out so she could audition?

Richard: We talked about the pros and cons of this all night. Would we have to move? Would I quit my job and try to get a teaching position in California? Would I commute, fly back and forth, while we rented an apartment in LA somewhere? What about school for Annie? Hundreds of questions, and we had no answers to any of them.

Celeste: We finally decided to do the audition, which might result in nothing, of course. She might not get the role. If she did, then we could make decisions.

Richard: If she did get it, she'd earn enough money to pay for any college in the country that would accept her. And Celeste could do her writing, which was starting to take off, from anywhere. LA might be a good place for her career.

Interviewer: And you became Celeste Rousseau, romance writer extraordinaire.

Celeste: I don't know about the extraordinaire part, but that is my pen name, yes.

Interviewer: You've published twenty-seven novels so far, and six have been turned into movies. You've given Nicholas Sparks a good run for his money.

Celeste: Well, yes, but TV movies, not any big Hollywood productions. Lifetime, Hallmark, A&E. It all became decently successful. And being in LA, with the connections we made through Annie's job, that definitely opened doors for me, no doubt about it.

Richard: As usual, Celeste is way too modest.

Interviewer: So Annie got the part, and you relocated to LA.

Celeste: Annie got the part. The audition was just a formality. They knew they wanted her from the start. Did a screen test, read some lines, took some photos, offered her a contract. They didn't even audition anyone else.

Richard: We kept our condo in Chicago, and I kept teaching here. We rented an apartment in LA Actually, Burbank. Celeste and Annie moved, I flew out some weekends, on breaks and summers. Filming would only take a few weeks out of the year, so it wasn't full-time, year-round. At least we didn't think it would be.

Celeste: We thought this might last a year, maybe two. But it became the highest rated sitcom on any of the networks by the second year. They kept offering more money for Annie to renew each year.

Richard: I couldn't leave my post at the university here. I was an associate professor and due for full professorship and tenure within another year. So, we kept it going.

Celeste: With Annie's schedule, and then there were commercials and such when the show was in hiatus, and talk shows, interviews, that sort of thing, it quickly became clear this wasn't going to be three or four months in LA then go back home. It was a full-time job being Schuyler Jones.

Interviewer: How did you handle her schooling?

Celeste: At first, I tried to get her into a school in the Burbank area. But the schedules wouldn't line up. I talked to other stage and screen mothers. Most hired tutors or put their kids into private schools that worked around production schedules and provided tutors as needed. She might be in school all summer when most kids are out, because that's when the show was on hiatus.

I didn't care for any of the options, so I homeschooled her myself for the first year. Then I hired a tutor to be with her on the set. She would take classes when she wasn't needed for shooting. Often, she had to be on the set six or eight hours of the day but was actually working only about an hour or two, so plenty of time for schooling during the day rather than waiting for her to come home at night and try to teach her when she was exhausted.

Richard: We'd been teaching her ourselves since she was born, of course. She was reading at age three. By the time she started *The Family Crest*, she was reading Mark Twain and Jack London, so reading a script and memorizing lines came very easy to her. The producers and directors all loved that about her. She'd read a script one time and have all her lines memorized. She was a natural at acting and at taking direction. She could cry on command, with actual tears, which I found amazing because she never cried in real life. No matter what.

Celeste: Yes, she was always a very steady, even-tempered child. Except for that first plane trip.

Interviewer: Your only child, right? No siblings?

Celeste: Only child. And maybe because of that, she felt like a tiny adult by the time she was six. Rarely had time for friends. Hung out with adults all the time, at home with us, on the set with the cast and crew. Homeschooled and tutored, not in a classroom with other kids much. I worried that childhood was passing her by.

Richard: But she never seemed to miss it. She was enthralled with acting, with filming, with reading. She could connect to adults and talk to them on their level.

Celeste: It was always funny when some adult would talk down to her like a child and she'd set them straight.

Interviewer: Precocious.

Richard: It wasn't even precocious. It was just mature. It felt a little unnaturally mature, but that's the way she was.

Celeste: By the second season – Annie's seven years old – she's giving the director suggestions. Giving tips to the older kids. And not in a rude or irritating way. They actually listened to her. I think they all forgot she was a kid. They started inviting her into script meetings by the time she was ten.

Richard: And by season two, she was getting offers for movies. Got a few bit parts, then a couple more serious parts. Nine years old, she played the daughter who discovers her father is a serial killer in *Paper Cuts*. Big, serious role in a big, serious movie.

Celeste: But there was only so much time, and we were afraid she was working too hard. She kept up in her schooling. More than kept up. She was completing two grades a year sometimes.

Interviewer: How did she become religious, discover this faith of hers? And when did that happen?

Richard: We aren't religious and don't attend church, but we discussed spiritual things at home. We are spiritual people, but we don't ascribe to any particular man-made religion.

Celeste: But she had an abiding interest in these discussions very early on. She would ask pointed, probing questions, sometimes that we couldn't answer very well.

Interviewer: Such as?

Richard: The one that really stands out in my memory, I think she was four years old, and she asked me where we come from. I thought she was asking about where babies come from, and I thought that might come best from Cel. As a woman, she could probably answer that better and in an age-appropriate response that would satisfy Annie without getting too detailed. If I started answering that question – the professor in me – I'd be talking about DNA and conception and genetics. I was at least smart enough to know that's not what Annie wanted to know.

Celeste: He tells Annie, "Go ask your mother." Typical male response. Ha!

Richard: Well, you're the romance writer.

Celeste: Annie asks me, "Where do we come from?" I asked a few questions to try to gauge exactly what she wanted to know. Like where do babies come from? Where does our family originate from?

She was like, "No, where do people come from? Where did the world come from?"

I pulled Richard back into the conversation, and the three of us sat down. "Well, the world has been here a long, long time. Millions and billions of years. And there were animals, and some of the animals changed over time – started walking on two legs instead of four, started forming families and tribes and clans, and..." I didn't know where I was going. How to answer this in a way a four-year-old would understand.

Richard: And Annie said, "No, I know about evolution." Although she probably didn't pronounce evolution quite right. "I mean, where did the first animals come from? How did they get here?"

I tried explaining this as best I could to someone her age, even if she was quite intelligent. Tried to keep it simple in a way that made sense to her but was still at least somewhat accurate. I didn't want to fill her head with fairy tales.

Celeste: And no matter what Richard told her, she would follow up with, "And where did that come from?"

Richard: It turned into a two-hour discussion of the Big Bang Theory, chemical reactions, single-celled organisms, whatever. She seemed to understand everything, but it didn't satisfy her. And I'm an English lit professor, not a science guy.

When it was finally time to put her to bed, Cel and I were exhausted.

She seemed to forget about it after that. I was afraid we'd wake up in the morning to a new barrage of questions, but she moved on to things that interest any four-year old, maybe played with dolls or something.

Celeste: About a year later, she was five, I think. Yes, it was before she started filming *Family Crest*, we're at the breakfast table, all three of us, and Annie says, "I think Jesus made the Big Banged."

Richard: We were kind of floored, and we were laughing. We'd talked about different religions in front of Annie, and never in a ridiculing way, more in an academic mindset. People are always looking for explanations of things they don't understand. An overarching plan. Something, or someone, who is in control. That's a natural human reaction.

Celeste: I'm sure we'd mentioned Christianity, along with many other religions, in our discussions. We'd probably mentioned Jesus. But there'd been no big discussions. I wasn't even sure where she got the idea that Jesus caused the Big Bang.

Richard: As we chuckled over it and tried to figure out how to answer her without being demeaning to anyone's religion, Annie got this very serious face. A bit perturbed. Like how dare we laugh at her serious statement.

Celeste: I finally said, "Some people believe that a god created the universe. We believe that it happened naturally, but people believe lots of different things."

Richard: Annie relaxed and said, "Okay. Well, I believe Jesus made it bang naturally." Then she went on with her breakfast and started talking about something completely different.

Celeste: It was such a matter-of-fact, clear statement of what she believed. After she was out of the room, we had a huge belly laugh. Five-year-olds can say the funniest things sometimes.

Richard: Didn't hear much more about it, then when we asked her what she wanted for her sixth birthday, she said she wanted a Bible.

Interviewer: And you bought her one?

Celeste: Yes, we bought her a Bible, a Koran, and the teachings of Buddha.

Richard: She read some from all three of them, then put the Koran and Buddha on the bookshelf. The Bible went on her nightstand, and she'd read it every night. She'd come out and ask me what this word meant, or how to pronounce this name, or ask "How did Moses make the sea split open?" Things like that.

Interviewer: How did you answer her?

Celeste: We would explain how the Bible meant it, and then we would provide a more rational-based explanation. For example, the Bible says God opened up the sea. If something like this actually happened, it could have been an earthquake that caused it. Or, more likely, this is a made-up story to illustrate a point, to give the people of that day a history they could relate to, like Greek mythology.

Richard: She'd nod and say, "Oh, I see." Then toddle back off to bed to read more.

She came out a few minutes later and said, "Or maybe God caused the earthquake." Then back to bed.

Celeste: We weren't going to tell her she was wrong, or this was all fake, or anything like that. We would listen to her questions and try to answer them truthfully and clearly. She would figure it out on her own after a while. She would lose interest eventually, like kids always do.

Interviewer: Only she never did.

Richard: That's an understatement.

Celeste: While we aren't believers like she is, I can't even express how proud I am of her and her accomplishments. For a believer, she is so meticulous and analytical and even scientific in her studies of religion and Christianity. While she found her own path with her faith, I feel like we had a lot to do with how grounded she is in her approach.

We would never ridicule Annie for her beliefs.

Richard: And she has never condemned us for ours.

INTERVIEW #9

**"I've been called the Redneck Philosopher, a highly
offensive term. I am not a philosopher."
~ Slade Bennington**

Slade: Are you hungry? We've been talking for hours.

Interviewer: No, I'm fine. But if you are, we can take a break.
    Slade: No need for a break. I'll just ring up room service.
[Slade grabs the child's pink and purple walkie-talkie on his desk] Mandy,
come in.
    Mandy: *[child's voice over the speaker]* Mandy here. Over.
    Slade: Can you make me a sandwich, sweetie? Over.
    Mandy: Yes, Papa. Be right there. Over.
    Slade: Thank you. Over and out.
    Now, where were we? Oh yes, you'd asked me about my philosophy.
I don't consider it philosophy. It's common sense, which isn't very
common these days. It's the stuff that's right in front of us. It's the stuff
everyone knows but does their best to ignore and avoid.
    It's like my rebirth brought it all into focus, clarified things, but it
was all stuff I already knew. Stuff everyone knows. I just point it out
and people either go, "Ah, you're right, I knew that," or they get angry.

Interviewer: Why would people get angry?
    Slade: When you point out the obvious to someone, they can get
angry. Because they knew it and they're mad at themselves for not
accepting it. They feel attacked by the truth, and you can't fight against
the truth when you know it's true.

Interviewer: You've been called the Redneck Philosopher.
    Slade: Now that's an offensive word.

Interviewer: Redneck?

Slade: No, philosopher. A philosopher is someone who thinks about thinking. Someone who studies thinking. Can you imagine anything more useless?

I think about life, and then I do something about it. That's called living. I try to help others who've been caught up in themselves. We aren't meant to live internally. We live as a single organism that's part of a bigger organism. Like coral.

[Six-year-old Mandy walks in with two slices of bread on a paper plate, mustard spread on one piece, mayonnaise on the other.]

Mandy: Here ya go, Papa.

Slade: Thank you, dear.

[Mandy walks up and gently slaps a slice of bread to each side of Slade's face, condiment side to skin.]

Mandy: There, now you're a sammich. *[Runs out of the room giggling uncontrollably.]* I made Papa a sammich, I made Papa a sammich!

Slade: That's the third time she's done this. It's her favorite joke now. So, I play the straight man, set her up, and let her think I'm surprised every time.

Can you hand me that towel?

INTERVIEW #10

"Fiction contains more truth than nonfiction.
Or at least it's easier to digest."
~ Slade Bennington

Interviewer: Let's talk about your books and writing. What inspired you to write that first book, your memoir?

Slade: There was no plan to write a book. I was just bored. I was trying to remember what all happened. I had a notebook, a pen, and the use of my arms, so I started writing to fill the time, to take my mind off the pain. I had a lot of time on my hands in the hospital. Can't stand TV. Didn't have many visitors. Matt came when he could, but he was working and taking care of Mom.

I wrote down everything I could remember about the event. I wrote down everything I could remember about Jolene so I wouldn't forget about her – the good and the not-so-good times. I wanted to memorialize her in words.

Then Mom died, so I started writing about her too. At first, it was anger. A release. Purging. But the more I wrote, the more sympathetically I began to see her. I saw her come out of the shadows of her addiction and maybe saw the true person of my mother for the first time in my life.

Then it all started pouring out. Mostly journals, random notes and thoughts, no coherent order or organization or plan to turn this into anything. Matt kept bringing me new notebooks and more pens. Then he brought me a used laptop he'd picked up at a yard sale.

By the time Matt took me home, I had a couple hundred thousand words. I'd retyped everything from my handwritten journals into the laptop. But I wouldn't let Matt see it. It was just for me. Just my personal exercise. Or exorcise.

Interviewer: That's a lot of words – two good books' worth. How long did it take to write all that?

Slade: Did all that in about six or eight months, I think. Finally, it felt like I hit the end of the purge. Everything about my life, the life event that night, and everything that transpired since, all the things that had gone through my mind. How my perception about everyone had changed: Mom, Jolene, Matt, my friends, girlfriend – now ex-girlfriend. Couldn't blame her a bit for disappearing.

After Matt bugged me for weeks, I finally printed out a copy. Had to send him to the store to buy more paper and twice for printer ink.

He started reading through it – skimming mostly, Matt's not much of a reader. But he kept saying I should put it out as a book. I knew better. First, it wasn't organized into anything like a story, and who would be interested in some redneck who drove his car into a ditch, killed his little sister on the way to Planned Parenthood, and burnt off his face and legs?

Interviewer: How did this turn into a book?

Slade: Several months later, Matt started dating this chick who worked for the *Star-by-God-Telegram*. They met when she called to do a follow-up story about the crash. Chelsea fancied herself a writer. At some point, they were talking about books – hard to imagine Matt having a conversation about literature, I know. But she was writing a book and hoped to be the next Great American Novelist. Actually she had written three or four novels and had a literary agent, so she was pretty good. Nothing sold to a publisher yet. Matt mentioned my writing, and she wanted to see it.

I said no. It wasn't meant for anyone else to read. It was like a diary or some deep groaning from my soul, not intended for public consumption. I'd had hard enough time letting Matt read it.

But Chelsea was sweet as can be, and Matt really liked her, so I caved just to help Matt get laid. Printed out fifty pages or so for her. She took them home. Brought them back the next day and she'd splattered stuff on several of the pages.

She apologized profusely – which it wasn't a problem since I could print out more pages – but she started crying. I kept trying to tell her it was no big deal, no need to be so upset over spilling something on it. But she said it was the story that was making her cry, and she didn't spill her drink on the pages. Those were tearstains.

Well, I love making women cry, so I gave her fifty more pages.

Pretty soon, she was wanting to organize it and edit it. Said there was an important story to tell, and she thought she could help me find an agent. She agreed to do a bunch of work for no pay unless I made some money on it. I didn't go for that deal. It wouldn't be fair to her. It wouldn't sell and I didn't want her doing all this work for nothing. I finally got her to agree to $500.

After it did sell, I sent her some more money so she wouldn't feel cheated. It never would have happened if not for her.

Interviewer: How much more did you pay her?

Slade: That's between her, God, and the IRS.

She edited the whole thing down to about 120,000 words, organized it, cleaned up the writing. Then she handed it off to her agent. Her agent only handled fiction, so she passed it on to the nonfiction editor in their agency.

We signed the contract for representation about a week later. My agent – Liv with Farraday & Associates – made a bunch more suggestions on changes that Chelsea helped me make.

Interviewer: Liv? Olivia Farraday? She's probably the most successful literary agent in the country.

Slade: She is now. Not sure that was true before she signed me up as a client. But yeah, that's her. I named a villain after her in my sci-fi books years later. I hope she's forgiven me for that.

Then Liv auctioned the darn thing off. Three different publishing companies wanted it and kept upping the ante.

When Liv called with the final offer, I couldn't even process it.

I've known a few writers, before and since. Most were high school English teachers who wrote on the weekends. Maybe they'd get a short story published in some obscure magazine for fifteen bucks. Or they self-published a novel and sold twenty-nine copies. They would do readings at the local library with three obese women in the audience. Or, like Chelsea, they were really good, and they wrote novel after novel and never landed a book deal until they eventually gave up.

And I got a contract for my scribbling with an advance that had more digits than I earned in a year when I was working full-time. So Matt and I bought a house.

Interviewer: What was it like when the book came out and it took off?

Slade: I still have trouble believing it. Why were all these people so interested? The publisher set me up for a national book tour. TV morning shows. Newspaper interviews. Hit the bestseller lists on *New York Times* and *USA Today*.

Every place asked for an author photo to go with stories, so we sent out author photos. Not many publications actually used them. Probably put their readers right off their bacon and eggs. Some of the TV shows even preceded my interviews with a "graphic content" warning to viewers. Get your kids out of the room or you'll give the little shits nightmares, that sort of thing.

Took about six months or more, but then the royalty checks started coming and I had to hire an accountant and an attorney and an investment adviser. Then the Hollywood guy called.

Interviewer: What about your second book?

Slade: In the middle of all this brouhaha – book tours, interviews, meetings with studio executives and lawyers – Liv calls me up at ten o'clock one night and tells me I need to get busy writing another book. Strike while the iron is hot. Make hay while the sun shines. This from a woman who tells me I use too many clichés.

I didn't have a second book in me. I didn't have a first book, just all my thoughts that spilled out when I was bedridden and hooked up to a morphine drip. Other people turned it into a book. I wasn't a writer. And what else did I have to write about? I'd written the story, such as it was.

I'd kept writing, but it wasn't anything that could be made into a story, even by someone as talented as Chelsea. I'd started my musings about life and how it works. How it doesn't work. Much of that was in my first batch of writing, but it was all the stuff Chelsea had chopped out to get down to the story. I was just filling pages again with these random thoughts.

I called up Chelsea. Her and Matt had broken up, gotten back together, broken up again, I don't know how many times. But we started talking about how to pull all this together into an inspirational book, some sort of "here's how I see life and how to make the best of it when things turn to crap." She wasn't sure it was possible but agreed to help me out since I'd made it worth her while the first time. She quit her job as a copy editor at the newspaper, and we moved her into the spare bedroom so we could work all night. I didn't sleep much, and Chelsea was used to working the night shift.

She traveled with me on book tours so we could work on the manuscript on the road. She came out to LA when I was on the set with Randall doing the movie.

That kind of forced Chelsea and Matt back together, which was my ulterior motive anyway. They've never gotten married but they're still together in that same house. They did eventually replace all the cabinets with normal heights.

I emailed Liv with the synopsis and an outline as we got closer.

Interviewer: What was her reaction?

Slade: Absolutely hated it. Cursed me out. Said I was trying to ruin her career. She wanted a follow-up story, not a self-help book to sell on the shopping networks.

Chelsea and I worked real hard to put more real-life examples from what I'd been through into the book to illustrate the points, give it some type of narrative arc or whatever they call it. Then I sent it to Liv even though she wasn't speaking to me at the time.

Interviewer: And?

Slade: Didn't hear from her for three weeks. Just ignored me. Then she called. She had a contract already, but the publisher was going to assign an editor to me to rewrite it. It was a good contract. Very good. The publisher liked it better than Liv did.

I worked with that editor for months. Then I sent the whole thing to Annie. Seventeen-year-old Annie. She ripped it to shreds and told me what it needed. I told Liv and the editor that I was going to revise it. Liv nearly fired herself as my agent. The publisher threatened to take back their advance, so I wrote them a check and sent it back. They never cashed the check though.

I rewrote it with Annie's input and Chelsea helping every step of the way.

Sent it back to the publisher and asked if they still wanted it or if I was free to shop it to a different publisher.

They doubled my advance. They timed the release for right before the movie came out to take advantage of the studio's promotional campaign.

That's when all hell broke loose.

INTERVIEW #11

**"I wouldn't have picked 'Highway to Hell' as my
theme song, but the kids dug it."
~ Slade Bennington**

*Interviewer: Those were some chaotic times during the second book tour. The
movie coming out. People asking you for help and advice.*

Slade: It was nuts. I started a regular book tour, just like before. I
was better known now, so bigger crowds, bigger venues. Instead of a
bookstore with twenty people, it was a college auditorium with three
hundred. A hotel conference center with six hundred.

Texas Tech out in Lubbock had me scheduled for the performing arts
auditorium that holds four hundred. About a week out, they moved it
to the Buddy Holly Hall, which holds something like two thousand.

The day before, they had to move it to the basketball arena. The
publisher overnighted two thousand more books for me to autograph
and sell. The college provided a staff to handle sales. When they
introduced me and I wheeled out on stage, they had laser lights and
music blaring like WWF wrestling or something. I wasn't real excited
about "Highway to Hell" being chosen for the intro music, but the kids
dug it.

These kids were screaming and cheering. I roll up front and center,
clip on my microphone, and start talking about perspective in life with
my monotone voice. Probably the most boring lecture these kids ever
heard in their entire lives, and that's saying a lot since they had to sit
through college professors every day. But they didn't seem to care. I
signed books and took pictures with those kids for four hours. When I
couldn't write my name anymore, we had to close up shop and turn
people away.

Interviewer: The book tour in California is when things got really crazy.

Slade: California was crazy to start with, but yeah. I was talking to
Annie one night and she asked why I didn't charge admission if there

were this many people coming. I said authors don't charge admission for readings and book signings. You want to draw people in to buy your book.

But Annie said, "The reason meet-the-author sessions are free is because no writers can draw an audience. Not like this. Charge admission and give them the book for free."

I ran that idea past Liv, who thought it was terrible, but she ran it past the publishing company's publicist and marketing team. Given the situation, they thought we might be onto something. Annie insisted that Liv get all the credit for the idea.

All these book clubs and reading groups in California wanted us to come, so we started charging a hundred dollars per person plus expenses, including travel costs for me, Chelsea, and a publicist.

We thought that might start to reduce the number of requests we were getting or the size of the crowds, but we thought wrong. Seems like charging for it made it more important, more urgent for people to attend.

Churches invited me. Last time a church invited me anywhere was when I was ten, and Oakhurst Baptist Church invited me to not come back to Vacation Bible School. An unfortunate trash can fire in the boys' bathroom.

When I say churches were inviting me to speak, I don't mean the little Baptist and Methodist churches on the corner. I mean those gawd-awful glass and steel cathedrals in LA and Houston and Chicago. One pastor sent his personal jet to pick us up and fly us out. I think he was impressed that I could make more money than he did.

We charged those churches a hundred and fifty per person.

Interviewer: You cut this very lucrative book tour short.

Slade: It got to be too much. Chelsea wanted to go home to be with Matt. Poor girl was having a nervous breakdown. It was too much stress on my body, and I started getting sick. Doc said I needed to stop, come back to Fort Worth for some tests. There's a few things that have never quite worked right since the crash. They flare up now and then, and Doc gets all worried.

We curtailed the schedule and planned to return to Texas the following week. That's when the troubles broke out at the Forum, so we cut it all off immediately and got the hell out of Dodge.

INTERVIEW #12

"For most of history, anonymous was a woman."
~ Virginia Woolf

The following are excerpts from interviews with four people who agreed to speak with me only on the condition of anonymity. As a journalist, I've always tried to avoid quoting anonymous sources. Anonymous sources are often invaluable for background information or details that you can then verify elsewhere. Allowing someone to speak – to criticize someone – under the cloak of anonymity goes against my ingrained journalism training.

There are limited exceptions to the legitimate use of anonymous sources. After checking out their stories, and finding how they all confirmed each other's facts, without any of them knowing the others, I believed they were all telling me the truth as they see it. They were from four different professions, four different parts of the country, and never attended any of Slade Bennington's courses at the same time. As best as I could ascertain, none had ever met or spoken with any of the others.

The main factor that persuaded me to protect their anonymity is that all of them felt strongly that they would be irreparably harmed in their careers or personal relationships if their names were revealed. Guaranteeing their anonymity was the only way they would speak to me, and I felt it was important for their voices to be included.

I conducted multiple interviews with each of these sources over a period of months. I present the pertinent excerpts from these interviews with this caveat to the reader: always be wary of anonymous sources. Take them with a grain of salt and see if you can determine the person's motivations.

I've combined answers under a single question or topic to avoid repetition and to organize the information in a more readable format, but each interview was conducted one-on-one, not in a group.

The interview subjects are (not their real names):
Shelby: *executive with a major motion picture studio.*
Danielle: *licensed psychologist from a major midwestern university hospital.*
Frank: *commercial airline pilot and former US Air Force officer.*
Vicki: *former sex worker, former leader of a Slade Book Club, currently a motivational speaker.*

Interviewer: How did you first meet or hear of Slade Bennington?

Shelby: I first heard the name when his book was acquired for a film. I read a brief paragraph about it in *Variety*. It wasn't my studio that was going to make this movie. But I thought it sounded interesting. I'd never heard of him or his book, which was apparently a bestseller, but I had missed all that somehow. After his second book came out, I snagged a copy to see if it was something our studio or one of our production teams might be interested in, but it really wasn't the kind of book to turn to film – it was more of a motivational, self-help book, not like his first book, his life story, which was fairly dramatic.

I found the book interesting, but it didn't really grab me. Probably because I was reading it looking for a movie angle and I was disappointed. But when I heard Slade was coming to LA on his author tour, I thought I should go see what all the hoopla was about.

I didn't meet him until two years later. I was going through a divorce, and he was conducting one of his "Find Your True Self" seminars locally. I was at a low point in my life. I'd just lost my job, husband was a serial cheater, and now we were in a bitter child custody battle. I'd heard from friends that his courses had completely changed their outlooks on life, so I thought, *Why not?* I gave it a try.

Danielle: I'd read both of Slade's books and found them fascinating from both a professional and personal standpoint. As a psychologist, I didn't see anything new or groundbreaking in his books, but I liked the way he personalized his experiences and distilled them into his perspective, wrote a very down-to-earth sort of "here's what I did and what I learned, maybe this will help someone else too." He never talked down to the readers, and he didn't claim to have some revealed truth that everyone had to accept. It was very pop psychology, but from an "ordinary guy under extraordinary circumstances" point-of-view. The thing that always came across to me was this "aw shucks" humility that felt very real, not a put-on.

About twelve years ago – it had been years since I'd read his books – he was giving a speech in Chicago. I decided to attend, more from a professional standpoint than anything I hoped to personally glean from his course. Was there some way he presented things that would help me with my patients? And yes, I had that nagging curiosity to see him in person – the celebrity, the notoriety. The crowds and hysteria that surrounded him early on had receded somewhat, although he still drew large crowds for this type of event. There was this bit of rock star vibe attached to him still.

After the speech, I very impulsively signed up for one of his courses. My name and the word 'impulsive' had never before been used in the same sentence. It all seemed to speak to me personally for the first time. I'd always separated my personal and professional lives, but with Slade, the two quickly bled into each other.

I would lie in bed awake at night reviewing the things he'd said, and I could hear his voice saying them. I'd drift off to sleep and then hear his voice the moment I woke up. It was strange – I'd never experienced anything like this before and didn't know what to make of it. He had this soft, southern gentleman accent, a trace of that Texas drawl, but a sophisticated, almost aristocratic tone, not that stereotypical southern Bubba accent. His voice is mesmerizing at times, and it doesn't sound like the voice that should be coming from his face.

After the course – a six-week series of lectures with homework – I signed up for a one-on-one session with him. Thirty minutes for $5,000. I know, I couldn't believe it either. But I wanted to meet with him and discuss some things that I knew he would be able to help me with more than any of my doctor colleagues. Things I'd never told anyone, or even admitted to myself, and never would until I met with Slade.

Frank: I was in the military when I first heard of Bennington. My wife told me about his book during a phone call when I was deployed to Afghanistan. Just sort of in passing as she told me about her day, what she was doing, the kids' progress in school, that sort of thing. It wasn't anything earth-shattering or alarming, just a casual, "Oh, here's a book I'm reading," comment. She said it was interesting, but it didn't sound like the kind of book I'd read. About some guy who'd nearly died in a car wreck and came out all messed up but struggled through it to make something of his life.

A couple of years later, we were living on an air base in Japan, and the base exchange had a display at the front door with his newest book, which Amy – my wife – decided she wanted since she liked his first book so much. Apparently, this book was some sort of advice book or something, and she became obsessed with it. Reading it over and over, highlighting portions, writing notes in the margins, constantly wanting to read a passage to me. It sounded like pabulum to me, but I didn't want to piss in her corn flakes so I tried to listen and understand why she was so excited over this.

A few months later, the Department of Defense was sponsoring Bennington to go on a world tour of military bases to give motivational speeches to the troops. Like the military couldn't have found amputees and paraplegics of our own. Amy was jumping up and down excited to go see him. I couldn't care less but figured what the heck. She wants to go, we'll line up a sitter, grab some dinner at the O Club, and make a nice evening of it.

We went, and I still didn't get it. The community center had an overflow crowd, standing room only, in violation of all the fire codes on base. A couple thousand people or more crowded into the auditorium and the lobby, a place that shouldn't have held more than six hundred tops.

Amy acted like she was at a Bon Jovi concert or something. I tell ya, it was strange to see. This guy with no legs and a scarred-up face, strapped into a wheelchair so he wouldn't fall out, sitting there talking about happiness and contentment and life's purpose, all that sort of stuff, and the crowd was mesmerized. Hanging on his every word. Sometimes he'd stop talking before finishing a sentence, and the whole crowd would finish it for him. Quotes from his book or something, and everyone there, my wife included, had them memorized.

People cheered him. Oohed and aahed over his supposed insight or wisdom or whatever. People would wave their arms over their heads and sway back and forth when he told them to. It felt like the revival services at the Pentecostal church I had to attend when I was a kid. It definitely had the feel of a religious gathering. I kept waiting for people to start speaking in tongues or break into a chorus of "Our God is an Awesome God." I'd never seen anything like it.

When he finished his talk, he invited people to come to the table on the side where he would autograph books. At least his arms worked. Amy insisted, although I wanted out of there as quick as possible. It was cold outside, so I agreed to go warm up the car while she waited in line to get an autograph.

I waited in the car for two hours.

When she finally came out, she had a handful of pamphlets and wanted to talk about flying back to the states to attend one of his courses for thousands of dollars. We didn't have that kind of money, but I decided to wait a day or two to have that conversation with her. She was so pumped up, it would have caused a fight.

Vicki: I was a professional sex worker in Las Vegas when Bennington's movie came out. After our shift dancing at Top Hat's, a couple other girls and me went to the theater to catch a late-night showing. Ya know, we needed some time to unwind.

Interviewer: What kind of sex work did you do?

Vicki: I'd started with the basics, ya know, street corner hooking on Van Buren Street in Phoenix when I was fifteen. After I got beat up by my pimp a couple of times, and he threatened to kill me, I left town on a Greyhound bus for El Lay, figured I'd hit the big time.

That turned out to be a huge mistake. Got involved with some bad influences, some drugs and stuff. Before long, I was living in a group home with a meth lab in the garage. Made one good friend, and she died from an overdose a month later. That's when me and Greyhound headed for the bright lights of Sin City. Best decision I ever made.

When I turned eighteen, I got to go legit. Got clean off drugs. Got healthy. Joined a gym, switched to an all-organic, vegan diet. Did yoga and meditation. Landed a gig at one of the high-end brothels outside Reno, in Lyon County.

Made a few films during that time and saved up a ton of money. Moved back to Vegas and got a job as an exotic dancer and part-time escort and companion. But I managed my own business, set my own hours and rates, and was very choosy about customers.

It was during that time my girlfriends and me went to see the Slade movie. After that, I was hooked. I bought his books and devoured them. Then I found out there was a local book club that was reading and discussing his books, so I joined.

I've always been kind of a natural at organizing and leading things, so within a couple of months, I was named president of the book club. We tried to move on and read other books, but everyone, me included, kept coming back to Bennington's books for more discussion. People were talking about how they were applying his lessons to their daily lives. We just started weekly Slade discussions.

A few months later, Bennington was scheduled on his book tour to make a stop in Vegas. Well, I took that bull by the horns and contacted his agent. She put me in touch with his publicist, and Bennington agreed to come to our little book club to read a portion of his books to us, talk for a bit, and answer questions.

There were about fifteen of us that met in the back corner of a Barnes & Noble, and the others couldn't believe I was able to get Bennington to come see us. I mean, he had two other stops in Vegas, and they were both at hotel conference centers with hundreds of people.

When he wheeled into the bookstore, we were in our space waiting for him, all set up with books for him to autograph, but word spread quickly that he was in the store. Other customers came over. I swear, before it was over, there were a couple hundred people there.

And when he talked, it was like he was looking right into me. Inside my soul. Speaking directly to me like there was no one else in the room. When he left, I was shaking.

INTERVIEW #13

**"If I can handle Slade riots, I can handle
your company's sales meeting."
~ Chelsea Mandrake**

Interviewer: How did you meet Slade?

Chelsea: I was working at the Fort Worth newspaper as a copy editor when this story came across about him. One of our reporters did a follow-up story about his car accident, the one-year anniversary of the crash, it might have been. I did some fact-checking and read the original stories in the paper about it, his sister dying and all. I thought, *What a horrible thing.* And his injuries were horrific. I sent a note to the reporter asking if he had any photos of Slade to go with the story. A picture is worth a thousand words, and this story cried out for some art – before and after shots.

But we were short-staffed – just had some layoffs, and it was fall, so all the photogs we had left were busy with high school football. The reporter had finished the story and was going on his two-week unpaid furlough. It was tough times at the paper. I told the editor I'd see if I could get pix.

I called Slade and he put me in touch with his brother, Matt, to see if they had any. I went to visit them. I'm not a photographer, but I checked out a camera to take with me. Matt and I went through a bunch of photos, and Slade rather reluctantly agreed to let me take a couple of shots of him.

Turns out that story, and my photo of Slade, made our front page.

Slade was an interesting guy, but Matt and I hit it off. I didn't think much more about it until Matt called me a few days later. I guess he'd kept talking about me until Slade made him call and ask me out. He was so shy. It was cute but irritating.

The rest is history, as they say. I was over at Matt and Slade's place a lot. All three of us were in our thirties and none of us had ever been married. Matt and I started dating. Slade became a friend.

Then Matt brought up the idea of me helping edit and organize Slade's writings into a book. I read a few pages and jumped at the chance. But I had no idea how massive a job that was going to be.

Interviewer: What were the book tours like?

Chelsea: At first, that was fun and exciting. Then it got overwhelming. I traveled with Slade all the time, organizing meet-and-greets, setting up venues, making sure the books were there, the seating was arranged properly, coordinating everything from microphones to refreshments to hotel rooms. I'd never done that type of work before, but because I started on the ground floor and it grew, I guess I grew with it.

Now that's my business. My company. Mandrake Events, LLC. It's what I do. If I can handle Slade riots, I can handle your company's sales meeting. And I've got a staff of four, so I don't travel much anymore at all. Most of the time, I sit in my office and do conference calls and finance stuff on the computer all day.

Interviewer: I understand you started out to be a novelist.

Chelsea: Oh, yeah, that didn't really work out. But I write songs now. Country songs. Play at open mic nights at a few places. I've got a YouTube channel with a dozen subscribers. That hasn't worked out either, but that's okay. It's my creative outlet and I enjoy it.

Interviewer: Talk to me about this Slade riot. Los Angeles Forum, right?

Chelsea: Yes, during that second book tour. Things had gotten out of control, absolute hysteria. I started warning Slade that we needed to back off. It was too big. We needed to bring in some professionals to organize things. It was way out of hand, and I didn't have the expertise or any staff.

He agreed. We canceled some dates that were already planned and stopped adding anything to the schedule. Informed the book publisher that we were cutting everything short. But the Forum event was too big and too late to cancel.

When word got out that we were canceling events, everyone decided to go the Forum instead, thinking it would be their last chance and there'd be plenty of room.

There wasn't. Place was overfilled, police and fire marshals were overrun. Forum staff lost all control. There was a giant crowd outside trying to get in. We couldn't even get to the place to get Slade inside. There's like 10,000 people inside, plus 20,000 more outside, pushing, shoving, fights breaking out, and we can't even get to the performers' entrance. We were expecting maybe five thousand.

We tried for over an hour and then I had to call the head of the Forum and tell him we were leaving. It was too dangerous. They started making announcements over the PA system for everyone to go home, and that's when the shit hit the fan.

Our van was surrounded by a mob. Thank goodness they didn't know it was Slade inside. They would have torn him limb from limb. There were so many people swarming everywhere, we couldn't get out of the parking lot.

I knew we were going to die. And the publicist was in absolute hysterics. But Slade held our hands and just kept telling us all would be well, and our driver managed to pick his way through the crowd without running over anyone. He kept threatening to hit the gas and plow through them, but Slade was so utterly calm and told him not to hurt anyone.

We got out of there right before the shootings and fires started.

Interviewer: Twelve people died that night.
Chelsea: It was horrible. We didn't find out how bad it had gotten until a couple hours later when we checked into a hotel and turned on the TV. Watched it all from the news helicopter footage.

We got sued, the book publisher got sued, the Forum got sued, the police got sued. Everybody sued everyone.

Interviewer: How did Slade react?
Chelsea: He was so calm during the whole episode, but afterwards, I've never seen him so despondent. Angry, even. For weeks. I was in the room when he called his publisher and told them he wouldn't be doing any more book tours for them. They threatened to sue him, and he just told them how much money he had made for them, and they were to use their profits from his book to set up a fund for the victims and families or he'd take his next book to a different publisher.

And they did. And Slade gave them all the credit for being such great, compassionate humanitarians. Then he matched everything they spent dollar for dollar, but never publicized that at all.

That's just the kind of person he is. He'll probably get mad at me for telling you that.

INTERVIEW #14

"Happiness is the roof; sadness, the floor. Contentment is the beam that keeps it all from crashing into the basement."
~ Slade Bennington

Interviewer: You've stated that one of the big problems people face is the desire for happiness, that happiness isn't the goal. What is the goal then?

Slade: Life will always have happy moments and sad moments. That's a given. If your goal is to be happy all the time, you will be sorely disappointed. The rough times will destroy you. You're setting yourself up for failure with an impossible target.

Even our founding fathers recognized this. They didn't say that happiness is a fundamental right. They said "the pursuit of happiness" is a fundamental right.

Contentment, on the other hand, is being satisfied with yourself and your life regardless of circumstances. You enjoy the happy moments more and recognize they are temporary. You can endure the sad bits, knowing they don't last forever and that you will get through them, that better times are around the corner.

Contentment levels you out. Eliminates the high highs and the low lows. You still ebb and flow – you're not just a robot with a single setting.

Interviewer: You've written a lot about your situation. How does that apply here?

Slade: I'm always using myself as an example because my life is the only example I have to draw on. In my previous life, I was healthy, had a decent face, two eyes, four limbs. I could pee standing up. I had a few girlfriends. I had my own apartment at age sixteen. A job. Enough money to eat, pay the rent, and buy some pot.

I wasn't old enough to buy beer, but I could get pot any time. Does that make any sense to you?

And I was miserably unhappy. All the time. I blamed my mother and her addictions. At eighteen years old, I was raising my five-year-old sister. Loved my sister with all my heart, but that's a huge burden to put on a teenage boy, not quite a man. I knew it was the right thing to do, but it's hard to be a single guy and want to go out with friends and party and date and have a girl spend the night when your little sister is there, depending on you to cook dinner and make sure she gets her homework done and goes to bed at a decent hour and gets up in the morning so you can fix her breakfast and get her to school on time. And if she was sick, how was I supposed to go to work? I lost three jobs because I had a kid to raise. I got a small taste of what single mothers must go through.

So, I blamed my mom. I resented my sister at times, even though she was the most important person in my life. I was mad at my brother for making me take her, even though I knew it was the right decision.

Then, I'd get a new job and I'd be happy. It would pay more than the job I lost. I got a new car – new to me – and that made me happy. I got a new girlfriend and she made me happy. Jolene got straight A's in seventh grade after nearly failing sixth grade. That made me happy. I got a new dealer who had better pot, and that made me really, really happy.

None of those things lasted. The happiness is always short-lived. A month later, I still had that car, but it didn't make me happy. I hated the boss at my new job. Jolene was getting on my last nerve. My girlfriend dumped me for a jock. My dealer got busted. Life was terrible again.

And when something good and something bad happen at the same time, the bad overpowers the good. You don't see the good when you're in the middle of something bad. When your toilet breaks and floods the bathroom with muck, you're not too excited about the new car sitting in your driveway.

We live our lives swinging from one moment to the next, from high to low, life is grand, life is terrible. If you live like this, the terrible will always win out.

Interviewer: What do you do about it? How do you achieve this contentment?

Slade: It's all about seeing the big picture. It's balance. It's a process, but it starts with a mindset. You must see the big picture. Then, you must make the right choices, but recognize that we all make wrong choices at times and that's just part of life. Learn from them. Don't beat yourself up over them. Don't shift blame and try to find someone else at fault for everything that goes wrong. Most of what goes wrong in our lives is due to decisions we've made. Learn from them and move on. Recognize your own frailties and faults, and accept them as part of life.

Sometimes what goes wrong in our lives has nothing to do with decisions we made or anyone else – it's just life. Shit happens. It's how we deal with it, how we approach it, that makes the difference in our own lives and in those around us.

Perspective is everything. I had that life moment that gave me perspective. It can all end in the blink of an eye.

I lost my sister and all I remembered were the good times, the love I had for her. I remembered her smile, not her tears or our screaming matches. I lost my car, and it didn't matter at all. I moved from pot to morphine. The whole idea of a girlfriend disappeared from my life. I lost my mother, and I could suddenly see the struggles she had as a single mom raising two boys and then a baby girl years later. Her illness – mental illness – her addictions and her pain. She was a good person but she lost her way. Some due to her own bad decisions, but that didn't make her a bad person. She loved us. She just wasn't capable.

I lost my legs and most of my face.

I realized all that I had wasted, all that I'd lost. But that grief only lasted a moment – I realized what all I still had. I was alive again. A second chance. How many people get that? Jolene didn't.

I had my mind. My arms. Doctors and nurses and therapists and counselors swarming over me to take care of me. I had my dear brother to help me with his brand of tough love, exactly what I needed. I had so much more than most people ever have, even after all I'd lost. In excruciating pain, pain I didn't know was possible to survive, I was surrounded with the good in life.

I saw it. I found a new perspective. Balance. Happiness and sadness are part of life. Death and loss and grief are part of life. Live it. Accept it. Be content with whatever you have, with whatever life throws at you, with whatever station you're in at the moment. That moment will pass. Happy moments pass. Bad times fade.

Life is good. And then it ends. Be a blessing to everyone you come into contact with while you're here, and the blessings will return to you a thousand times over.

Interviewer: When did you see all this? In the hospital? While you were recovering?

Slade: I saw it as I carried Jolene to the road. She was conscious, talking to me, but I knew she wouldn't survive those injuries. So I carried her and held her and talked to her. She knew she was dying, and she was content. She smiled and told me how much she loved me.

She told me to stay strong. The last thing she said to me as they loaded her in an ambulance and sprayed my legs with a fire extinguisher was, "Live. You live. Make it count."

I knew right then that I was going to survive, but my life was going to change dramatically. Things would never be as they once were. I saw life as it really is and I accepted it.

This peace washed over me that I've never been able to explain. God. The universe. The whole thing spread out on a tapestry in front of me and I saw it. I saw it all. I accepted my role in it.

Interviewer: If you could go back in time and change it, what would you do differently?

Slade: Nothing. I wouldn't change a thing. If I'd kept my legs, if my face hadn't melted off the front of my head, I never would have seen this or I wouldn't have accepted it. I never would have met Annie. I never would have had these three girls that are my unending joy.

Do you have children? Would you trade your legs for them? In a heartbeat, you would.

That is contentment. That is life.

INTERVIEW #15

"Slade is the writer, director, and star of his own movie.
He is his own plot. Whether the ending will be satisfying
is yet to be determined."
~ Randall Kleifisch

Interviewer: You've known Slade for more than twenty years, both professionally and personally. Tell me about your relationship.

Randall: Yes, I've known him since before we started preproduction on his life story.

I wanted him involved from the beginning: working with our script writers, casting, everything. He was so matter-of-fact about everything, very low key, but very insightful, especially for someone who knew nothing about movie production.

I've worked fourteen-hour days with him at my side for years. I've had countless dinners and lunches with him. Probably hundreds of phone calls, teleconferences. I've read all his books.

To this day, I still feel like he's someone I just met and haven't yet gotten to know. But he's never been anything but helpful, professional, and courteous.

Interviewer: You've directed or produced how many movies based on Slade's books?

Randall: Five, so far. I'm not sure if he's going to write any more books or not. If he does, we have first right of refusal to evaluate for potential film treatment.

There was his first book, his memoir about the accident and how he overcame those horrific injuries to rebuild a life.

Then there have been the four sci-fi pieces. Was originally planned for a single book, but it caught on like wildfire, so Slade turned that into a trilogy. Then he followed that up with *Volume IV*.

It feels complete to me. But then, *Star Wars* felt complete after the third film, and that's still going. There's even been talk of the studio licensing the characters and turning our script writers loose rather than waiting to see if Slade decides to keep it going.

Interviewer: Do you have a personal favorite?

Randall: That's like asking who your favorite child is. I love them all equally, of course. But his life story – the first movie – will always have a special place in my heart. It was the first true story I'd ever done. It made Slade famous. It made Schuyler even more famous than she already was. I earned my only Oscar – so far – with that piece. It was truly a dream come true to make that film.

Interviewer: What did you think of Slade and Schuyler's relationship early on, during the filming? What can you tell me about their initial meeting and friendship from that time?

Randall: It was wonderful. It was sweet. Slade is a very intelligent, interesting guy, as I'm sure you know. As you also know, his appearance can be disconcerting when you first meet him. The fact that Schuyler, as a teenage girl, was able to look past all that and befriend him speaks to her maturity at that age. And it wasn't befriending him out of compassion or pity or being polite. They really hit it off. I'd catch them sitting in the breakroom talking, or with books spread in front of them. He would discuss her homework with her. I would walk in while he was telling her about his sister or his mother, or she was telling him about her entire education, from first grade on, being with tutors on the set of TV shows and films, or her favorite books.

Interviewer: My understanding is they were just friends at first, and the more romantic or intimate relationship didn't begin until a few years later. But why do you think they were so enamored with other from the start?

Randall: They both had bits missing, maybe, in different ways, and yet they are the two most grounded people I've ever known. They'd been damaged and they had healed. When they found each other, they just clicked. They each knew they'd found a rare gem. As completely opposite and different as they are from each other, maybe they are two puzzle pieces from the same soul.

Interviewer: I've not thought of Annie – Schuyler – as damaged in any way. She seems like she's been the poster child for having your act together since she was a kid. How do you mean?

Randall: Oh, I don't want to speak out of school. I have nothing but the highest admiration for Schuyler. What an amazing, incredible woman she is. She was an amazing, incredible child, teenager.

But I think if you take any child, from the time she is three or four years old, put her in a television studio and make her an international star by the time she's six, never attend a regular school a single day in her life, have very few friends her own age, hang out with adults all day long, something can be missing. I think she was very lonely, or at least very alone. Maybe she was fine with the solitude, but it matured her much too quickly. I think she missed out on some things.

With Slade, she found a friend. Someone she connected with, and I don't know that she ever had connected with another human being in her entire life. She can be very distant, closed. No siblings, no classmates, no riding bicycles in the neighborhood. She was so well known by the time she was six or seven years old, she couldn't go anywhere the rest of her life without her parents or adult guardians. Security systems. Bodyguards.

Interviewer: Bodyguards?

Randall: Armed bodyguards in New York City when she was fourteen years old doing the Broadway musical *Lolita*. So many threats were made against her, and against the play. She either got pedophiles who wanted to meet her in person or Puritans who wanted to kidnap her to stop the play. Death threats. Protesters would throw eggs at her when she stepped out backstage to sign autographs. One creep grabbed her and tried to pull her into his car, but the bodyguards intervened and beat him to a bloody pulp. The cops just stood back and watched, and no one complained about it either. Well, the guy catching a beat-down might have complained, but no one was going to listen to him.

I'm sure all this was quite traumatic, but when I met her, she seemed to have pushed it all aside, or stuffed it inside. Like nothing had ever happened. She was a mature young woman at sixteen years old who wanted to be taken seriously as an actress.

Interviewer: And she was.

Randall: Oh, she certainly was. To see her blossom on the set was a sight to behold. And I was glad she and Slade hit it off. Oh, I know, there were some rumors – maybe more callous jokes than rumors – about them. I knew that wasn't the case. For one thing, Schuyler was much too mature and sensible, and Slade was much too gentlemanly and caring. For another thing, because Schuyler was underage, she was never left alone. She had a minder, a tutor, her parents, me, and a whole cast and crew around. Slade and Schuyler were never alone or in private together, so I thought the jokes were tasteless and reprehensible. I don't know anyone who took any of the rumors seriously. Vulgar locker room talk.

Interviewer: Men can certainly be that way at times with the locker room talk.

Randall: Oh no, all this gossip and innuendo came from the women. Professional actresses, some famous. I think Schuyler made them feel very insecure.

Interviewer: When did you first become aware that Slade and Schuyler had taken their relationship to the next level?

Randall: That wasn't until several years later. Actually, not until they announced their engagement. So that was, what, five or six years later. I was a bit surprised, but not at all shocked. It made perfect sense, in fact. I was quite happy for the two of them, but I knew they would be facing yet another round of public scrutiny, rumors and gossip, crude and cruel jokes.

Interviewer: How did you feel when Schuyler announced she was leaving acting for good?

Randall: Simultaneously heartbroken and totally understanding. She called to tell me before she made it public. I had seen it coming. I tried once, very briefly, to talk her out of it, then I stopped myself. I knew there was no talking her out of it. And no reason I should want to talk her out of it. She was making the best decision for herself, for her life, for her happiness. Why would I want to talk her out of that? Only my selfish desire to direct her in her next film to win a Best Actress Oscar. Her talent was abundant, but if her heart wasn't in it, and it wasn't, then my only reaction had to be complete support and understanding, as much as I knew the world would miss her.

For several years, I entertained the notion that she would change her mind and make a comeback, but over time, that hope faded.

Interviewer: Did you ever attend one of Slade's courses or seminars, or have any sessions with him?

Randall: Oh no. That sort of thing isn't for me. I read his books, of course, and it's all very interesting, but not my cup of tea. I know many,

many people who did though, and he brought a lot of light to a lot of people. Slade is probably the most insightful person I've ever met when it comes to human nature, to reading people's emotions.

He has a rather uncanny knack for knowing what you're feeling before you even know it yourself.

INTERVIEW #16

"Love is the only true thing, and people lie about it all the time."
~ Slade Bennington

Interviewer: Your first book was the story of your life and overcoming the accident – or not an accident, a life event, as you call it. A story of human drama, which made for a great film adaptation. Your second book was quite different from your first. More of a philosophical look at life, although I know you dislike the term philosophy. Where did this second book come from? What was the inspiration?

Slade: No, I didn't think of it as philosophy. I just needed to get down in words the insights, the illumination, the clarity I'd received when I was reborn. All the truths I could see so clearly. Nothing new or revolutionary – all stuff that everyone innately knows, but we ignore it. We push it to the side because we're so wrapped up in our immediate, selfish lives.

You know how you wake from a dream and you can remember it for a moment, but then it fades and you can't recall it? You can't get it back. That's what I feared at the time. I saw things clearly and needed to write it all down before that knowledge faded into the shadows again.

Interviewer: You often reference shadows, a recurring theme through all your books. Explain the symbolism.

Slade: Not symbolism so much, but an accurate description of how it was revealed to me. We live each day in the shadows. We see ourselves and our immediate surroundings within our own light. We see what affects us directly. Others move in and out of the shadows as they interact with us, and we only see how each person and each event impacts our lives. This is a result of complete selfishness.

Now, there's nothing inherently wrong with selfishness, as odd as that may sound. We must feed ourselves, have a place to live, earn money to buy things we need. The next level of selfishness is to care for our immediate family. They are the ones inside our light.

But for everyone we interact with, our immediate internal thought is how will this person improve my life at this moment? If there's nothing in it for us, back into the shadows they go.

What we don't see is they are doing the same thing. They live within their own light, and we exist only in their shadows. Everyone is doing the same thing, and so we all live in little light bubbles, out for our own benefit alone.

If one person expands their light, focuses their attention on how to positively impact others, they may be viewed as a philanthropist, or a humanitarian, or a nice person. But they will be taken advantage of because everyone else still lives in their own light bubbles.

Except... except if you know. If you see.

The key is to gradually expand your light. See others how they see themselves. Find the light path to them. Connect your lights and take care of each other. Selfishness fades, and yet it doesn't. All that you do for others comes back to you because they will care for you as well. You improve your self-interest by bringing others into your light.

Interviewer: That sounds like philosophy to me. Or religion.

Slade: That doesn't make me a philosopher, and I'm certainly not trying to create another religion. There are plenty of those around to choose from. I just try to expand my light and show others how to expand theirs.

Interviewer: You have a pretty large group of followers. Some have referred to them as a cult.

Slade: I want no followers. I'm no cult leader and I want no cult. I only wanted to share what I saw. If it helps someone else, wonderful. If another person finds it boring, or psycho-babble nonsense, that's fine too. They will have to find their own way, as I did. But these groups started as book clubs – readers who enjoyed my books and took it upon themselves to form groups of like-minded readers.

Interviewer: Do you think they took it too far? Forming groups that study your words like scripture, adding their own interpretations and dogma to a movement based on your books. I've visited some of these groups, and they have your photo hanging on the wall or set on the table in front of them when they meet. I visited a home of one of your adherents who had three photos on the wall: Christ, Obama, and you.

Slade: Ah, yes. The new Trinity. Jesus, Barack, and Slade.

Look, many people have taken my thoughts and found some inspiration or motivation, some solace, some meaning in life. Others took my words as a starting place, a jumping-off point, and made their own way. That's fantastic but has nothing to do with me. I didn't encourage them or support them. Well, not anymore. The first year after that book published, I went on a book tour. That included meeting with dozens of book clubs and reading groups. These started off normal enough, like any author on a book tour. But within a few weeks, they had grown to something like what you see in those old films of the Beatles' first tour of America, or the pope visiting Buenos Aires.

I was glad to have touched so many in such a positive way, but it took on a life of its own. Some of those book clubs started sending me photos – they turned their meeting rooms into Slado-Masochist shrines. I stopped touring and stopped giving interviews. My publisher wasn't happy, but I pointed out how many books we were selling, so they shut up.

Interviewer: And no more philosophy books for you?

Slade: Ha! Nope, that's when I switched to science fiction. All grounded in my worldview, but fiction, for entertainment purposes only. Beach reads. Something to keep my mind busy and bring in an income. And a few million people have taken my novels and ascribed some deep meaning to them.

It's kind of sad, really. Looking for symbolism, hidden truths, secret formulas to a meaningful life in a novel about a human falling in love with an alien who is a spy for her planet, sent to Earth to infiltrate the United Nations, not realizing it wasn't the world government they thought it was. And the alien falls in love with the human race despite, or because of, all our foibles.

There's no deeper meaning here other than love is the only truth.

The media didn't help. Played me up to be the next L. Ron Hubbard, creating a new religion out of science fiction, starting a cult, holding some psychological power over millions of the faithful. That was ludicrous.

Interviewer: A lot of celebrities, actors you knew from your time working in Hollywood plus Annie's connections, flocked to you for advice and guidance. Life coaching, some called it. Spiritual guru, some said.

Slade: My personal favorite was Shaman to the Stars. *Heh.* I forgot who said that first, but I nearly fell out of my chair laughing. Then some reporters started using that title unironically.

I was trying to help some friends, some of Annie's friends. Once again, the media got it completely wrong and played it up into something it wasn't. I tried to tamp this back down, but it quickly got out of control. It tore through the entertainment industry like a wildfire in Silverado Canyon. Eventually, I shut all that off. They can believe whatever they want, but I wanted no part of it and certainly wasn't going to encourage it.

I still believe there are ideas in my books that can help people, but they weren't intended to be a set of doctrines for others to follow. I was documenting my experience, how I found my way out of a troubled life in the midst of a traumatic experience, to give hope to others so they can also find their way. Everyone has to find their own way. Your way might not be my way.

Interviewer: The New York Times reported last year that there are more followers in these groups than there are active members in the Episcopal Church.

Slade: Does that surprise you? It shouldn't. Annie predicted the end of the mainstream Protestant denominations ten years ago. So far, her predictions have a lot more merit than mine.

Interviewer: Let's talk about Nora Campo.

Slade: I was afraid you'd bring her up. I'd rather not, but I promised you transparency when I agreed to these interviews. Can I get you a beer first? I need a beer. Too bad Doc says I'm not allowed to partake anymore.

I will talk about Nora. But not yet. Let's put that off for another day.

INTERVIEW #17

"Ironic that you need training to pretend to act natural."
~ Slade Bennington

Interviewer: After the second book tour, you started your courses and individual sessions.

Slade: A few people I'd met on the movie set had contacted me and wanted to talk. A few more contacted Annie and asked if she could put them in touch with me.

At first, it would be a phone call with a friend or acquaintance who was having some particular life issue and wanted my take on it. But word started to spread, and the requests kept stacking up. That's when Annie suggested I put together a seminar or class or something. Let things settle down then do something organized. Charge enough to keep it to a smaller group, not a mob.

I started thinking about this and sketching out some notes. Annie, with her natural teaching abilities, was absolutely instrumental in putting this together in a coherent way. We got Chelsea involved again to help plan the sessions, getting venues, publicity, a website – she is so incredibly talented with the organizational stuff. Chelsea kept insisting that we raise the amount we were planning to charge and market it to celebrities, politicians, professional athletes – people who could afford it. And they were the perfect target audience because they need the help more than anybody.

The individual sessions came about a year after we launched the courses due to demand. Some of the people who came to the courses kept asking to meet with me privately.

Annie was always coaching me on how to do public speaking. I was awful at it from the start. She helped immensely in that regard. Her acting experience was crucial in getting me to the point where I could sit on a stage and talk to people naturally. That did not come naturally to me.

Ironic that you need training to pretend to act natural.

Interviewer: You'd planned to do this tour of courses for a year. How long did you do it?

Slade: We toured for three years. All over the country. Then to Europe. Then a USO tour to military bases overseas. I did that one for free.

Then I said I was done with the travel. No more. We set up a home base in Fort Worth and said if you want to take a course, you have to come here. I was done with being on the road all the time. It's exhausting, and by then, Annie and I had decided to get married. She didn't want me traveling that much. She wanted a home with a husband.

Interviewer: Her idea again to set it up at a single location?

Slade: Absolutely. She's brilliant with things like that. That also gave Chelsea time to stay at home with Matt.

When we bought this place, I suggested we build a conference center here rather than paying for a hotel or convention center. Annie put her foot down on that one though. Stomped that idea like a rotten grape. Said she didn't want people coming to her home. So we started renting a conference center in Dallas. Home is our safe place. Our escape from the craziness of the world. Our private abode. Don't mix work and home, she said. Home is more important than that.

As usual, Annie was right. Once the kids started coming, I was glad we didn't have people coming to our place for sessions.

Interviewer: Your teachings, your beliefs, don't quite line up with Annie's, do they?

Slade: No, of course not. Do any two people believe exactly the same thing? We complement each other's viewpoints rather nicely though.

Interviewer: Annie is very religious, a devout Christian. Do you believe in God?

Slade: Oh, absolutely. I'm just not as certain about God's identity as Annie is. I think she's onto something, but everyone has to find their own path. Seems to me like God is big enough to create more than one path. That path always seems to be in the shadows, though, doesn't it?

Interviewer: How long did you teach these courses at the conference center?

Slade: About ten years. Until Nora. Still do the occasional one-on-one session, but only for existing clients. Not taking on anyone new. I go out and give a talk somewhere once in a while, but I've cut those way back too.

Interviewer: What do you say to people who contact you and request a session?

Slade: I tell them to buy my damn book and figure it out for themselves like everyone else has to.

INTERVIEW #18

"There's a sucker born every minute, and that minute was mine."
~ Shelby, movie studio executive

Interviewer: Did you find his books, courses, or sessions helpful? And what changed in your opinion of him?

Shelby (studio executive): My first thoughts were what an extraordinary person he was, and the crowds that he was able to draw. I really kicked myself for not being on top of his first book to get it for our studio. Paramount made a fortune on that, and several people launched highly successful careers from it. He was a national obsession. But I could see why after hearing him, after going to his courses. I scheduled a single one-on-one session with him, knowing it would be a one-time thing only. Three years and five one-on-one sessions later... yeah, he's not cheap, but I kept convincing myself that it was worth it, and that I'd only need "just this one more session" to get my shit together. I always felt on the verge of some major breakthrough.

But it never quite came. Reality eventually set in that I had pissed away a lot of money on a manipulative charlatan. He'd just say the same things over and over, ask the same questions, and then make you feel like you weren't trying hard enough if you weren't getting enlightened.

There's a sucker born every minute, and that minute was mine.

Danielle (psychologist): At first, it was helpful, although I couldn't quite put a finger on how or why. I felt good about life after a course, or after a session, or after rereading his book. It all seemed to make so much sense – even more sense than the profession I had studied for years and practiced for a couple of decades. I began to doubt psychology. No, Slade never said anything derogatory about that. Just doubts that grew in my own mind. Slade was supportive of psychology, counseling, therapy – he recommended it to many people.

But I always felt like what he had to say was more real and more important than anything I'd learned in school.

It was during a one-on-one session – and we had several – that he point-blank asked me: "Are you gay?"

I denied it, stuttered, stammered a bit, then said I wasn't sure, then – while he waited for me to answer truthfully – I said yes. I came out of the closet right then. I admitted to Slade something I'd never even admitted to myself.

He smiled at me and said, "That's wonderful."

I said, "You think it's wonderful that I'm a lesbian and my family is going to disown me?"

He said, "I think it's wonderful that you are discovering your true self. It's about time, don't you think?"

I called my parents and my brother that night to tell them. My dad was like, "You're just now seeing this, or did you think we didn't know?" Mom said, "That's nice, dear. Did you meet someone?"

My brother said he always knew there was something wrong with me and hung up. We never spoke again. He died of cancer a few years ago. Even when he was in hospice, he refused to take my calls.

No matter what I feel today, I'll forever be grateful to Slade for seeing right through a facade I'd had up for so long that I didn't even know the real me anymore. Maybe I'd never known the real me. That, of course, led me to my relationship with Margo. We've been together ten years now.

It feels to me like I got my life together due to Slade's help, and then he changed. Maybe I didn't need him anymore. Maybe I'd used him as my excuse to get my life together and gave him too much credit.

But after I came out, he began to seem very shallow, self-centered to me. His core teachings sounded like discount-store motivational tapes, a B-grade Tony Robbins with a mesmerizing voice and face that's hard to look at but harder to look away.

I had trouble seeing what I'd seen in him before. Maybe I'd moved on. While there was this great, momentous epiphany in my life because of him, or guided by him, I look back now and I have no idea why I was so enamored with his teachings. At the time, it had felt like I was getting a personal audience with the Dalai Lama. It was definitely his charisma, his persona, more than his actual teachings. He just has a way of living rent-free inside your head.

Even after I'd stopped going to any sessions with him, after I'd moved on and decided Slade wasn't all that he'd professed to be – or that I'd built him up to be – I couldn't get his voice out of my head for months.

Actually, his voice still shows up once in a great while.

Vicki (motivational speaker): His teachings turned my life around. But then he nearly destroyed my life. I read his books several times. I listened to him speak every chance I got. I had saved up so much money – in my line of work, I knew I'd have to retire by the time I was thirty or so – I was set for life with everything safely invested. Planned on opening a business of my own, maybe a really nice brothel or high-end escort and companion service.

I would dream about Bennington's words, his voice. Go to sleep thinking about something he'd said or written, and wake up thinking about something else he'd said. Eventually, the book club wanted to move on to other writers, but we'd just come back to Slade.

We read and discussed and analyzed his books repeatedly. We came up with lists of important points and teamed up with accountability buddies to check in with each other throughout the week. We had memorization contests.

And then, Bennington announced a seminar at the MGM Grand. I couldn't pass that up.

If his books were the gateway drug, the seminars were meth and crack cocaine rolled into one. Then the personalized, individual sessions – pure heroin.

I would have been better off if I'd just stuck a needle in my arm and put an end to it. I couldn't stop. I quit working. I flew around the country to attend his seminars, and I'd always try to schedule a one-on-one with him if he had any slots open. When he moved his seminars to Texas, I flew to Texas a few times. Then I moved to Texas.

Why? I'd never wanted to live in Texas. But life didn't seem worthwhile unless I was reading his books for the umpteenth time, attending a seminar, or planning the next trip to a seminar. And those individual sessions were a rollercoaster. I mean, the excitement and anticipation leading up to that one-hour meeting with him, being in the same room with him, talking to him. Listening to him. Knowing he was listening to me. That man could see inside my soul and say things that blew me away. I'd leave feeling so rejuvenated, so high on life.

But that high gradually faded. Each time, I didn't get as high as the time before, and the high didn't last as long. Instead of thinking that maybe it wasn't as good for me as I'd imagined, just like with drugs, all I thought about was how to get more.

During one of our individual sessions, maybe the tenth or twelfth one, I suggested that we should see each other socially, especially since I'd relocated to Texas. Maybe we could hang out. Maybe we'd be good for each other.

I practically threw myself at him and damn near proposed.

He brushed me off. I don't think that had ever happened to me before. I assumed the fire must have burned off more than just his legs, but I didn't even care about that. I just wanted to be with him. Take care of him and learn from him twenty-four/seven.

It wasn't a month later that I heard on the news he was marrying that actress.

I'd never had my heart broken before. And I swore right then, it would never happen again.

He'd bled me of almost my entire life savings. Made me entirely dependent on him for emotional support and for my own personal value, my self-esteem. I worshipped the ground he walked on and then it became so clear, so obvious, that he didn't care for me one bit. I'd dedicated my life to him, and all he was dedicated to was the next time I'd pay him to make me feel good about myself.

But eventually, I put my life back together. I moved back to Vegas and now I do motivational speaking to women's groups on how to avoid toxic partners, how not to fall in love with narcissists, and how to keep the man in your life sexually pleased.

Frank (airline pilot): The arguments over Amy flying to the states to attend one of his courses were the worst fights we'd ever had up to that point. I eventually put my foot down and said no, we didn't have the money. But I agreed that the following year, when we were scheduled to be transferred stateside, we'd try to get her to one of those courses. I saw how important it was to her, but I didn't understand. I couldn't understand. Seemed like a huge con game to me. Pay someone tons of money so they can tell you the goal in life is to be happy. Keeping my five grand would have made me happy.

I made the mistake one day of asking Amy why she was so unhappy in life that she needed to pay this guy that kind of money – my hard-earned money. I literally risked my life for my paycheck, and this is what she wants to spend it on. She came unhinged at that point. Like she was an opioid addict and I'd threatened to flush all her pills down the latrine.

We held on for a while, but that was the break. That was the beginning of the end. We owned a house in Virginia and sold it during our divorce. She got $70,000 cash from that deal.

A year later she was asking for more alimony and child support. Come to find out she'd spent all of that settlement money on sessions with the Crispy Christ.

INTERVIEW #19

"How could I possibly control someone else's mind? I can barely wrangle my own."
~ Slade Bennington

Interviewer: While you have many supporters, you do have a few detractors, in addition to Nora Campo's parents. This, of course, is to be expected for someone so much in the public eye. But there is a common thread that runs through those who oppose you: that you hold some sort of spell over your followers, some kind of mind control or even use brainwashing techniques. There have been rumors that you exercised this mind control over the teenage Schuyler Jones – Annie – and groomed her for a period of years to become your wife.

Slade: That's an easy explanation for some as to why Annie would choose a man like me as a husband. Yes, we've heard those bits of gossip. I've seldom seen anything piss Annie off more.

Interviewer: She strikes me as a strong, intelligent woman who controls her own mind.

Slade: She gets the angriest because no one has ever suggested that perhaps she brainwashed me into marrying her. She told me, "Why do they always think you have the ability to dominate my mind, but no one ever gives me enough damn credit to believe it could be the other way around?" Then she stomped her feet and left the room. The only time I've ever heard her cuss.

Interviewer: But what of these accusations? There's Nora, of course, and the allegations her parents made. I've spoken with several others – former followers of yours, clients, I guess I should say – who said pretty much the same thing but refuse to go on the record or speak publicly.

Slade: I said it before. Sometimes the truth makes people angry. I can't be responsible for how someone reacts to the truth. I merely present it. Sometimes the truth doesn't turn out the way you think it should.

Lots of people over the years have publicly criticized me, and I haven't detonated any explosive device I'd secretly implanted in their brains while they were under my hypnotic spell. I don't even defend myself against them. They are free to have their opinions of me, and their opinions are as valid as anyone else's. I'm not going to criticize anyone who criticizes me. If I'm going to write books, give speeches, make movies... criticism goes with the territory. My books have more than five thousand bad reviews online from people who hated them. Granted, there are tens of thousands of five-star reviews, but my point is that nothing and no one is going to be equally liked or admired by everyone. Name the best-selling singer of the past year, and in five minutes, I'll find you a thousand people who can't stand the sound of her nasally, whiny voice.

I don't take any criticism or disagreement personally. All I do is express my opinions. And they are allowed to express theirs.

Interviewer: You've never sued anyone for making these claims about you?

Slade: I thought about it once or twice, but I let it go. Now, if I really could control someone's mind, I would sue every one of them and I'd have a sympathetic judge and I'd win every case because I could worm my way inside the jury's feeble minds, now wouldn't I?

Interviewer: You've also been criticized for the fees you charged – $6,000 for one of your seminars and one-on-one sessions at $10,000 an hour.

Slade: I've also put all my books out there in paperback – around fifteen bucks – and digital books for less than ten. I've put some classes online for free. I do my best to make my message available to everyone who is interested, regardless of their financial situation.

The seminars – absolutely, I charged a decent sum, which around ten thousand people saw fit to pay, and there were thousands more on a waiting list when I stopped doing the courses. Out of my fees, of course, were staff salaries, travel costs, lodging, renting the hall, meals provided to all attendees, and so on. It always sounds like a lot of money, but I paid all expenses out of it. Any remaining profit went to the foundation. And sometimes there wasn't any remaining profit. If any event fell short, I made up the loss out of pocket.

For the one-on-one sessions, think of it this way. A pipe bursts under your home. You could buy a book on plumbing and some tools and see if you can learn to fix it. You could even watch a video on YouTube for free. Or you could call a professional plumber and pay a hundred dollars an hour to get the job done right.

Interviewer: You charged a bit more than a hundred dollars an hour.

Slade: I was trying to fix lives and minds and hearts. They are a bit more valuable and complex than a toilet. Unless, of course, your toilet is broken. Then that becomes the number one – and number two – priority.

But it was supply and demand. Had to raise the price to keep the crowds down to a manageable level, or we'd have been overrun again.

ARTICLES #2

"The surgery was a complete success."
~ Dr. Bituin Ramos

Nine years earlier
Los Angeles Times, Jan. 14

Actress dies following controversial surgery

Nora Campo, 24, noted film actress, stunt performer and athlete, died Tuesday in Manila following a controversial elective surgery to amputate both of her legs.

Ms. Campo had announced her decision to have both legs surgically removed to "achieve clarity of life" after participating in a series of life-coaching sessions by Hollywood guru, author and double amputee Slade Bennington.

When no US or European doctor would perform the surgery, Campo located a doctor in the Philippines who agreed to her request. According to a statement from Dr. Bituin Ramos, the surgery was a complete success, but Campo died of cardiac arrest two days later.

Campo is best known for her action roles in movies based on Bennington's science fiction novels, in which she played a brash Brooklyn high school student turned vigilante alien hunter.

Bennington could not be reached for comment. His publicist provided a one-sentence statement that said Bennington had tried repeatedly to talk Campo out of her decision, and that he and his family are devastated by the news of her death.

***

Eight years earlier
Variety magazine, Jan. 14

Actress's family sues Bennington for wrongful death

The parents of actress Nora Campo have filed suit in federal court against Hollywood guru and life-coach to the stars Slade

Bennington. Ms. Campo died one year ago today after surgery to amputate both her legs.

According to court documents filed by the Ocampo-Devlin family attorney, Mark Devlin and Rosaria Ocampo-Devlin are seeking actual and punitive damages of $250 million. The suit alleges that Bennington coerced and manipulated a mentally ill and emotionally fragile Campo into believing she would become "enlightened" if she had her legs removed.

INTERVIEW #20

"Bennington doesn't have any legs. He shouldn't have any arms either. Then he could slither in the grass like the snake he really is."
~ Rosaria Ocampo-Devlin

Interviewer: Ms. Ocampo, would you take a few minutes to tell me about Nora, about her as a young girl, a person? Help me to get to know her, not just the actress and celebrity the whole world saw on the screen or the news stories surrounding her tragic death at such a young age.

Rosaria: Yes, yes, I would love to. I love to talk about my Nora. She was my angel from the day she was born.

Interviewer: Where was she born?

Rosaria: In our little village about an hour from Pili.

Interviewer: Where is Pili?

Rosaria: It's the capital of Camarines Sur, in the Bicol region.

Interviewer: This is in The Philippines?

Rosaria: Yes, yes. A tiny farming village.

Interviewer: Tell me about her early life, her childhood in this little village, and how you came to America.

Rosaria: We didn't know it, I didn't know it at the time, but compared to everyone here, we were very poor. We always had food and we had a small house, so we didn't want for anything. But you work every day to have enough food to eat tomorrow, you know. It's a very different life. And there's no one to help you, no government to help you. So you don't think about that. You just think about working today to eat tomorrow.

I married when I was fourteen. My father made an arrangement with a man from the next village. And I married. Nora was born when I was fifteen. This is normal. Here, this sounds too young, but to me, it was normal. No problem.

But my husband, Nora's father, he do bad things to Nora when she was three. I didn't know, I didn't know at first. But then I got suspicious. She had stopped eating and was crying a lot, and she had really bad diaper rash. I wanted to take her to the doctor, but my husband said we couldn't afford it, just put some cream on it or something.

It didn't get better, and so when he was driving to Pili and would be gone for his job for all day, I walked to the doctor. I had to carry Nora she was in so much pain. The doctor looked her all over and asked if someone had been touching her down there in a way you're not supposed to touch a baby. I was horrified to even think that, and I said no, no way, it must be something else.

But on the way home I began to get suspicious of my husband, if he had done something like this. Could he do something so evil? I ask myself that question over and over on the walk home, and by the time I got home, I answer myself with yes, yes he could.

I vowed to never let Nora out of my sight again. I told my husband about the doctor but I told him the doctor said it was bad diaper rash or allergy to soap. I didn't say anything about what else the doctor said. But he became angry and beat me for taking her without his permission, said the doctor cost too much money. But that confirmed my answer of yes, yes he could do something like this.

Not three weeks later, something woke me up in the middle of the night. Some noise. I reached over for Efren —

Interviewer: *Efren?*

Rosaria: My husband. Efren. I reached over and he was not in bed. I slipped into the other room where Nora slept, and he was beside her on her mat with his hand under her blanket. It was dark, but there was moonlight coming in the window and I could see what he was doing. I grabbed a knife from the counter and I pulled him up by his hair and stabbed him in the neck.

Interviewer: *You killed him?*

Rosaria: No, no, unfortunately he did not die. But the police came and took him to the hospital in Pili, then they took him to the jail. I have cousins in the jail. They work there, I mean. Not in jail like criminals. My people are not criminals.

Before the trial where I would have to testify, and the doctor was going to testify, someone finished the job for me. They never found out who. Some other prisoner who didn't like child molesters, praise Mary and Joseph. We never had to see that evil man again. God will take care of him with justice.

Interviewer: Is that when you moved to America?

Rosaria: No, no. We had no money, and with my husband gone, there was even less. I worked odd jobs where I could, but we had to move to Pili so I could find work. I got a job as a bartender so I had to work nights. I paid an old neighbor woman to watch Nora. So we were doing okay, but it was hard life, you know. Yes, yes, it was hard life.

Interviewer: When did you meet Mark Devlin?

Rosaria: Mark came into the bar one night with some friends of his. They had been diving at the coast, then came to the city. One of his friends lived in Pili, another American. They had been in the Navy together, at Subic Bay many years earlier. The friend had married a local girl and stayed, moving to Pili with her. Mark came to visit his friend.

We talked a lot for the few days while Mark was in town, and then he went home to America, but he wrote me letters. He wrote emails every day, but he also wrote me love letters by hand and mailed them. We made plans for him to come visit again. We fell in love through our letters and when he came again, we knew we were to be married.

He loved Nora too, and she adored him. I asked Mark if he was going to move to Pili like his friend. Then he could be with us and also have a friend in the city. But he said he couldn't move here, would we move to California with him? He was still in the Navy, and an officer, so he had to go back.

So I said yes, yes, Nora and I will move to California with you. And so we did.

Interviewer: How old was Nora?

Rosaria: She was six when we moved. So she don't remember lots about the Philippines. She don't remember... she didn't remember her father, Efren, at all. At least not when she was awake. But sometimes I thought there was something broken inside her mind because of him.

Interviewer: What do you mean, broken? In what way?

Rosaria: She could be a normal little girl, having fun, playing, helping me in the kitchen. Then sometimes she would get very quiet and sad, and she would stare at the wall for hours. I couldn't get her attention away. If I shook her or grabbed her, she would become terribly frighten and begin to cry. So when she had these spells, I would leave her alone and in a while she would seem to wake up like nothing was wrong, but she didn't even know time had passed.

She would be helping me make dinner, and then she would sit and stare at the wall. Mark and I would eat, clean up the kitchen, put everything away. I'd make a plate to warm up for her later. Then she'd come around and she didn't understand when we had eaten. The last thing she remembered was helping me peel potatoes.

Interviewer: I understand Mark got Nora involved in athletics.

Rosaria: Mark had been a Navy SEAL. He was a runner and very athletic. He did Iron Man competition. He ran marathons. He would go out to run and take Nora with him. She would run beside him, and when her little legs got tired, he would put her on his back and run with her. He said it was good training for him. Then when he ran a race without Nora on his back, he felt lighter and faster.

But soon he didn't have to carry her. She ran with him the whole way. We put her in gymnastics class when she was seven. Mark taught her martial arts – he is black belt in Tae Kwon Do. He got Nora weights to lift when she was older. She ran a marathon when she was fifteen. She played in many sports in high school. All-State in track and field. When she was nineteen, she was on TV for the first time when she won that ninja show. She won for all of America and then traveled to Japan and was on TV again.

Interviewer: How did Nora meet Slade Bennington?

Rosaria: After *Ninja*, Nora decided she wanted to do stunts for the movies rather than go to college. She got a job at a studio and she would do the dangerous stunts for the famous actresses.

One movie, the director was Mr. Kleifisch. He really like her, and he ask if she wanted to be more than a stuntwoman, but to be an actress. He found out she won the ninja show, and he thought people would really like her. So he gave her a small part in the movie. She did stunts for the star, and she had a few lines as a different character. Then he gave her a bigger part in another movie. Then no more stunts for other people.

He was doing that science fiction movie of Bennington's book, and he ask Nora if she ready to be a star. She agreed, but only if she could do her own stunts.

Mr. Kleifisch told her she could do some stunts, but that insurance wouldn't let her do most of them because they would be paying her so much money as a star.

I was so proud of my baby.

Interviewer: Had the spells she'd had as a child gone away? Or did she still have those?

Rosaria: They had gotten better. She still had them, but less often and shorter. When she was little, it might be two or three times a week. By the time she was in high school, maybe only once every couple of months, and it might last only ten minutes instead of an hour.

Interviewer: Did you ever take her to a doctor for these spells?

Rosaria: Oh yes, yes, many doctors. Lots of tests. They did brain scans and MRIs and blood tests and spinal taps and I don't know what all. They thought she might be having seizures so they checked her for epilepsy and other things. They never could find anything. And in all those years, she never had a spell at the doctor or hospital so they could see.

Most doctors said they thought it was all in her head, psychological, not some physical thing in her brain. Some wanted to do counseling or medication. Others said that if she wasn't hurting herself or anyone else, they thought she might grow out of it and better to leave it alone.

So that's what we did. We made sure she was safe. And she started growing out of it at puberty. It didn't go away completely, but it was better.

Interviewer: Back to when she met Bennington?

Rosaria: Oh yes, yes. She was making this movie with Mr. Kleifisch, and Mr. Bennington was always there on the set. She would call me every day to tell me about her exciting day, meeting all these stars, being in a movie. She was on cloud nine every day. I've never heard her so excited and happy in all her life.

And she told me about Mr. Bennington. How he looked. That scared her and made her nervous at first. She told me he was nice to her but he made her nervous.

Then one day on set she had a spell. It was time for her to do a scene or something, but she was just sitting on the floor staring at the lights. She called me that night and told me that Mr. Bennington came up beside her in his chair and put his hand on her shoulder and sat next to her and whispered to her, and it calmed her down and she came out of her spell. He got her an orange juice and then she was fine and went back to doing her work.

She said he was amazing and made her feel so much better. She had a couple more spells, and he would talk to her quietly with his hand on her shoulder and she would get better within a couple of minutes.

She started talking to him more, and she told me she was no longer scared of him, that he was incredibly nice and smart and comforting. He asked her where she went during these spells and if she could remember what she was thinking about right before she went.

Then she stopped having spells at all. She said he had healed her, cured her, with his words. I asked her what he said, you know, so I could do the same. But she couldn't remember. He just talked to her during a spell, and she would come out of it and feel fine. She never had another spell after that. She turned twenty-one while making that first movie.

We were very happy about that, and happy that she had met Mr. Bennington, that he was able to do this for her. She spoke of him all the time. She would come home to visit and all she wanted to talk about was Mr. Bennington. After a while, it became irritating. But it made her happy and she wasn't having any more spells. She said she was going to some classes that he did on living life clear or something like that, and that was all she wanted to talk about.

Then she was meeting him in private sessions to talk more. This made me nervous, although everyone said what a nice person Mr. Bennington is.

Mark was more nervous about this than I was. The way she talked about him all the time and paying him money for these classes, a lot of money. He thought she was being taken advantage of.

If we tried to ask her about these things, she would become angry and refuse to talk to us. She wouldn't come visit for a few weeks and she wouldn't call me every day like normal. So we backed off. We were happy for her but still concerned.

Then she invited us up to her apartment in LA for a dinner to celebrate – they were making a second movie from the next book and her role was getting even bigger. Mr. Bennington had written a much bigger part for her character. We were all excited about that for her, but later, looking back, it seemed like he did that on purpose to make her depend on him more.

At dinner, it was Nora and me – Mark couldn't go because of a deployment – Mr. Kleifisch, a couple of other actors and other people. And Mr. Bennington and his wife. That was the first time we ever met.

I tell you, it was hard to eat dinner with this man across the table from me. He was very hard to look at. I'm not trying to be mean, but it will make you lose your appetite to see a person so scarred up.

But by the end of the evening, I had grown to like Mr. Bennington. My bad thoughts about him let up. He was very nice and treated Nora with great respect in front of me. Everyone there seemed to love him.

And his wife, Annie, she's the most beautiful woman I've ever seen, other than my Nora, of course. She was very polite but a bit standoff. Like she didn't really want to be there. She used to be an actress, you know, but she quit. She seemed like she didn't really like all these people much but put up with them because of her husband.

I don't understand how a beautiful woman like that would quit being a famous actress and marry a man that look like him.

Interviewer: Nora wasn't the only actor enthralled with Slade. He seemed to have this effect, or this type of relationship with lots of actors and celebrities. Did that make you feel better about it?

Rosaria: It made me feel better. I thought if all these older and experienced people were such close friends with Mr. Bennington, it must be fine. He must not be taking advantage of our little Nora. But that made Mark more suspicious. That became a bad point between Mark and Nora, and they had been so close since she was six years old. They got to the point they couldn't talk to each other at all, or even be in the same room, and that broke my heart for both of them. And it was all because of how obsessed she was with Mr. Bennington.

And by then, I thought it was Mark being too tough on her, too tough on Mr. Bennington. He'd never met Mr. Bennington, and I thought he was being unfair. That caused problems between me and Mark too. I couldn't choose between my husband and my daughter. I love them both and wanted them to get back to how they used to be. But any talk of Mr. Bennington, and Mark would become so upset he'd have to leave the room. He didn't trust him, but he couldn't say why.

Interviewer: Did you notice any other behavioral changes in her during this time? Mood changes? Anything concerning, in hindsight?

Rosaria: It was mostly positive at first. Other than the conflict with Mark and her obsession with Mr. Bennington and his classes. Her attitude was positive, excited about work, about life. She worked very hard. Constant. She was filming, or training, or rehearsing, or running marathons, or going to Bennington's classes.

She started writing during this time too. Journaling, she called it. Like a diary.

Interviewer: Do you have those?
Rosaria: Yes, yes. I have them all.

Interviewer: Would you be willing to share them with me?

INTERVIEW #21

**"The things that are most difficult to talk about are
the most important things to talk about."
~ Slade Bennington**

*Interviewer: You've never spoken publicly or to any interviewer about Nora
Campo. She said she wanted her legs removed so she could "see with clarity,"
or something like that. "Free my true self from the confines of my body" was
another statement she made.*

*She was also quite clear that her decision was due to your teachings in the
"Free Your Self" seminars, of which she was an avid follower. According to her
family, she attended seventeen of your group courses, six classes per course, at
a cost of $1,000 per class. Plus, more than a dozen one-on-one life-coaching
sessions for $10,000 each.*

*She paid you nearly a quarter of a million dollars to change her life, and
her life-changing decision was to amputate her legs to be like you.*

*Tell me about Nora and your relationship to her, and what you said to her
that made her choose to remove her legs.*

Slade: There are two important things to remember.

First, please remember that I had more than a thousand clients
during that time period. That included dozens, maybe more than a
hundred, repeat clients who attended multiple seminars and private
sessions. Most were actors, CEOs, politicians, doctors, attorneys,
professional athletes, and highly successful people from various
professions. I had six psychologists as clients. Three mega-church
pastors. The freakin' vice president of the United States.

Not one, not one other person besides Nora, took what I was saying
the way she interpreted it.

Interviewer: Did you ever try to talk her out of it?
Slade: Numerous times. I tried to call her. Flew to LA to try to
see her in person. Sent her emails and text messages. I spoke with her
parents, her manager. I mean, at first, when she announced what she

was going to do, I didn't think she was serious. I thought it was some publicity stunt, or she was being metaphorical. When her mother called me, I realized what was happening. She was really planning to do this.

Interviewer: What is the second important thing to remember?

Slade: Nora had severe mental health issues. I was trying to help her, and I tried repeatedly to get professional help for her that was beyond my capabilities. I try to give people good advice, but I'm not a doctor, not a psychiatrist. I have often, in my interactions with clients, recommended them to counseling. As I did with Nora. Over and over.

When filming began on *Volume III*, I called Randall, who was executive producer, and begged him to somehow force Nora into getting the help she needed. Told him he needed to have an intervention, tell her she wasn't going to be allowed to be in this film if she didn't get help. He promised he would try but that there was no way he could pull her off the project at this point. And he did try. She seemed to get better.

She made it through filming that movie, was seeing a counselor, even attending church with her mother. Then she abruptly told her manager she wasn't going to act anymore and sent out a press release about her planned surgery.

Interviewer: She always pointed to you as the inspiration, that it was your teachings that inspired her to do this. What did you say to her?

Slade: The same things I said over and over to thousands of people. To millions of people. It's all in my book. Learn to see life clearly. See yourself clearly. See others clearly. Eliminate the obstacles that prevent you from seeing clearly and being your true self, living your true life.

Interviewer: Let me read to you a few lines from the handout material at one of your seminars, which was adapted from your book.

***

When I had legs, I went wherever I wanted to go. I avoided places I didn't want to go. I went places I shouldn't. Skipped places where I should have been. I went, with my healthy legs, to unhealthy places and hung out with unhealthy people. My legs carried me to very selfish places.

I was constantly on the move, on the go, on the run. Running from myself. My true self. Running from God. Walking away from those who needed me. Walking away from those who loved me.

With my legs, I drove. I drove fast. I drove recklessly. I drove with abandon.

With my legs, I killed my beloved sister.

Once my legs were gone, I had to depend on others. On those who loved me unconditionally. I could go nowhere on my own, trapped in my body, strapped to a bed, unable to go to the bathroom alone or clean myself.

Without legs, my body was captive. And that freed my mind. I was able to think clearly for the first time without the distractions my legs provided.

***

Interviewer: *Do you think passages like this might be what drove Nora to her decision that ultimately took her life?*

Slade: Charles Manson got the idea to commit murder from Beatles' lyrics. Teenage boys committed suicide after listening to Black Sabbath songs. A young man walked into a church and killed twenty-seven worshippers because he'd seen another young man do the same thing on the news.

Are any of these logical, rational decisions made by healthy minds being unduly influenced by music or CNN?

No.

What I taught was, in context, clearly metaphorical and metaphysical. Not literal. Not to be taken literally and everyone knew it.

Interviewer: *Nora didn't.*

Slade: Everyone but Nora.

I also wrote and spoke about how losing one eye clarified my sight of the world and the people around me, allowed me to focus on love of others rather than my selfish desires. I've talked about how losing my face focused my attention on my inner self, my true self, rather than the shallow, temporal surface. If you're beautiful, how do you know if someone truly loves you or if they only love the way you look, or they lust after you, or they want a trophy wife or arm candy?

And you didn't hear about anyone cutting out their eyes or burning off their faces, did you? The thousands who attended my lectures, the millions who read my books. Not one eye gone missing.

In my course, I even quoted Jesus from the scriptures, who said the same thing I was saying: "If your eye offends you, then pluck it out. If your hand causes harm, cut it off and cast it into the fire."

Jesus was being symbolic here too. You didn't see any of his disciples going around lopping off their hands and gouging out their eyes. They knew what he meant. My clients knew what I meant.

Interviewer: What did you mean?
Slade: I meant to take a hard look at your life and find the obstacles that are getting in the way of your contentment, interfering with your ability to love others, to love yourself, and get rid of those obstacles. It might be things like pride, selfishness, insecurity, material wealth, status, fame, whatever. It might be a toxic relationship or a job or debt. It might be drugs or drinking or shopping or pornography. It's anything that prevents you from seeing outside yourself to truly see others, and to see inside yourself at the real you.

Interviewer: You stopped teaching your courses after Nora died. Why?
Slade: I immediately canceled all scheduled courses. Told everyone it was temporary, that I needed time to process Nora's death. I said I'd reschedule courses in the near future, but I needed some time off.

I kept putting it off after that. The time wasn't right. The time will never be right. It's been almost ten years now. There will be no more courses.

Interviewer: That hasn't stopped others from following in your footsteps. Um, sorry.
Slade: It's a cliché. No worries.

And yes, there are groups out there and self-appointed leaders who teach the principles outlined in my books. I can't stop them. I've made it clear to everyone who asks that I have nothing to do with them, I do not support them or condone their actions, they aren't doing it with my permission, and I certainly do not receive a penny from it.

Interviewer: Other than the ongoing book sales these courses generate for you.
Slade: All of which is donated to charities. We live very modestly. Have small trust funds, and I do mean small, set up for each of the kids.

Everything else either of us has ever earned is donated to the philanthropic foundation. Annie handles that, along with a board of directors and a team of accountants who publish public financial records every year.

Interviewer: There's nearly a billion dollars in that foundation now.

Slade: And more than $100 million a year is donated to various causes – all charitable, civic, and educational. None political. Never give a dime to any politician.

Interviewer: Why not?

Slade: It just encourages them. Politicians are the one class of criminals that makes me reconsider my stance on the death penalty.

Interviewer: Have you spoken with Nora's parents since her death?

Slade: Immediately after, yes, by phone. I spoke with Nora's mother, Rosaria. What a sweet woman. I wanted to console her, to grieve with her, but she consoled me more, I think. Mark couldn't even come to the phone. I think he was too broken up over it.

Then the lawyers got to them, and my lawyers prohibited me from talking to them. That's a big problem with lawyers. They don't want people to work things out, to forgive each other, to get over holding any animosities. There's no money in that. My lawyer said that if I called them up and said, "I'm sorry for your loss," their lawyer could take that as an admission of guilt of something.

Interviewer: If you could talk to Nora one more time, is there anything you'd like to say to her now?

Slade: I talk to her every day. We have forgiven each other.

NORA'S JOURNAL

"And if thy right hand offend thee, cut it off, and cast it from thee, for it is profitable for thee that one of thy members should perish, and not that thy whole body should be cast into hell."
~ Jesus Christ

Ten years earlier
Nora Campo's journal – selected excerpts

Day 1: *Day one on the set for V-3 today and I thought this would be a good time to start my journal like Slade recommended. So excited to start filming finally. Preproduction takes forever and isn't much fun, mostly meetings. Fortunately, I'm not needed at most of them. Even more excited to see Slade again. Hoping he will be there. I need to talk to him. I need to hear his voice and his words again. Life is the bomb!*

Day 6: *It's so different without Randall directing. He moved up to exec producer and hired this other guy to direct. He's done some famous movies so I guess he's good, but I don't like him as much. I don't dislike him. I'm comfortable with Randall. He took me under his wing. Ken just barks orders and doesn't look at me much. It's harder without Slade here. I thought he was going to be here. He's always been here for our other films. It's different without Slade and Randall. It's not bad. It just feels like a job now.*

Day 29: *Did a video chat with Slade today. He's not able to be here right now due to some other project, but he said he would be out in a few weeks. I really needed to hear his voice. I've been struggling with so many things. He's able to guide me through the process of dealing with all this crap. Brett keeps coming onto me even though I've made it clear I'm not interested. Alyssa really doesn't like me. Very condescending. I think she doesn't believe*

I'm a real actor and I don't belong here. Ken rolls his eyes and mutters under his breath, like he can't stand me. I'm doing a terrible job, I know. Randall knew how to get the best out of me. Ken expects me to know how to do it and expects me to know what he's thinking. I'm not measuring up. I'm in over my head. I was ready to blow up at Ken today but I held my tongue. I don't know what he wants from me. Slade was able to talk me through it. I'll be much more confident tomorrow, and Slade said I should ask Ken to have a ten-minute sit-down and tell him how I'm feeling and ask him what he wants me to do different. I'll see if I have the nerve to do that. He's not very approachable. I might have to talk to Slade one more time before I can do that.

Day 47: Ken screamed and cursed at me on the set today in front of everyone. I wanted to die or hide in the corner or go home to see my mom and curl up in her lap and cry. I tried to reach Slade but he wasn't available. I talked to Mom and she said to go ahead and cry, then go back tomorrow refreshed, but not to let anyone talk down to me. Stand up to him. But if I was Ken, I would have cussed me out today too. I couldn't get anything right. I don't think I'm cut out for this. I hate to let Randall and Slade down, but I don't think I want to do this anymore.

Day 63: So excited! What a great day! No time, will write more tomorrow. Off to dinner with Ken and Randall to talk about the next project and we haven't even finished this one.

Day 64: Ken is phenomenal. Took me a while to get used to him, or maybe him to me, but it's clear he's an even better director than Randall. Randall said the secret to success is to always hire people better than you, to surround yourself with people smarter than you. Can't wait to talk to Slade again.

Day 71: Slade showed up on set today for the first time. He only stayed a little while, but he talked to me privately for about 15 minutes. Helping me keep my head straight dealing with Ken. I can't stand that ass. Slade says rise above. Be a pro. So I will.

Day 88: Found out today that photography is being extended a week and we'll be reshooting some scenes because Ken didn't like the way they came out.

Day 89: *Not just reshooting scenes. New scenes too. New scenes that were written this week. This is going to take forever and I want to be done.*

Day 104: *I can't believe it. I really can't believe I did this. Why? Why would I do that? I wasn't even drunk. Well, not that drunk. Why did I ever let that greasy, fat, hairy asshole talk me into sleeping with him? And he's the director. Jesus. When I first started working in H'wood, I always swore I'd never be that person. I'd never be taken advantage of like that. I'd never use sex to move up or make the right connections. If Harvey Weinstein had cornered me in a hotel room, I'd have removed one of his eyes. Dad taught me how. So why? I just gave in. He's been flirting for weeks, then yells at me all day, then wants to buy me dinner and drinks and talk about tomorrow's scenes and he's a completely different person. Nice, I thought. Nothing but professional until it wasn't. And I did what? Went along. Don't make waves. He can help or kill my career. I don't even care. How do I tell Slade? He's going to be so disappointed in me.*

Day 127: *It's a wrap, finally. Wrap party tomorrow night. Should I even go? I guess I have to.*

Day 128: *Slept with Ken again. I need a shower. Maybe two. Why? Sometimes it's just easier to say okay.*

Day 151: *Finally found the nerve to tell Slade that I've been seeing Ken. He treats me well – doesn't yell at me like he did on the set. He's actually very nice, very smart. Well respected – everyone likes him. Except me, apparently. So why am I dating him? Slade said he must be fulfilling some need, and he didn't mean sex. Some void, some space, some emotion of mine that being with Ken serves. I need to find out what that is and then I can deal with it. Fix that broken part from the inside out, from my mind, instead of using Ken as duct tape to hold it together. Slade is flying out next week and we'll have a few sessions to see if we can figure out what's wrong with me. Or maybe we could find something about me that's right. I doubt it though.*

Day 155: *Met with Slade twice today. 8 a.m. and 3 p.m. I invited him to have dinner with me and Ken so Slade could see us* *interacting. Ken doesn't know why I'm meeting with Slade. He probably wouldn't like it if he knew I was trying to find out how to dump him.*

__Day 156:__ Dinner was interesting. Things are starting to get clearer.

__Day 157:__ Met with Slade twice more today. He's flying back to Texas in the morning. I need some sleep. Maybe a week's worth. Crawl into fluffy pajamas and set the alarm for next Tuesday.

__Day 160:__ Ken called and broke up with me. I'm really mad that he dumped me while I was trying to figure out how to let him down gently. But shouldn't I be relieved? Why did I scream at him? Why am I crying? Can't reach Slade. Need to call Mom.

__Day 208:__ I've learned so much the past couple of months. I have always relied on the physical – running, gymnastics, sports, weight training. Ninja. Stunts. Action films. I've never let my emotional self take the lead. The physical me is in the way of my spiritual growth. Thank you, Slade! You saved my life. You are giving me my real life maybe for the first time.

INTERVIEW #22

"Saying nothing sometimes says the most."
~ Emily Dickinson

Interviewer: Is this Mark Devlin?
Mark: Yes, who's calling?

Interviewer: Robb Grindstaff here. I'm working on a book about Slade Bennington and —
Mark: I have nothing to say. Nothing fit to print.

Interviewer: If I could just ask you —
[click]

> **Author's note:** *Over a period of six months, I also left two voicemails for Mr. Devlin, Nora Campo's stepfather, and sent three emails and one registered letter. He never responded to any of my requests for an interview.*
> *I asked Rosaria Ocampo-Devlin if she could speak to Mr. Devlin about agreeing to be interviewed, and she informed me that they were in the process of getting a divorce. Rosaria was moving back to the Philippines to be with her elderly mother in the village outside of Pili.*

INTERVIEW #23

"I think it's going to be a blockbuster."
~ Randall Kleifisch

Interviewer: Tell me about Nora Campo.

Randall: What a tragic, tragic story. Such a shame. Such a waste. Beautiful girl, extremely talented. Very headstrong. Insisted on doing her own stunts. We'd let her do a few, but nothing dangerous. Extraordinary athletic prowess. But a very troubled young lady.

We tried – I tried – to get her the help she needed. I'd seen flashes of her emotional or mental health issues during previous filming, but on *Volume III*, she seemed strung out. I even required her to get a drug test at one point, which she became almost violently angry about. But she took it and passed. I required her to see a counselor, with a report from the counselor direct to me on her fitness to continue filming.

Once she saw how serious I was about this, she relaxed a bit. She went to the counselor. She moved her mother to LA into her apartment, so she had some family support. Things were very strained between Nora and her father by that point. Everything settled down. Nora's mood and behavior improved.

Interviewer: Behavior? Can you be more specific?

Randall: Early on in filming *Volume III*, Nora was on edge all the time. Anyone said anything to her, she would snap at them. Sometimes a curse-filled stream of venting at the whole crew. Throwing things. Smashing things. Or sitting in the corner crying, holding herself and rocking back and forth.

Ken Riegel was directing, and he called me several times saying she was impossible to work with. So I'd go down to the studio and meet with Nora. Or meet with Ken. Or both of them together.

Slade had called me beforehand to give me a heads-up. I knew Nora had been seeing Slade for his guidance, but he told me this was beyond his depth – she needed professional medical attention. He was "just some guy with a few ideas about life" is how he put it. But I called Slade a couple of times to get his advice and to keep him informed.

As soon as he could, he flew to LA to meet with her on set. That seemed to help. I don't remember the sequence of events exactly - it's been a few years - but that might have been when she started taking her situation seriously, started seeing the counselor, moved her mom in. And the rest of the filming went off without any major issues. We were even discussing preproduction for *Volume IV*.

Interviewer: And what did you think of Nora and Ken's relationship?

Randall: I try to stay out of my cast and crew's personal lives. But I did call Ken up one day and asked if he thought this was a good idea. I mean, one day he's calling me to complain that she's out of control. A couple months later, they're dating. And he's the director. She's a star - not the lead, of course - but a major character with a tremendous following from the first two films, and we planned to make her the star in *Volume IV*.

Interviewer: What did Ken say?

Randall: He said it was nothing serious and nothing to worry about. Just a casual fling that wouldn't last and wouldn't interfere with production. I gave him a stern warning that it better not, and it didn't. At least not with *Volume III*. Nora kind of threw a wrench into *Volume IV* though.

Interviewer: How so?

Randall: *Volume III* had been written as the end of the trilogy, and the lead character dies. *Volume IV* was developed after that with the whole idea that Adele - Nora's character - takes the new lead role in the sequel to the trilogy. We had to completely start from scratch to find a new actress for a character that Slade developed specifically for Nora.

That, of course, was a minor, insignificant thing compared to the personal tragedy and grief her parents, all of us, had to deal with.

Interviewer: When and how did you learn about Nora's plan to have her legs amputated?

Randall: Same as when the whole world learned, when she fired her publicist and sent out a press release on her own. It was all over the news, the internet, everywhere within minutes. I thought it was a hoax. I first saw it on Twitter. I thought someone had hacked her account, that this was someone's cruel idea of a joke. But then there was a link to the news stories. She'd confirmed it with a reporter from *People* magazine.

Interviewer: What did you do?

Randall: I called her immediately. I didn't even text her first. Left her a voice mail. I left her a voice mail and a text message every hour for the first couple of days, I think. I don't know if she was avoiding me or if she had so many calls and texts, she couldn't get to them all.

I called Slade. I called her mother, Rosie, I think it was. The dear woman was beside herself. I asked where Nora was and said I would come see her right now. She didn't know where she was. She had disappeared two days before she sent out the press release. No one had heard from her other than the one call she made to *People*. Slade chartered a plane to get to LA that day.

I called the police. Told them it was a mental health emergency. We didn't know where she was or what she was going to do, but she was in a state to do serious self-harm. The police, being the police, didn't seem that interested, so I called the police chief. He's an acquaintance – and he got the ball rolling. I also called a private detective I'd worked with as a technical adviser on some films, and he immediately began tracking her down.

A few days later, he discovered she'd already flown to Manila.

He contacted our embassy there. They were virtually no help whatsoever. Extremely disappointing.

Slade paid for a round-trip airline ticket to fly Nora's parents to the Philippines that very day. But it was already done.

We received word of Nora's death before we could get her parents to the airport. We were all too late. Such a heartbreaking situation. I've cried myself to sleep over Nora many times, and the fact that I couldn't help her. I didn't do enough. I should have done more.

And what kind of doctor would do that for any amount of money?

Interviewer: What's your take on the claims that Slade uses some sort of mind control or brainwashing techniques on people?

Randall: I think that's highly overblown. Yes, I know there are people who are quite dedicated to Slade and hang on his every word. He's charismatic. He has a way of drawing you in, and drawing things out of you – emotions, feelings, thoughts. He's a very empathetic person. He can sense what you are feeling, feel it himself, if you will, so he can relate well to everyone on their own level, about whatever issue they are dealing with.

Interviewer: Some blame him for Nora's death. Others wonder why Schuyler would leave acting to marry someone in Slade's situation or condition. They believe, or at least express a concern, that he was able to somehow manipulate them into these decisions, that perhaps they were impressionable or vulnerable and he took advantage to plant ideas in their minds.

Randall: Let's start with Schuyler. Anyone who has ever met Schuyler for more than five minutes, if that long, would realize that impressionable and vulnerable are not adjectives anyone would use to describe her. I can't even fathom anyone being able to manipulate or control her choices in life. Quite the opposite, in fact. Schuyler has a way of coming up with an idea and then making you think it was your idea. I've been on the receiving end of that bit more than once. She's very good at it, and that talent has served her well.

Nora is a different story altogether. Very troubled, looking for something to latch onto. She found it in Slade, but her mind took it to other places. There was certainly no motive for Slade to try to convince Nora to cut her legs off. That makes no sense at all.

I spent many, many hours side-by-side with Slade, alone and with other people. He's very compassionate but still an objective, rational person. He truly cares about people.

Interviewer: He does have a way with people. He also has a way to get people to part with rather large sums of money to take his courses or get counseling sessions with him.

Randall: His services never came cheap. Virtually everyone I've ever spoken with about it said it changed their lives – for the better – and that his work was worth every penny. And if anyone didn't think so, they never had to spend more money or time with him. So many people would take his courses and sessions repeatedly. And there was no secrecy about it – not like some cult where you can't discuss it or you have to abandon your family and friends. People talked about it all openly. This wasn't *Fight Club*.

Interviewer: What's next for you?

Randall: I'm working on a docu-drama about Nora's life.

We've signed Siena Lopez to play Nora, which closes the perfect circle. Siena played Adele – Nora's role – in *Volume IV* after Nora died. In this, Siena will play Nora, and she will play Nora playing Adele. She's absolutely brilliant.

I think it's going to be a blockbuster.

INTERVIEW #24

**"His voice would appear in my head, and I'd
sign up for another $10,000 session."
~ Anonymous**

Interviewer: What's your opinion or experience with the allegations that Slade uses some sort of mind-control or brainwashing techniques?

Shelby (studio executive): Lots of people – me included, obviously – are always looking for something, some answers, some sort of secret to life. That makes people very susceptible to latching onto someone like Slade or anyone who has some apparent answers. Slade was very good at playing that role and very good at monetizing it. And many of us, thousands of us, willingly threw our money at him like he was a Chippendale dancer. Oh, bad analogy, I guess. He took advantage of people who willingly let themselves be taken advantage of. Not sure I can put all that blame on him.

But how else can you explain Schuyler Jones marrying him? Or that Campo woman saying he told her to have her legs amputated? That was really freaky. Glad I got out of that cult before he convinced me to do something like that.

Danielle (psychologist): I've thought about this for many years. He definitely knows how to play to a crowd, and he knows how to manipulate you on an individual basis. I don't know if I'd describe it as mind control, but he is very casually manipulative. He knows how to get you to open up and talk. That's a good thing, a critical thing in my profession. Without any professional training, he's one of the best at this I've ever come across. Maybe it's something physical – his physical appearance – that draws this out of you. He's rather shocking to look at when you first meet, but the longer you're around him, that all fades away. He has a way of looking at you, asking you a question, then waiting for you to answer, like listening to you and hearing what you have to say is the single most important thing in the world.

Then, when it's time to sign up for the next course or session, he's very good at a soft-sell approach. He is never hard sell, pressure tactics, or anything like that. It's all very subtle. "You have made such amazing progress. I believe you are so close to a life-changing breakthrough. Do you think you can take it from here on your own? Or do you think one more session might be what the doctor ordered?"

He never countered price objections or negotiated. "Oh, I completely understand. It is expensive, and I know people have limited funds and other obligations. It's totally up to you if you think you can afford it and if you think it's worth it or not."

I'd go home and lie in bed, unable to sleep, worried about finances and spending that kind of money, but then his voice would just appear in my head and make all the right arguments on why I needed to sign up for another $10,000 session.

The next morning, I'd call and set another appointment, then worry myself half to death for the next month about whether I should cancel and not waste the money. It is perhaps the closest thing to an addiction that I've ever known personally. I could suddenly relate to my clients who are addicted to opioids or gambling or sex. You know it's harmful, wasting money, but you need just one more hit. Dopamine is powerful stuff.

Frank (airline pilot): He completely took control of Amy's mind and life. Rational thought, which was never Amy's strong suit, flew out the window when it came to all things Bennington. All she wanted to talk about in the last year of our marriage was Bennington said this, Bennington said that. She would throw these quotes of his at me like that would win an argument, as if I'd say, "Oh well, if Bennington said it, it must be true. I repent for being a heathen and will do as he commands."

By the time we divorced, she was completely wrapped up in him and his classes. To the detriment of taking care of the kids, getting a job, saving any money, paying her bills.

I eventually went back to court and got full custody of the kids and got the alimony reduced. The judge agreed that she had abdicated all parental duties and financial responsibilities. She was angrier that she wouldn't have any more money to spend on his classes than over losing custody.

I don't understand the pull, the attraction. I attended that one speech he gave. I read some of his book, trying to see what Amy was seeing. It never connected with me. Maybe there's a certain flaw in the minds of some people, like Amy, that he takes advantage of, gets inside their heads. Once there, it was clear that he was in total control. He creates an obsession in some people.

I don't understand it and never will.

Vicki (motivational speaker): Absolutely. After my experiences with him, I studied this, how it works. How someone can get inside someone else's head and manipulate them. Brainwashing and mind-control techniques that actually work.

It was eye-opening and quite scary. Most of the articles I read on the topic sounded like they were written about – or by – Slade Bennington. From his books, which tell you most of the problems in your life are your fault, to the seminars where all newcomers are welcomed and made to feel loved, which makes you want to please everyone there by being fully devoted to Slade, to the one-on-one sessions where he keeps probing your mind and your emotions until he finds just the right buttons to push.

And then he presses those buttons to get you to do whatever he wants. Write him another check. Spend your own money to go start another book club. Stop doing the work that you'd made a good living from. Abandon your own life plans. Cut your damn legs off.

And when he's done with you, you're tossed aside for someone younger and prettier and richer. I guess after he married that rich bitch, he didn't need my money anymore.

Interviewer: What advice would you give if someone close to you expressed an interest in diving into Slade Bennington's program?

Shelby: To each their own, I say. If someone asked my opinion, I'd give it. Not really worth the kind of money he charges, and I'm not sure it really works for everyone. Maybe it does for some. But set a budget for how much you're willing to spend and stick to it. Be ready to walk away. Don't get sucked in. And don't go cutting your legs off.

Danielle: I'd give a very blunt assessment, largely but not wholly negative, and give plenty of warning. But if someone was insistent, I'd advise them to always keep a certain skeptical distance.

Skepticism, however, is difficult to maintain when face-to-face with Slade Bennington.

Vicki: Don't be a fool like I was. If someone you care about has gotten involved with this charlatan, you need to schedule an intervention. Same as if they were hooked on drugs. I managed to get out alive. Not everyone has been so lucky.

Frank: My advice would be to run as fast as you can, with your hand firmly on your wallet, while you still have legs to run on.

INTERVIEW #25

"Slade can give a speech now and people don't burn the place down or start shooting, so that's an improvement."
~ Chelsea Mandrake

Interviewer: What's your take on the people who claim Slade is manipulative or uses some kind of mind control over people?

Chelsea: They're fucking idiots, that's my take.

Interviewer: And people like Nora?

Chelsea: Look, there are seriously disturbed people out there. You can't blame someone for having a mental illness. But you can't blame Slade for her illness either. I mean, where were her parents? Her manager, her agent? All the people surrounding her that should have been watching out, caring for her, protecting her? They were all too busy making a lot of money off her. Slade kept trying to help her and kept trying to get others to help her. But he didn't live in the same state. He didn't live in her house. Where were the people who saw her every day?

I'm not blaming them either. I'm saying that to blame Slade makes no sense when there were other people much closer to the situation and they couldn't stop her either.

And I need to correct something I said earlier. Slade was really upset over the Forum situation, but when Nora died, that was the worst I've ever seen him. He pretty much locked himself away and refused to see or talk to anyone for a month. We were all really worried about him. Annie protected him, wouldn't let any of us near. Not even Matt. Not until Slade said he was ready to see people again. And not until Annie agreed that he was ready.

Interviewer: How did that affect him?

Chelsea: He came out of it stronger than ever before. But he was changed in ways I can't quite put a finger on. I'm not sure he's ever gotten over it.

Interviewer: Do you still do any work for Slade?

Chelsea: No, now we're just family. Slade's business got to be more than I could handle at the time, and we didn't want business to interfere with our family relationship, so we agreed that he'd hire a professional company to handle all his travel and arrangements for his courses after the Forum. Then he shut most of that down after Nora. I started my own company doing the same thing, but on a much smaller scale.

Things have returned to some semblance of normal. It's been a few years. He can give a speech now and people don't burn the place down or start shooting, so that's an improvement.

INTERVIEW #26

**"Death threats don't bother me none. Been there, done that.
Got the T-shirt. It ain't so bad."
~ Slade Bennington**

Interviewer: You've had your share of death threats over the years. How have you handled those?

Slade: Well, most of the time, you can safely ignore them. Especially on social media. Everybody wants to kill everyone there. It's the Shootout at the Not-OK Corral. Downright cancerous.

There have been two instances that were deemed serious enough to pay attention to.

First – and this had to be more than twenty years ago – a woman kept stalking me. Coming to my house all hours of the night. Said she needed to talk to me. Told her to call and make an appointment at the office, I don't do drop-ins at my house. By the third or fourth time she showed up at three a.m., Matt chased her off with his trusty Mossberg. It was never loaded, but it got rid of paparazzi and crazies pretty quick.

She started calling after that, all hours, day and night. Emailing long diatribes that made no sense. Seemed mentally ill, but not dangerous in any way. But I had to refuse her request for an appointment, and eventually I blocked her email and her phone number. But she'd get a new email address and a new phone number and start up again.

Then, when I kept ignoring her and blocking her, her emails got more and more agitated, angry. Angry at me for refusing to help her, but she needed some serious meds, ya know. Not a little chat to try to get life priorities straight.

We contacted the police, but she hadn't done anything illegal or threatening.

And then she did. It started with emails saying that if I wouldn't meet with her, she'd kill herself. Then she'd kill me first. That's when the police finally got involved. They picked her up and she was in and out of a mental health facility in forty-eight hours. Then she left a note on my front door, written in her own blood, apparently, telling me I was going to die. Down to the specific date and time of my death.

Police picked her up again. This went on for about a year. I got a restraining order, but ya know, if you're schizophrenic and think a guy with no legs is chasing you, a piece of paper from a judge doesn't suddenly make you go, "Oh, wow, what was I thinking?"

They finally got her committed to a facility indefinitely as a danger to herself and others, and I never heard from her again. I hope she got the help she needed and that she's doing well.

Interviewer: What was that like, having someone coming to your house, threatening to kill you?

Slade: I never took it that serious. I was more concerned she would hurt herself. I didn't really see her as capable of actually committing violence, just these violent words that bounced around in her head that she couldn't control.

Matt, on the other hand, seemed pretty set on blowin' her head off if she ever banged on our door in the middle of the night again. He started keeping that shotgun loaded until I made him stop.

Interviewer: Do you remember her name? Maybe I could track her down and find out how she's doing?

Slade: No, man. No need in picking at a scab.

INTERVIEW #27

"When the FBI is scratching their collective heads and getting nervous, that tends to put you a little on edge."
~ Slade Bennington

Interviewer: What about the second death threat?

Slade: This one was a little more pernicious. Is pernicious the right word? I should have my editor here.

Maybe it was because I'm married and have kids, so I'm protective of them. When you're young and single, you tend to think of yourself as immortal. That won't happen to me, sort of thinking. Especially since I'd already died once. What else could happen to me?

Interviewer: When did this threat happen? What was different about it?

Slade: About three years ago, I think. Yes, Mandy was three years old.

It's different when you've got responsibilities – people you love and you're responsible for their safety. It hits you a little different. Someone kills me, that doesn't bother me. Hurt my family and there will be hell to pay. And even if someone kills me, well, that's taking a father away from my girls, so that's hurting them. That would make me angrier than me dying again.

And this time, we didn't know who it was. The first one, she emailed me, gave her name, showed up at my house. We could take some preventive actions.

This one – anonymous notes left on Annie's car in the grocery store parking lot. Same note left on her rental car in the faculty parking lot at Harvard – in Cambridge, Massachusetts, for crying out loud. Letters in the mail with no return address. Cops got the notes and letters – no fingerprints. That really set off the alarm bells. Someone was being careful to not be tracked down or identified. Someone rational. Smart. Smart is much scarier than crazy.

Next was an envelope addressed to "Your father" that was pinned to Jo's backpack while she was at dance class. Her backpack was in her locker – with a combination lock. Fortunately, she didn't open the letter. Just brought it home to me. Thought it was from the instructor, maybe the monthly invoice was due.

It was another threat from this same person.

That's when we contacted the FBI. They worked with the dance studio. There were security cameras at the entrance. The cameras had malfunctioned for about fifteen minutes that day – inexplicably and during the time Jo was in class – so there was no video of who might have broken into her locker. There was no forced entry – someone knew her combination. No one remembers seeing anyone or anything suspicious. This is a small dance studio, not some huge complex where someone could slip in and out unnoticed.

Then we got phone calls at night telling me I was going to die for what I did. Voice was computer-generated. Phone number was spoofed. FBI was recording and tracing and couldn't get anything. Calls appeared to come from different states and even other countries. Caller would start by saying, "Good evening to the Bennington family and the Federal Bureau of Investigation." He – or she, I suppose – was toying with them.

Interviewer: What did they say you did that you needed to die for?

Slade: Never did say, so I couldn't even apologize.

When the FB of I is scratching their collective heads and getting nervous, that tends to put you a little on edge.

We already had pretty good security at our place here. I mean, we've got thirty acres out in the country and we're pretty self-sufficient when it comes to personal defense. But we hired a security company, installed some round-the-clock perimeter defense, a gate guard at the end of the drive. Had security go with Annie and the girls anywhere they went – dance, music lessons, grocery shopping, church, whatever.

Interviewer: How did the girls take it?

Slade: Jo and Evvy were none too happy about the restrictions, of course. They listened to me and understood it was serious, but I didn't want to frighten them either. Just taking extra precautions for a short time to be safe, but there is never anything to fear. They were ten and twelve years old.

Mandy was only three, so we didn't really talk to her about it. She was never out of our sight anyway. That was about the time her night terrors started. She must have picked up on the tension.

Interviewer: What was Annie's reaction to all of this?

Slade: Like everything. Annie always takes things in stride. She'd had some experience with this type of thing when she was a kid, so she was able to talk to the girls about it very calmly. "Here's what I went through, here's how I handled it, it all worked out fine, just give it a little time." That sort of thing. I think Jo and Evvy handled it better because they knew their mom had gone through the same thing when she was about their age. Sort of a mother-daughter bonding thing. "I had death threats at your age too." How many moms can have that talk with their girls?

Interviewer: Was she worried?

Slade: No, not really. Cautious. We were all cautious. But not worried. I assumed it was some nut job who was really good with high tech stuff and liked trying to frighten people. Or thinking he might get some money to go away.

Interviewer: Did they ever catch him? Or her?

Slade: No, no idea who it was. It just stopped.

When that happens, there are several possibilities, according to the agent-in-charge. The guy could have died. Maybe committed suicide. He might be in jail for something unrelated. Or a mental institution. Or maybe he started taking his meds again. Or his mother pulled the plug on his internet connection in the basement. Mainly, he wasn't getting the response or attention he wanted, the FBI got involved, and he decided the game wasn't worth it anymore.

Interviewer: How long did this go on before it stopped?

Slade: We got letters and phone calls for about four months. Sometimes every day, sometimes a week would go by without hearing from him.

Then it was two weeks. Then three. After a couple of months with no contact, and no leads, the FBI began to think it had subsided or possibly ended. They kept in contact. We had a device on our phone to record and track any calls, although they'd never had any success tracing any of them. We were to call them if we received any letters or notes. Local sheriff increased patrols in our area, which meant they drove by every four or five hours instead of not at all.

But nothing ever came again. Gradually life went back to normal, although we've implemented some additional security measures that are permanent.

Interviewer: Such as?

Slade: Oh, I won't talk about that. But don't show up here unannounced, I'll tell ya that much.

INTERVIEW #28

**"Slade could put out a Sudanese cookbook and it
would be a number one bestseller."
~ Liv Farraday, literary agent**

Interviewer: What's it like being Slade Bennington's literary agent?

Liv: Besides frustrating? It was extremely rewarding. And frustrating. Did I mention frustrating?

Interviewer: Was?

Liv: Yes, I'm not his agent anymore. Still handled by my agency, but when he started writing science fiction, I handed him off to our sci-fi/fantasy specialist, Paul Dobbs. Paul retired a few years later, and now Alanna Rossi reps him, although apparently he's not sure he wants to write any more books now, which is very frustrating.

Interviewer: We'll come back to the frustrating part. How did you first meet Slade?

Liv: Another agent in our firm at the time had a client. She had a fantasy series he was representing but never was able to land a contract for. Dragons and swords were big that year, and every publisher was inundated with dragon stories. She was an exceptional writer, it was just bad timing.

Interviewer: This was Chelsea Mandrake?

Liv: Yes, that's the one. Chelsea contacted her agent to recommend this book she was helping edit, said she thought we should take a look. Based on her recommendation, the agent looked it over, and he was impressed enough to forward it to me since I handled all our nonfiction authors at the time.

I read it in one night and offered him representation the next morning. The rest is history.

Interviewer: You knew it was something special then.

Liv: Special. Powerful. Heart-wrenching. Tragedy and loss. Survival against all odds. Redemption and a new purpose in life. Everything you could ask for. The writing wasn't the best and it needed work, even though Chelsea had already helped him revise it some. But it was this magnificent story, and Slade had this incredible voice. You can't teach a writer voice. They either have it or they don't. If they have it, editors can fix the rest.

That actually leads right to the first bout of frustration I had with Slade. I hired an editor to revise the book for him, to get it into good enough shape that I could sell it. Then I put feelers out with about half a dozen of the top publishers. Had four of them immediately interested just from a synopsis and a sample. That turned into an auction within days – that rare situation where more than one publisher wants the book and they start bidding for it. That almost never happens, but this was the perfect storm.

So we sign the contract. Slade got an unheard-of advance for an unknown person, not a celebrity at the time, and for a first book. Not like an advance for a famous celebrity writing tell-all memoirs, but pretty darn good.

The publisher assigned an editor who worked with Slade for a couple of months to make more changes. Then, when that was all done, Slade calls me one day and says he doesn't like the new version after all the changes were made and wants to go back to the previous version. I told him you can't do that. He said cancel the deal then. I said you'll have to send back the advance, including my commission, and the publisher could sue him for breach of contract.

At first, he said fine, cancel it and he'd write a check. But I guess he had twenty-four hours to think about it, and probably already spent the advance, so he backed off. He wanted to make a few more changes and tweaks. The publisher agreed if he could get it done in two weeks. He got it done in one.

His editor at the publishing house called me and said the changes made it even better, but don't tell Slade that or he'd want to make more changes. We were beginning to learn how to deal with him.

Interviewer: When did the book take off?

Liv: With some good promotion and marketing, and a book tour set up for Slade, it did well right out of the gate. Nothing earth-shattering, but we got him on some local TV shows. His physical appearance seemed to draw attention to the book. Then we got him on some national morning talk shows, and it started growing even more.

His royalties more than paid back his advance in the first year and it continued to sell for a while longer, so he did great. Hit the top ten lists for a few weeks. Got a lot of favorable reviews. The *New York Times* called it "moving, touching, funny and heartbreaking." Which pretty much sums up Slade all the way around. Except they forgot "frustrating."

Interviewer: How did it go from that to the mass hysteria of a few years later?

Liv: Some movie producer read the book. Passed it on to his studio people. They read it. Passed it on to their acquisitions people. They decide they want the film rights. After Slade hung up on them a few times, they were able to track me down.

We negotiated the film rights, and then it took a while – it always does – but Paramount starts production. Movie was scheduled for release in two years. I call Slade and tell him he needs to write a second book. We'll time the release with the movie. They've got big names directing and starring. This was no B-movie. This was the big time.

Slade says no, he's not writing another book. He said he wrote his life story and nothing else has happened yet. I tried pitching him ideas on how to write a sequel, a follow-up, what's happened since. He said he didn't have anything to write about.

I called Chelsea to see if she could prod him, give him ideas, anything. She said he was writing every day. Had computer files and notebooks stacked up on the end table. I may have even encouraged her to steal his files and send them to me. Okay, I wasn't serious, but he needed to get on the stick.

Interviewer: Strike while the iron is hot.

Liv: Absolutely. In our business, you can't let windows of opportunity like this pass you by.

Chelsea talks to him and lets me know he is chewing on how to turn his ideas and ramblings into a book. Just like the first time. So that was great. With absolutely nothing in hand, not even a synopsis or a sample, the publisher agrees to take it and offers a million-dollar advance if he delivers a publishable book on time. But no pressure!

Interviewer: How did Slade take that?

Liv: He didn't. Said he was writing, it might turn into something, it might not, but he wasn't signing any contract, not even for a million dollars, that would put him under "undue pressure to be creative" if he didn't feel like it. I finally got him to sign a letter of intent and first right of refusal to keep the publisher on the line.

Have I mentioned how frustrating Slade can be?

The publisher was basically like, "We don't care what it is, we'll be able to sell it. Get us a pile of shit and we'll all make a lot of money."

Interviewer: And when you got it?

Liv: It was a pile of shit. I called him. I flew him to New York to meet. This wasn't even a book. It was a "when life hands you lemons" collection of thoughts. Chicken Soup for Amputees. I told him I needed a story, not a rambling feel-good manifesto.

He said this was what he wanted. But there was no story. No one would buy this junk.

I reworked it. Sent it back to Slade and Chelsea to rework some more, begging them to add some storyline to it that would at least tie it all together. Once they'd done that, I sent it to the publisher, and they kept their end of the bargain. Their editor revised it some more, working with Slade for several months.

Then Slade says no, he's not happy with it. He's going to completely rewrite it. There was no time. It was still a pile of crap, but it was scheduled for layout, promotion, and release. It would sell, and it would be the last book he would ever sell.

But apparently that actress had his ear, and she was full of ideas on how to make it better. And he thought she was some genius. I had ten years' experience at the time. The publisher and the editor were the best in the business. But some teenage screen queen was going to make it better.

He put his foot down and actually returned his first advance check. Ready to walk away. I had to beg the publisher to give him one month.

What he sent me a month later was completely reworked. Same stuff, but in a very different form. The thing that hit me right out of the gate was that all the editing that had been done had edited his voice right out of it. Schuyler put his voice back into it. She reorganized it. She found that single unifying theme that led to a narrative arc that would pull readers in and keep them hooked. She rewrote the opening paragraph for him, and it was a killer.

The publisher barely noticed – they had a manuscript ready to go on time, so they were ecstatic. I don't know if they even read it again.

I knew we were sitting on a breakout book, but I had no idea it was a time bomb ready to blow.

Interviewer: The crowds, the hysteria that surrounded this release –

Liv: No idea it would do anything like that. How could anyone know? You never know, and I'd never seen anything like that before. An author gives a reading, and it feels like a rock concert. It was damn scary. And it got scarier.

Interviewer: Slade may be frustrating, but he has a certain charisma or attraction, doesn't he? Do you have any explanation for that?

Liv: None whatsoever. He's a gentle guy, very intelligent and thoughtful, soft-spoken but very stubborn. And given his physical appearance, the thought that thousands would want to come see him in person never crossed my mind. The thought of people rioting when he didn't show was the furthest thing from my mind. I figured he'd sell a million of these books and talk to audiences in the hundreds.

When it took off, I was pleased, to say the least. By the time they'd rented the Forum, I thought it was out of control and dangerous. I had no concept of how bad it had gotten until the publisher called me and said their publicist, who was traveling with Slade, wanted a SWAT team with a helicopter to rappel in and rescue her.

Interviewer: After the book tours ended, things settled down?

Liv: At first, then things took on a life of their own. Without Slade. The book kept selling. It stayed on the bestseller list for 163 weeks. His first book rejoined the bestseller list, even hit number one for a few weeks after the movie came out, and then again after the Oscars. Slade outsold the former president's and first lady's memoirs combined that year. The movie was the number one box office hit.

Nobody in the publishing business, I mean nobody, saw that coming. It was exciting. It was sheer terror.

Then Slade goes into hiding for a bit, then he's part of the in-crowd, then he's the Shaman to the Stars and married to the biggest name in show business.

Interviewer: But no more books of this type?

Liv: No. I tried once. Asked if he would consider writing a follow-up based on the seminars he was giving. He rejected the idea outright, and I didn't push. I'd learned when his mind was made up.

Then he calls me one day. Actually, it was night. Like after midnight. Said he'd written a science fiction novel and wanted to know if I could sell it. He thought he should put it out under a pen name, but I told him his name was the one and only thing that would sell it.

I handed him off to Paul, who said it was quite good. And that turned into three more books and four more movies.

Slade Bennington is the most successful author of an entire generation, in both fiction and nonfiction. If he put out a Sudanese cookbook, it would be the biggest seller of the year.

And Randall Kleifisch would figure out a way to turn it into a movie with at least two explosions.

INTERVIEW #29

"Sometimes a mother just knows these things."
~ Celeste Schuyler-Jones, aka Celeste Rousseau

"People can change, and not for the good,
when they become famous."
~ Dr. Richard Jones

Interviewer: When and how did you meet Slade Bennington?

Celeste (Annie's mother): I'd read his book, the first one, when it came out. What an extraordinary story. When Annie's agent called her to audition for the part of Jolene, I was super excited.

First met Slade on the set during filming. I was so anxious to meet him. And what a gentle soul.

Richard (Annie's father): Yes, on the set. A gem of a human being.

Interviewer: What were your thoughts about the relationship between Annie and Slade at the beginning?

Celeste: I thought it was wonderful. Annie really connected with him. His appearance didn't faze her, which we had tried to instill those values in her, so I was rather proud of her for that. And he was very helpful to her on the set. They became friends.

Richard: I agree with Cel. He was quite gracious with Annie, spending time with her, talking. You could see a connection.

Interviewer: What were your reactions to the famous kiss at the Oscar award ceremony?

Celeste: I was hugging Rich and had my back turned. I saw it later on the video. I thought it might have been a little inappropriate of her, but it was a bit of overexuberance.

Richard: It was an exuberant moment. Didn't think much about it. There was a lot of typical Hollywood gossip afterward, which I found rather absurd.

Interviewer: And a few years later, what was your reaction to their engagement announcement?

Celeste: It didn't really surprise me. We'd known Slade for six or seven years by then. We knew they were best friends and stayed in constant touch. And it seemed right. I had a feeling. That mother's intuition. Sometimes a mother just knows these things.

Richard: Well, I don't have mother's intuition, so it did surprise me. Some people asked me if I had any concerns because of the age difference or Slade's disabilities, but we knew him as a person, and none of that even crossed my mind.

I knew there might be some difficulties in how others would perceive them or treat them, no different than a mixed-race couple might face. And they were so much in the public eye. Those were my concerns – how they would deal with the notoriety and how people might treat them, how the media would portray them.

Interviewer: How did they handle that?

Richard: Slade never even seems to notice, or he pays no attention whatsoever. Annie doesn't tolerate it. She's never tolerated any hatefulness like that.

Interviewer: How did you react to Annie deciding to leave acting and show business behind?

Celeste: I was supportive, even though there was a small part of me that was disappointed. Not disappointed in her. I completely supported her decision, but then I'd find myself thinking, "Oh, I was going to be the mother of the greatest actress in Hollywood." And I'd realize how selfish and self-centered that was of me to think something like that.

Instead, I have this wonderful, intelligent daughter who has made quite a name for herself in her chosen field of study. I couldn't be prouder. And what a great mother she is. What phenomenal children she is raising.

Richard: Those grandchildren are the best part of our lives. We don't get to see them as often as we'd like, but that's about to change.

As far as the acting career, I was relieved. I was so proud of her success in show business, but it can really take a toll on a person, on who they are. People can change, and not for the good, when they become famous in the entertainment industry. I didn't like what I saw in the people who surrounded her. Slade provided a rock, a foundation that helped keep her grounded.

When she left acting and married Slade, yeah, a weight lifted off my chest. Profound relief.

Celeste: Yes, I can't wait to see more of our grandkids. And more of Annie and Slade, as well. Rich is retiring after this semester, and we're going to move south to be closer. Get out of Chicago. Get out of the Chicago winters.

Richard: But we're really not the country types, like Annie and Slade, living out in the hinterlands like that. We like to be close to restaurants, entertainment, theater, that sort of thing.

Celeste: We're looking at a condo in Dallas, and we'd only be an hour from the kids. And Annie brings Slade up to Dallas for doctor appointments every couple of months, so I'll be able to take her to lunch or shopping, some mother-daughter time.

Richard: We also like Austin, but that's a little farther drive. Still closer than Chicago, of course.

Interviewer: Is there anything else you'd like to make sure I know about you, Annie, Slade, anything at all I haven't asked that you wanted to add?

Richard: Can't wait to take the grandkids to the Shakespearean Festival in Dallas next year.

Celeste: And to be clear, Rich is retiring. I'm not. My newest book will publish next spring.

Richard: I think it's one of the differences in our career choices. I've taught the same courses and topics year after year. It doesn't change much. Cel, on the other hand, can dream up a brand-new story every few months, so it's always new and exciting for her. I finally hit the wall and realized teaching English literature no longer excited me after forty years.

Celeste: Maybe you'll have time to write something you want to write.

Richard: Maybe. We'll see. Or maybe I'll have time to read all of your books, and all of Slade's.

Celeste: And you can read Annie's too.

Richard: If I start having a problem with insomnia, maybe.

Celeste: Oh, Rich, stop it.

INTERVIEW #30

**"We are responsible for doing the right thing,
not for other people's reactions."
~ Dr. Annamarie Bennington, PhD, aka Schuyler Jones**

Interviewer: You and Slade have been through some periods of significant turmoil, but you've also seen long periods of relative tranquility. Where do you see your life at the moment?

Annie: I live with Slade and three daughters. What is this tranquility you speak of?

Life is always turmoil and tranquility at the same time. Life is finding that balance regardless of circumstances.

Interviewer: Balance. Contentment. Now you're sounding like Slade.

Annie: Or Slade sounds like me.

Interviewer: How much of an influence on Slade's work, on his philosophy or outlook on life, do you think you've had?

Annie: Profound, I hope. As much as his influence on me. When you're married for sixteen years, your lives become so entwined there's very little separation in some ways. In other ways, we're still two quite different people. But that balance in life is something I learned to seek early on, something my parents worked hard to instill in me.

When I first met Slade, I'm not sure he'd quite reached that point. He saw balance, contentment regardless of circumstances, as important, saw that it was the key. But he hadn't yet figured out how to achieve it or maintain it. I lived it but had a hard time explaining to someone else how to find it. He kept interrogating me on the topic, forcing me to actually think about how I worked to maintain that contentment in life.

As the two of us talked, early on during filming, he was writing his second book, trying to get his thoughts together in a way that would resonate with others, that could help others. He was picking my brain and finding things that matched with what he felt, what he saw.

We'd debate different aspects endlessly. I'd play devil's advocate to force him to think things through, to come up with the best way to phrase something, the best way to explain a concept. I'd learned those dialectic skills from my father and from a couple of tutors, so I put them to good use with Slade.

Interviewer: Sounds like you were a significant influence in Slade's thinking, in his concepts that he has written about and taught.

Annie: Not so much influencing his ideas, but I think our discussions and debates helped him refine them, polish them, find the rights word in the right order to present to others. They were his ideas, not mine. Perhaps, over time, he blended some of my thoughts in with his, just as some of his thoughts blended with mine. But I didn't change my beliefs to conform to his, and he didn't change his to match mine.

We were largely on the same wavelength to begin with. I had a few years head start on him.

Interviewer: Even his literary agent said you, as a teenager, had a major and positive impact on his second book. That your revisions and edits made it much better.

Annie: That wasn't hard. It was a disorganized mess, and parts were incongruent, contradictory.

Interviewer: But Chelsea had worked with him to revise it before that, as well as his agent and a professional editor.

Annie: It wasn't poorly written. Chelsea had worked miracles to turn his notebooks full of ramblings and musings into an actual book manuscript. But it was missing a unifying theme and continuity.

I don't think his publisher even cared at that point – they just wanted a book out by the time the movie hit theaters because they knew it would sell. They wanted to cash in. They weren't interested in creating a profound book that could positively impact millions of people.

And it would have sold big, and then that would have been the end of it. The end of Slade's career. He wouldn't have gone on to reach so many people who needed to hear his ideas, his message. He would have put out a mediocre book that sold big for a year based on his name and temporary celebrity, then it would have been in the bargain bins at the grocery store. There would have been no courses or seminars or sessions.

Interviewer: And there would have been no Nora Campo and no death threats, no Forum riots, no Slade-worshipping book-club cults.

Annie: And we're right back to that balance in life. That there are highs and lows, terrific elation and horrific tragedy. We're responsible for doing the right thing. We're not responsible for other people's reactions to that, as difficult and heartbreaking as that can be sometimes.

Interviewer: Speaking of death threats, I understand you went through that as a teenager.

Annie: Ah yes, wonderful, beautiful, magical Broadway.

Interviewer: It was quite controversial, you appearing as Lolita. That does seem a bit risqué for you, especially when you were, what, fourteen?

Annie: Fourteen to fifteen, yeah. And it was definitely a sexualized role, lots of sexual tension in the play, but it was all very tastefully done. No nudity. I'd read the book, and then I read the screenplay before agreeing to do it. Once I'd read it, I jumped at the chance.

Interviewer: There was quite a backlash against that. Some called it soft-core pedophilia.

Annie: Critics said the same thing when Nabokov first published the book in the 1950s. Obviously this criticism came from people who never actually read the book or saw the play. Or they read only the opening chapters without following the story through to its conclusion. Or they are too dense to grasp the underlying themes and symbolism.

Interviewer: It definitely broke you out of the box you'd been in during the six years of The Family Crest.

Annie: That it did, and that was my intention. All the roles I'd been offered were extensions of that precocious, smart-mouthed six or ten or twelve-year-old. I was fourteen, so those roles didn't fit me anymore. Casting directors had me in mind for some part, then I'd show up and they'd say, "Whoa, who are you? Sorry, you're way too old and too tall for this part."

I didn't want to do sitcoms anymore. I didn't want to play the sulky teenage daughter of the lead in a sappy rom-com movie. And a five-foot three-inch lead actress didn't want to play mom to a kid who's six-foot-one. I wasn't going to do Hallmark junk. I wanted to be a serious actress.

Lolita on Broadway gave me that way to break out.

Interviewer: And then the death threats, attacks, and the pedophiles coming out of the woodwork.

Annie: Yes, all of that. Yin and yang. But I never felt unsafe. More amused by it all. Perhaps I wasn't old enough to know any better, didn't realize how dangerous a situation it really was. Or maybe it's my outlook on life and my faith that didn't let me get rattled.

Of course, all that created a lot of publicity buzz, which helped my career take off from that point. I was offered serious roles, eventually with Randall doing Slade's story. Everything works out for the best in the long run.

Interviewer: For a devout Christian, you seem to have an almost Buddhist approach to life.

Annie: From a philosophical standpoint, the two are not in conflict. There are hundreds of almost identical statements made by Siddhartha Gautama and Jesus of Nazareth.

Interviewer: What are the differences between the two religions?

Annie: The Buddha pointed the way to enlightenment and happiness. Jesus said, "I am the way. Follow me." It's a profound difference theologically and spiritually. But the life lessons each taught are nearly identical.

Interviewer: And similar to Slade's teachings.

Annie: Sladehartha, I call him. He hates that.

Slade's teachings are Slade's concepts, but yes, they are quite aligned with the similar teachings of Buddhism and Christianity. Slade does not, of course, claim to be the way like Christ. Neither does he claim to be the enlightened one like the Buddha.

He's a regular, ordinary guy who went through an extraordinary situation and came out on the other side a changed man. He wants to share his story and what he learned with anyone who might find it helpful to them in their circumstances. Everyone faces tragedy in life, and sometimes it's good to hear from someone who has been there and has a message of how they got through it.

The concepts are also very much in line with Stoicism and with Mussar from the Jewish tradition. I think that's the core message Slade tries to present. As he says, most of this is obvious if you open your eyes, which is why it's always viewed as revolutionary. Common sense is quite subversive.

Interviewer: Some have taken it much further than that.

Annie: That's on them.

Interviewer: You grew up in Chicago, then LA Worked in New York. Went to school in Rome and Paris. Now you're living on a piece of land in rural Texas, an hour from Dallas. How was that transition?

Annie: Yin and yang. Contentment. This place provides me with great serenity, peace, a connection to God's creation. A place I'd much rather raise my kids than any city on the planet. I can drive to the city or fly to any place in the world any time I want. I seldom leave here, but when I do, I can't wait to get back. This is my home, my family. My life. And those are my chickens over there, and my garden over there, and the girls are raising a goat over there.

Ever have barbecued goat ribs? They're wonderful. We'll have you over.

INTERVIEW #31

"Annie, get your gun. I've always wanted to say that."
~ Slade Bennington

Interviewer: I have an appointment with Slade Bennington. Is there a problem? What's going on?

Sheriff's Deputy: What's your name? I'll have to call in to get you cleared.

Interviewer: Robb Grindstaff. He's expecting me.

Deputy: Stay right here. *[makes a call on his cell phone]*

Okay, if you'll step out of your car and stand over there, she'll screen you. Anything in your pockets, empty into the tray. Do you have any weapons on you or in your vehicle?

Interviewer: No, no weapons.

Deputy: Okay, please unlock all car doors and open your trunk for me, then go see the deputy there with the wand.

Interviewer: Sure. What's going on?

***

Slade: Sorry about all that. With all the excitement, I forgot you were coming or I'd have had them wave you straight in.

Interviewer: What happened? They wouldn't answer my questions at the gate. I assume they aren't authorized to tell me anything and they don't know me from Adam, so I didn't really expect much from them.

Slade: Gunshots last night on the property. We've got a security guard at the gate at night, and he apparently decided it would be a good idea to do some target shooting at a bobcat about four o'clock this morning.

Guy's worked here for three years and never fired a round. Emptied his chamber last night. Sounded like a firefight.

Interviewer: What did you do?

Slade: Annie got the girls into the safe room then called the security company. They called 911 and tried to reach Bud – the guard. No answer.

Annie and I had taken our positions. Nothing more happened. Sat here for thirty minutes 'til the sheriff showed up. This is why you have to provide your own defense. You're responsible for yourself. No one else is responsible for you.

Turns out Bud dropped his cell phone out there somewhere while he was popping off at that kitty. Said he could hear it ringing but he wasn't leaving the guardhouse to go look for it in the dark with a pissed-off bobcat he couldn't locate, and he was all out of ammo.

Poor guy lost his job over it and he didn't even get the cat. Too bad, too. Nice guy. But nice don't overcome incompetence when it comes to defending my family. And he was obviously a poor shot, so we can't have that.

Company is sending someone else this evening. And the FBI will have someone here in an hour or so to check everything out, given the threats from a couple years back. I told them not to bother after we'd figured out what happened, but I think they like to find an excuse to come visit once in a while.

Interviewer: You have a safe room? Like a panic room?

Slade: Not a panic room. There is no panic here.

We decided it was a good idea. You don't really need to put that in your book though. Don't want to give away all our secrets.

Interviewer: And Annie is trained in firearms too?

Slade: We all are. All except Mandy, of course, although she enjoys it when we take her to the range to shoot a little .22 rifle.

Jolene is a crack shot, let me tell you. She has her own sidearm, a Smith & Wesson Shield, 9mm. She's very responsible, fully trained.

Evvy is a natural. Calm, steady. But she just doesn't like guns much. We don't push her. But she pushes herself to become proficient. I told her one day that if she really didn't like guns, she didn't have to shoot them. She said, "I want to make sure I'm good enough to protect Mandy if I ever have to." Now, who could ask for a more devoted big sister than that?

I asked her what type of gun she wanted me to buy her, and she said none. So I asked, "How you gonna protect your little sister if you don't have a gun?"

She said, "If things ever get so bad that I need a gun, I'll pick up one of yours off the floor."

Evvy can be one chilling young lady, let me tell you.

We're going to surprise her with the same as her mom's, a Sig Sauer P238. We got her one with a rainbow design. She loves rainbows. Annie's is desert camo. Hang on, let me show you.

Here. Feel how light it is. Nice rosewood grip on that cute little gun. Evvy can handle her mom's quite well.

Interviewer: Annie doesn't mind being around guns? Seems out of character for what I know of her.

Slade: She's quite the firearms aficionado, actually. But last night was the first time I ever got to use the line I've wanted to say for years.

Interviewer: What was that?

Slade: "Annie, get your gun."

Looks like I'll need to cut today's session short. FBI is here and they'll want to chat for a bit, I'm sure. Why don't you come back tomorrow, say nine a.m.? Annie and the girls will be at church.

Interviewer: We can do Monday if you prefer so you can go to church with your family.

Slade: I visit the doc up in Dallas on Monday. And church is Annie's thing, not mine. It bothers me when they tell everyone to kneel.

INTERVIEW #32

**"Everything points to the truth, even if there is
no way to understand it in our lifetime."
~ Dr. Annamarie Bennington, PhD, aka Schuyler Jones**

Interviewer: Does it bother you that Slade doesn't attend church with you and the girls?

Annie: Why should that bother me? He has his beliefs, I have mine. He's not an atheist or even agnostic. He has a different outlook on faith, his own approach. A different relationship with God. That's between him and God.

Interviewer: Being a renowned theologian, do you find it difficult to be a member of a church? You're probably more familiar with the Scriptures than your pastor is.

Annie: Oh, Billy – Reverend Thomas – he is an incredible pastor, and I'm so blessed to have him in my life. I may have studied religious texts all my life, but I still learn so much from him. I tend to focus on the facts, the historical record, the literature, the various translations, the society and culture of the day. I get very wrapped up in the minutiae and the academics of it all. Billy has a way of bringing it all home – bringing it to life. Bringing it to our lives.

He's one of the most genuine, loving, and compassionate men I've ever met. He doesn't speak down to anyone. He meets them where they are, physically and spiritually. He is a tremendous counselor. He keeps the entire congregation focused on what's important.

Interviewer: You attend a small church in a rural community. Why not one of the larger, more important churches in Dallas or Fort Worth?

Annie: This is where we live. These people are our neighbors. Well, such as we have neighbors. They aren't that close. It's only ten minutes to our church. Dallas is an hour away, Fort Worth even farther. I want the girls involved in church activities throughout the week, not an out-of-town trip once a week. It's the fellowship and relationships that matter.

I find a small church much more conducive to spiritual growth, a group of people who will hold me accountable in my daily life, who are there to support me as I am there to support them.

The large churches can be very cold and difficult to make those kinds of connections. And so many churches today are more political than spiritual, more about raising money than lifting hearts.

I study and teach religion. My church is where I meet God and fellowship with other believers.

Interviewer: And your daughters? They are following in your beliefs?

Annie: That will be up to them. They have to find their own way. I'll point a direction. Each person has to make that choice for themselves. I found my way early in life. Slade found his way much later. Many people never do find their way in this life, and you can't force it on them.

Interviewer: I understand that you chose Christianity at a young age, all on your own, not guided or pushed into it by your parents. How did that come about?

Annie: My parents aren't religious, but we talked about religion, spiritual things, and belief systems around the dinner table as far back as I can remember. From Greek and Roman mythology to the Native American beliefs to the Abrahamic traditions. We never went to church or anything, of course.

I don't remember any single moment or event when I suddenly decided to be a follower of Christ. I don't recall any piece of information that swayed me. There was no blinding light or vision or emotional conversion experience. It just was. He was with me from the beginning. I knew it all to be true, but I had to figure out how I knew. I wanted to learn everything about it. I took a very skeptical, doubting viewpoint – a trait from my parents, my dad in particular – to analyze everything and try to prove it wrong.

And yet, the more I doubted, the more I studied, trying to find the faults, the flaws, the lie – every question I had would be answered. Everything pointed to the truth. Even if there is never a way in my lifetime to understand it all. I knew. I always knew.

Interviewer: That must be a blessing to have that knowledge and confidence in your faith or spirituality. Many struggle with that their whole lives.

Annie: I'm not sure if it's been a blessing or a curse. It just is.

It's like falling in love with Slade. The first time I saw him, the first time I talked to him, I knew. I knew I loved him, and we would be married, have a family and a life together. It was clear.

I also knew – I was sixteen when we first met – that I would have to bide my time. Patience. It would happen when the ordained time arrived. I didn't know when that would be, but I couldn't force it. So, I marched on with my life, confident in knowing what my future held.

Interviewer: And is life with Slade a blessing or a curse?
Annie: Depends on the day.

INTERVIEW #33

"I nearly crapped my pants right there in the vestibule."
~ Rev. William (Billy) Thomas

Interviewer: Reverend Thomas, what's it like being Annie's pastor? That must be a little intimidating considering her knowledge of the Bible and religion.

Billy: Please, call me Billy. I'm not always the most reverend person in the room.

I first met Annie about ten years ago when I became the pastor here at Antioch Church. I had no idea who she was. Some young lady, a very tall young lady, strikingly attractive, who was one of the couple hundred members here. She was extremely gracious in welcoming me and helping me get settled in, introducing me to some of the other members.

Then I didn't see her again for a couple of months. I'd forgotten about her, frankly. I had met so many people in my first weeks on the job and had trouble remembering everyone's names. Going out and getting to know the community. Preparing sermons for Sunday morning and Sunday night services. Leading the Wednesday night prayer service. And people come and go – they move, they stop coming to church, they start attending a different church. I didn't think anything about it.

Then she shows up again one Sunday with her two little girls, and I remembered meeting her my first week. Didn't remember her name. I tell ya, for someone who is supposed to lead our flock, I have a terrible time remembering names until I meet someone several times. We introduced ourselves again, and she was just Annie, this young mother who attended our church on occasion. Nothing intimidating about that.

She was there every week and very involved, several times a week, for a couple of months. A quiet, serious volunteer worker in the church. Then she disappeared again for a couple of months. I finally asked one of the elders, "Have you heard from Annie, you know, the tall woman with the two daughters? I haven't seen her in a while."

And he said, "Oh, Dr. Bennington. She's teaching theology at Harvard right now. You know she's that actress, Schuyler Jones. Married to Slade Bennington, the famous author. They live a few miles out of town."

Well, I nearly crapped my pants right there in the vestibule.

Interviewer: That must have been pretty intimidating at that point.

Billy: It was for a bit. A few weeks later, the next time I saw her, I pulled her aside after the service and talked to her. I told her that if she ever thought I was teaching something incorrect, to please come to me. I asked if she'd be interested in reviewing my sermon outlines beforehand to make sure I wasn't making any mistakes.

Interviewer: What did she say?

Billy: She seemed genuinely embarrassed. Didn't want anything to do with that. Said she was looking forward to hearing my interpretation of things. She said God is so complex, none of us has the revealed truth, and that He is also simple enough to speak clearly to a child.

She also said she wasn't at church to hear theological dissertations, but to connect to God and His followers. She wanted me to teach her how to live a better life, be a better person, be a help to others, not expound on doctrinal theories.

Her words spoke to my heart, and I resolved to be that kind of pastor from that moment forward. I fail often, but that's where my heart is.

Interviewer: Have you met Slade?

Billy: Oh yes, we're great friends. I tell ya, that is one interesting dude. Annie and Slade have had my wife and me over for dinner countless times over the years. We'd have them over to our place, but we've got steps to the front door, not really set up to handle his chair. Slade and I will sit and discuss everything from God to football to fishing until the women tell us to shut up and it's time to go home.

Bea – my wife – and Annie have become fast friends. And I think that's saying a lot because Annie doesn't really seem to have many friends. No one close. Maybe because of her upbringing, being a child star and all that. She's friendly with everyone, but she can be a bit aloof. Bea just wasn't having it. Bea is like a second mother to Annie.

And those girls. Those wonderful girls. What a joy. Bea and I never were able to have any children, so no grandkids of our own. But those girls might as well be ours. Best huggers in the world.

Interviewer: You and Slade like to fish?

Billy: I like to drown worms. Don't often catch enough to make dinner for two. But Slade and I were talking about it one day, a few years back, and he hadn't been fishing since his accident. Well, I wasn't having that. I had to fix up the boat some way so's he could sit in it without tipping over or falling out.

I called him up one day and told him he had to get up early the next morning because I had a surprise for him. Said I'd pick him up at five. He said that wasn't early.

I pick him up, take him to the lake, help him into the boat, into a lifejacket, and strapped into a seat. Showed him how to unlatch it real quick in case something happened so he wouldn't be strapped into a sinking boat. Not that I've ever sunk a boat, but ya know, just to be extra cautious.

He acted like that was the most fun he'd ever had in his life. We sat out there on the lake for several hours. I caught a couple so small I threw 'em back. He landed a couple of striped bass worthy of mounting on a wall. Beginner's luck, I told him. He said it was a psychic connection with the fish.

When we're about ready to pack it in, the ranger pulls up next to us in his boat, says, "Good mornin', Reverend. Any luck?"

Slade is beaming and holds up his stringer.

Ranger says, "Can I see your licenses?"

Well, it never occurred to me that Slade didn't have a fishing license. Ranger made us let those fish go in exchange for him not getting a ticket.

Our next stop was Walmart to get Slade a fishing license.

We try to get on the water once a month now, weather permitting. He still loves to fish, but he's never caught any as big as that first day.

Interviewer: You ever try to get Slade to attend church?

Billy: Nah. He knows he's welcome anytime he wants. He'll show up on rare occasions, especially if one of his girls is in some program. And it's kinda nice having a good friend who doesn't go to church, ya know. I can bring along my snifter of Scotch on the boat and he's not gonna rat me out to the Ladies' Auxiliary, and if he drinks a beer, I'm not calling up his doctor to report him.

INTERVIEW #34

**"Annie was kind of standoffish at first, but I broke
her down with my famous banana bread."
~ Bea Thomas, pastor's wife**

Interviewer: Tell me about Slade and Annie.

Bea: Oh my, they are so special to me. Annie especially. If I'd had a daughter, I'd want her to be just like Annie. So smart, so beautiful, and what a wonderful mother to those girls. Those girls are so precious. I love them to pieces.

Slade too. He's a little harder for me to get to know, but he and Billy have become best buds. Billy so needed that too. He works all the time, and everyone he knows is a member of the church. It's hard to become really close friends with someone when you're their pastor.

Interviewer: Did you know of Annie back when she was an actress, Schuyler Jones?

Bea: I've never been much of a fan of movies, but I do like good comedies. I watched her grow up on *The Family Crest*. When I met her years later, I didn't know who she was. No idea that was her. Felt this instant connection with her. I found out later she was that darling little girl from TV. Maybe that's why I connected with her. It was like I'd known her for years. And I can sure see that girl from TV in Mandy, the youngest.

Annie was kind of standoffish at first, but I broke her down with some of my banana bread. And those girls just took right up with me from day one, so Annie had to come around eventually. Now, they're our family.

We get together some weekends to do canning and baking. I even gave her my grandmother's banana bread recipe.

Jo, the eldest, she comes over to my home sometimes. Even spends the night. She doesn't get to see her grandparents that often since they live so far away, so I've become her grandmother too. We'll sit up and talk. Mostly I listen. Teenagers need someone to listen to them without judgment.

I'm excited about Annie's parents moving closer, but also a little jealous that they'll get all the attention. I'm teasing. Can't have too many grandmas.

Interviewer: Tell me about Billy and Slade's friendship.

Bea: I've never seen Billy laugh so much as when he's with Slade. I think they're very good for each other. Billy, he's always worked so hard in his ministry. He cares so much about people that he never would stop to take time for himself. He worked all the time, and he worried that he wasn't doing enough. Never could stop to relax much. Yeah, he'd go off by himself to go fishing. But that was his alone time, his solitary time to meditate and think. He'd come back refreshed maybe, or maybe even more determined to work harder, to do more, to do a better job.

But he never seemed settled. Now, he does. He spends time with Slade and he comes back with a different attitude. More peaceful or something. I can't think of the word I'm looking for.

Interviewer: Contentment?

Bea: That's it. He's more contented with life, with himself, than I've ever seen him in our forty years of marriage. If I'd have known, I would have made him find a friend years ago.

INTERVIEW #35

"That would violate the sacred client-Shaman confidentiality."
~ Slade Bennington

Interviewer: Who were a few of your most famous clients?

Slade: That would be confidential – client-Shaman privilege, ya know. But some are publicly known because they made it public. It's all out there on the internet, but I won't mention any names.

Interviewer: We've talked about Nora, the most well-known case of a client of yours who had a tragic outcome. But can you talk about some of the successes of your counseling or seminars, without naming names or violating any Shaman-confidentiality rules?

Slade: There've been so many. Let me think. And it's hard to settle on one or two great successes, because success means different things to different people. Something that might seem minor to you or me might have been a tremendous, life-changing breakthrough for the person involved.

But there is one I'm thinking of. No one famous or anything. But it sticks in my memory as the yang to Nora's yin. And it was one of those cases where it didn't seem that deep a crisis to me at the time. A young man – in his late twenties – from New Mexico. That's all the identifying info I'll give. But he attended a book-signing event in Santa Fe the first tour, before everything got wild and crazy. He stopped by the table with his dog-eared copy of my book and asked me to sign it, said nice things about how much the book touched him, et cetera, et cetera. But he just seemed on the verge of tears. I'd seen this a few times by that point, and it was still just blowing me away that people were so affected by my story.

A couple years later, I'm in Albuquerque, right after the movie and the second book hit, so crowds were a lot larger, but it hadn't gone totally insane yet. And there's this guy again. I'm not sure how, but I remembered him, remembered his name, and I called out to him and asked him to come over and chat after my talk.

I signed another book for him – let's call him Jim before I slip and use his real name. He was tall and slender, so Slim Jim works. He was practically bouncing on his feet, and I was afraid if he smiled any harder, he'd split his face open. I hadn't yet realized how something so simple on my part could impact others.

He hung around the table where I signed books and we chatted a bit as the crowd thinned out. He leaned down and gave me a hug when it was time to go, and he was definitely sniffling a bit from crying or holding back the tears.

When I started doing the seminars, he wrote me a letter and asked me to come to New Mexico. I passed that on to Chelsea, she set up a weeklong course in Albuquerque, and she contacted Jim right away to let him know. I told her to sign him up at no charge since the whole event was his idea.

He was there, front and center, every day that week. He'd put on some weight – not quite as skinny as he had been, filling out nicely, looked like he'd been working out. He had a glow about him. If he was a woman, I'd have guessed he was pregnant or in love or something. Or some recent spiritual experience – just this lightness about him.

We would say hello and make a minute of small talk between sessions, on breaks and such. There were a lot of people there and a lot of work to do, so I didn't have time to just stop and talk to him for any length of time. But it felt like he had something important he needed to share with me, just biding his time for the right moment.

On the last day, I made sure to spend five minutes with him, thanking him for suggesting this conference. It was smaller than most of them we did – usually in LA or New York or Chicago. Even Denver, Phoenix, Philadelphia are all a lot larger than Albuquerque. But that made for a more casual, more intimate setting, and allowed for a lot more audience participation and questions. To this day, that was one of my favorite seminars we ever did.

So anyway, I thanked him for the suggestion, for coming, and then asked him if there was something on his mind he'd been wanting to say.

Once again, he instantly teared up, but with a smile, not with any sadness or pain.

He went on to tell me that his father had committed suicide when Jim was just five years old. When Jim was thirteen, his older brother committed suicide. He'd also had a grandfather and an uncle who'd killed themselves before Jim was born. And Jim had been in and out of counseling and treatment, on and off medications, suffering from clinical depression most of his life. He was terrified the darkness would overtake him one day and he'd kill himself, but he didn't want to die.

He said after he'd read my books, that fear dissolved. He knew he had depression, and continued his treatment, but he no longer had this irrational – or perhaps very rational – fear that he would be uncontrollably compelled by his illness to commit suicide because it seemed to run in the family. And he gave me another hug.

We exchanged phone numbers and email addresses because I wanted to stay in touch with him. And we did, for many years.

Interviewer: *Where's Jim now?*

Slade: He passed away recently. Cancer, not suicide. He had married, raised three children, had a successful career as an architect. He called me when he got the diagnosis – stage four, too far advanced to do anything about it by the time it was discovered. Pancreas, I think, or something like that. Docs had told him he had four to six months to live. He sounded just as chipper and happy as if he'd gotten a clean bill of health.

That's what living is supposed to be about. He wasn't frightened of death. He wasn't bitter that his life was ending before he turned fifty. And he'd been off any medications for fifteen years. He had embraced life and enjoyed his time on this planet.

His wife called me a month later. He'd taken a turn for the worse, was in hospice care, unconscious, and they would be removing all life support the next morning. She went on and on about how much I had meant to Jim, how my books had been a turning point in his life. She'd been his high school sweetheart, but they'd broken up in large part because of his depression and the mood swings that went with that. He'd called her to ask her out after he'd finished my second book, and he took her to see my movie – several years after they'd broken up. She had married and divorced in the meantime.

And they were never apart after that.

She invited me to the funeral, and I canceled a couple of speeches to be there. Beautiful service, a true celebration to honor his life. While we'd stayed in occasional touch over the years, I'd had no idea how successful he'd been and how much he had done for his community. A true hero.

Twenty years earlier, he'd been unable to sleep at night, gnawed by a fear that he would take his own life even though he wanted desperately to live.

That's what it can mean to find your true self and then connect your light to others around you.

Nora and Jim. Yin and yang.

INTERVIEW #36

"If I want to be around kids, I've got nieces. Kids are not Zen, man."
~ Matt Bennington

Interviewer: What's your life like today?

Matt: It's all good. Maybe not as good as I'd like, but better than I deserve.

Interviewer: You and Slade still close?

Matt: Oh yes. Brothers 'til the day we die. We don't see each other as often as we used to, of course. I mean, we lived in the same house for most of our lives. He and Annie bought that acreage when they got married, so he's over an hour away now. But we still see each other at least once a month, and we talk on the phone a couple times a week.

After they got married, Chelsea eventually moved in here with me. She's moved out a couple times, but she always comes back. So far, anyway. I haven't messed up so bad that she's left for good.

Interviewer: What have you been doing? Working?

Matt: About the time Slade and Annie got married, I bought that Pizza Hut I got fired from for delivering weed. Ran that for a few years – just pizza, no weed. Sold that and worked for Chelsea's company. I'd help with logistics, getting events set up, that sort of thing. I sort of retired from that after my back started acting up. Now I spend most of my time restoring muscle cars.

I'll buy some classic that needs a little TLC and put it back to its original glory. Then I'll sell it and buy another. Keeps me out of trouble and puts some cash in the bank. I don't need a lot. Just fun money.

Interviewer: Seems like a much calmer life today than ten or twenty years ago.

Matt: Boy, I'll say. Those were some crazy times. From growing up, to Slade's crash, Jolene dying, to him writing a book, then the movie and more books and more movies, and Slade getting all famous and shit. Now, it's like everyone is calm. Everything is Zen. I like Zen.

Interviewer: *No kids for you and Chelsea?*

Matt: No, we decided against that years ago, then it was just too late, but I don't regret it. If I want to be around kids, I'm the best uncle in the world to my nieces. Then, about the time they're getting on my last nerve, I can go home. Zen. Kids are not Zen, man.

Interviewer: *Is your Zen and Slade's contentment the same concept?*

Matt: Zen is shorter, easier to spell.

INTERVIEW #37

"One day I'll just be a memory. And then one day I won't."
~ Slade Bennington

Interviewer: What's your next project? More science fiction? More movies? Considering restarting your courses on contentment and seeing life with clarity? What's the next chapter in Slade Bennington's life?

Slade: Good question. I've been pondering over this exact situation. Annie and I have been talking about it. The answer is I don't know.

Interviewer: The Shaman to the Stars doesn't know what his purpose in life is?

Slade: Quite the opposite. My purpose in life right now, my current project, is being a father and raising these girls.

What I don't know is what the next project is going to be. And that's rare for me. I always seem to know what's next. There's always a project I'm working on, often more than one at a time, and I've always known what the next project is going to be and the one after that.

After Nora died, I stopped the courses. I've thought about restarting that. The world definitely could use a calm voice to talk about balance right now. But it doesn't feel right. And I like being home now. I don't want to travel. I don't want to go to LA I don't even want to go to the conference center in Dallas. Hell, I don't like to go to the grocery store.

And frankly, I'm not sure I'd draw the crowds I used to, at least not for the fees needed. It's been what? Nine, almost ten years. More than twenty years since my book came out. While I might think it's a work of classic literature, I'm not sure any publisher or reader is going to agree with that.

No more science fiction. I was only going to write one novel, and that was just for fun. I'd needed a creative outlet. Then it took on a life of its own. Publisher insisted on a trilogy, so that's what I did. Then the movies were rolling out, and everyone wanted another. A fourth book in a trilogy – that doesn't really make any sense. Especially since I'd killed off the main character at the end of *Volume III*. But they wanted another book, Randall wanted another movie, was going to make Nora the lead, and it would cement her career as a top female action star.

Nora's departure from this world ended a lot of things. I no longer feel any connection to that whole series or the characters. They'd not only taken on a life of their own, they left me. Flat moved out of my head. I was looking through one of those books the other day, and I couldn't even see why anyone would want to read it. Felt like someone else wrote it, and it was dull.

Volume IV is the worst thing I've ever written. It was forced. It didn't come from any creative side of my brain, such as that is. It came because everyone wanted another book so they could make another movie. I came up with an outline and then forced the words onto the page to fit the outline. Since I'd killed off the main character, and they wanted Nora to star in the next movie, I had to make Adele the lead character.

I'd always felt this deep, personal connection to my fictional characters. Like they were real people living in my head. Writing *Volume IV*, that was all gone. It really was pure fiction this time. Anyone else could have written that, and probably would have done a better job.

Interviewer: *It was still a huge success. And it made Siena Lopez an international star. The book couldn't have been that bad.*

Slade: And good for Ms. Lopez. I never met her. Never went to the set for filming that one. Took me a little longer to wash my hands of Hollywood than it did Annie, I guess. Everything takes me longer than it takes Annie.

Interviewer: *Now your purpose, your contentment, is raising your kids.*

Slade: Absolutely. There is nothing more important. And with Mandy just being six years old, that's going to be my purpose for several more years. But they grow up quick. So quick. They're gone in the blink of an eye.

One day, you're a teenager and think life moves so slow. Then you blink, and your kids are teenagers. And then, if I'm fortunate, my grandkids will be teenagers. Then I'll be a memory. And then, blink, I won't be.

It's all good. People think if they write a book, or make a movie, or have a hit song or whatever, that will somehow leave a part of themselves behind, and they'll always be remembered. But that's not true. My first book came out more than twenty-five years ago, the movie a few years later. Best-selling book, number one movie at the box office, Academy awards. You can't find that book anywhere in a bookstore these days. Hell, you can't even find bookstores. Netflix ain't playing that movie. There's a whole generation that's never heard of it. It's all gone in a flash.

Creativity and art are important, but they're more important to the individual who creates it. Our minds, our spirits, have this creative drive that needs an outlet. It doesn't matter if it's a commercial success or if no one ever hears your song.

I'm always telling Chelsea this because she thinks of herself as a failure. Never got one of her books published, never got a record deal for one of her songs. I tell her that's not what's important. People don't even remember what the number one hit record was from last year.

Writing it, singing it. That's what's important. If it touches someone in the moment, that's a huge success. That person might not remember that song a year or ten years from now, maybe not remember you or that moment. But in that moment, there was a connection between your light and theirs.

That's what's important, man. This moment. Be in it.

Interviewer: What's the best thing about being a father?

Slade: That moment when they have all finally fallen asleep and the house is quiet. I can sit here and listen to nothing. They're exhausting. They're loud. They cry. They whine. They want things. They want your attention, but when you try to give them attention, they want nothing to do with you.

Then, at the end of the day, when the little angels are all snuggled safely into blissful dreams, I think back over the wonderful day I just had with these magnificent creatures. I can sit here for hours thinking about them.

I'll also think about Jolene – my sister. You know, she'd be in her forties now. That's hard for me to imagine since she is sixteen for eternity.

How many people get to say they were given a second chance at being a parent? I was eighteen when Jolene moved in with me. I'd never had a father. Didn't know what a father was or what they were supposed to do. I tried to pretend I was a father. I was still in school, wanted to hang out with friends, have a girlfriend, work on my car. Instead, I was pretending to be a dad.

I was terrible at it too. And despite my worst efforts, Jolene was going to turn out okay. Maybe being an incompetent pretend father is better than none at all if you're trying, if you love them. Maybe if you love them, that's the only thing that matters.

Then I was given this great gift of Jo and Evvy to raise, and I got to partner with someone who knew how to do it. Annie had two grade-A parents. Her life was a little unusual, but she had rock-solid parents. Together, we were still making all the mistakes parents make. But we love them.

I think that's why Annie wanted another child. Why we have Mandy. Annie had learned a lot about being a mom and found out she was pretty damn good at it. We were a good team. So let's have another now that we know what we're doing.

I'm not sure it really works that way though. Every kid is so different. You have to learn how to be a parent all over again.

And in the blink of an eye, even little Mandy will be all grown up, moving out on her own, inflicting her own unique impact on the world.

After that, I don't know what my next project is. My next chapter. Like I said, I've always had two or three projects lined up for the future, like planes stacked up over DFW in a thunderstorm.

I don't right now. Nothing planned after that. No projects.

Interviewer: Does it bother you to not have a project planned or in the works?
Slade: Not at all. It feels like it should bother me, but it doesn't. Maybe it's my body telling me it's time to slow things down. Maybe I'll go fishing more often. Or take up ballroom dancing.

INTERVIEW #38

**"Change one thing in my life, and I'd be someone else,
somewhere else. Why would I risk that?"
~ Dr. Annamarie Bennington, PhD, aka, Schuyler Jones**

Interviewer: What's life like today with Slade, with your family, especially compared to the days when you first met and the first few years?

Annie: It's difficult to compare. It's a different life. Like those were different people in a different era. A different time, a different place. Another world. And yet, it's exactly the same. I'm still the same person. Slade is still Slade. But sometimes when I reflect on my time in the entertainment industry, and all that surrounded it, it feels like I'm watching a movie about someone else's life, not mine.

Interviewer: If you could get a do-over, what would you do differently?

Annie: I am getting a do-over, and I am doing it very differently. That's one of the biggest lessons Slade taught me. His life ended, and he got a do-over. As he puts it, you can start over any time you choose. Don't wait until you get burned. You might be a Jolene rather than a Slade.

Interviewer: How are you getting this do-over?

Annie: Marriage gives you a do-over, a new life with a partner. Children give you a do-over, new lives that you're responsible for. A change in careers, or a new job, a new place to live, all of those things give you a chance to restart your life.

But you don't even have to do any of those things. You just wake up one morning and decide. You decide to take charge of your life and you order your life the way you want it. You choose how to deal with challenges. You choose how to deal with challenging people. You choose the people you allow to be a part of your life.

Even if I had the chance, I wouldn't go back in time and change a thing. All the things that happen to us happen for a reason. All of my life brought me here, to this point, and there's nowhere else I'd rather be. No one else I want to be. No one else I want to be with. Change one thing at any point in my life and I'd be someone else, somewhere else. Why would I want to risk that?

Interviewer: What's next on your horizon?

Annie: I've been offered a full-time position on the faculty at Southwestern Seminary. But that's an hour and a half away, in Fort Worth. I'm not interested in that kind of a commute. I'm not interested in all of us moving back to the city or leaving this place. And I'm not going to rent an apartment there and live apart, only coming home on weekends, the way my parents had to do when I was young.

I'm talking to the school about some guest lecturer programs or seminars, as well as some online courses I can teach from home, and I'd only need to go to the campus once a week.

I have a place here I could teach from. When we bought this old farmhouse, we added the two studies – one for each of us – so we could each have our own private office to write, read, plan, think. Or pretend we're working when we need to escape the teen hormone drama.

The girls know they aren't allowed to interrupt either of us when we're in our studies unless the house is on fire.

Interviewer: Are you working on another book?

Annie: Yes, but I'm sure you'd find it quite dull.

Interviewer: Tell me anyway. You can kick me if I fall asleep.

Annie: In that case... I'm actually working on two simultaneously. When I get stuck on one, or get bored with it, I move to the other.

One is an analysis of all Old Testament prophecies about the Messiah, then matching them up with the life of Christ. It's been done before, of course – as King Solomon said, there is nothing new under the sun.

Slade says that too. He just phrases it differently.

But I want to add additional sources: historical records, non-scriptural literature from the ancient Hebrew times, archaeological information, that sort of thing.

The other book has a similar format. It lays out the story of creation alongside the most current scientific knowledge to show the two perspectives are not at all in conflict. There is no conflict between science and faith. The only conflict is man-made. Our minds have trouble reconciling the two, so people tend to divide up into two schools of thought that go from the extreme to the absurd: (a), evolution is real, therefore God does not exist; or (b) God is real, therefore He created the entire universe in six twenty-four-hour days about six thousand years ago.

Again, this isn't the first book to tackle this subject, but I'm trying to make sure I present the science as accurately as possible, and I'm including other ancient stories and literature that aren't in the Bible to paint a broader picture of how the Hebrews actually interpreted the creation story.

You still awake? You're fortunate I don't have my steel-toed work boots on.

Interviewer: I'm still conscious. Perhaps a little drowsy. Actually, these do sound interesting. Are these controversial subject matters for your intended audience?

Annie: I hope they'll be at least mildly controversial. Controversy is good.

Interviewer: Controversy sells.

Annie: Controversy makes you think. Theological treatises never sell unless you can get them on the required reading list for a course. And if I'm teaching the course, you can bet it will be on the list.

Interviewer: Do you ever autograph your textbooks for students?
Annie: I should start. I wonder if I can charge for that.

INTERVIEW #39

"Next time you'll know better."
~ Slade Bennington

"Real people can be monstrous enough."
~ Dr. Annamarie Bennington, PhD, aka, Schuyler Jones

Interviewer: I've interviewed you both separately several times, so it's nice to sit down with the two of you together. You're both going in different directions most of the time, it seems.

Slade: Life is busy, but Annie and I make sure we get time for just the two of us every day, just to sit and talk, or even if we're just laying in bed together reading after the girls are down for the night.

Annie: Of course, Slade falls asleep when we do that, so I have to keep elbowing him or reading something interesting to him. He starts snoring, and then I have to put his book away and take his glasses off.

Slade: Reading something she finds interesting, which might put me to sleep.

Annie: You like Aquinas though.

Slade: Yeah, but you start quoting Origen, and you might as well be putting me under general anesthesia.

Interviewer: Annie, do you read anything for pure entertainment, or are you always reading materials related to your work?

Annie: I don't consider it work really. I'm fascinated by the great thinkers – theologians, philosophers, historians. Yes, it relates to my studies, but it's what I enjoy. I find myself debating Calvin and Niebuhr in my head or wondering how a Jonathan Edwards would be received in today's world.

Slade: Now you see why I have no trouble falling asleep.

Interviewer: What about you? What do you like to read?

Slade: I've worked my way through all of Celeste's books. She's a great writer. And I'm a romantic at heart. Annie's the more practical realist. I like fiction – sci-fi, fantasy, romance, horror.

Interviewer: You read horror novels?
Slade: Oh yes, love 'em. King, Koontz, Rice. Shirley Jackson. Edgar Allan Poe, of course.
Annie: I can't read that stuff. Gives me nightmares.
Slade: When she interrupts to read me a passage from Origen, I'll wait about ten minutes and then read a passage to her from Lovecraft for revenge. Something particularly gruesome.
Annie: After all these years, I still don't know how you can read that kind of garbage. It can't be good for your mind or soul.
Slade: I find it helpful to confront your fears. Puts real life in perspective. No matter what trauma we may have faced, we don't have to contend with actual monsters under the bed.
Annie: Real people can be monstrous enough.
Slade: This is true. At least with horror novels, you can eventually defeat the evil. In real life, it never goes away.

Interviewer: What do you consider evil in the real world?
Annie: Humans. People. All of us. We are creatures of duality. Every person is born with the capacity for pure evil, and every person innately has the capacity for incredible love and compassion. Once someone has given themselves over to evil, that capacity for love can disappear. Like Hitler or a Charles Manson.
Slade: Or Marilyn Manson.
Annie: I don't even know who she is.

Interviewer: That duality of the human spirit seems to be the connecting point between both of your works.
Slade: Very true. Annie researches it from a faith perspective, then teaches that to others. I tried to get people to recognize it within themselves, to love themselves so they can make decisions to connect with others through love and compassion, to bring that to the forefront in their minds.

Now I just try to keep the girls from killing each other.

Interviewer: When you have an evening to just sit and talk alone, not reading, what are your favorite topics?

Annie: It might be more of the same, but more often, it's talking about what we did that day, the girls, the garden and animals, or plans to add another room to the house. Routine things like that. Everyday life.

Slade: We've talked about adding another bedroom, or even a separate guest house for visitors. Like when Annie's folks come down, they'd have their own little space.

Annie: But the girls will be growing up and moving out on their own in the not-too-distant future, so that will create a spare bedroom or two. Not sure a guest house would get enough use to make it worthwhile. Just another space I'd have to clean.

Slade: Nah, those girls are never leaving. Well, Mandy can't leave. Who'd make me a sammich?

Annie: I can't believe you keep letting her do that to you.

Interviewer: How do you see life in the future when the girls are grown and presumably on their own? Retirement plans?

Annie: I can't envision myself retiring. I just turned forty. I have a lot more work to do. I might go back to teaching full-time eventually.

Slade: Which is why Mandy can never leave. Who's going to care for me in my dotage? This is what you get for marrying an older man. You'll be spoon-feeding me and changing diapers again.

Jo: Shady Pines, Papa. Shady Pines.

Annie: Jolene, what are you doing here? I told you we weren't to be disturbed unless it's an emergency.

Jo: Well, it's a bit of an emergency. Mandy needs your help.

Annie: Can't it wait until we're finished?

Interviewer: No worries. We can take a break if you need.

Slade: What does she need help with?

Jo: I think you just better come see for yourself.

Slade: Okay, on my way.

Jo: Maybe you should all come. You're not going to believe this. You might even want to put this one in your book.

[We all make our way from Slade's study, down the hallway to Mandy's bedroom.]

Annie: Where is... How... What exactly are you doing up there, young lady?

Slade: How did you even get that way?

Annie: This is definitely your child. Not mine. All yours.

Mandy: *[laughter echoes]*

Slade: Do we get her out now, or do we take some pictures first?

Annie: Get her out before she gets hurt.

Jo: Pictures.

Evvy: Got my phone. Let me get a couple of shots before you get her out.

Slade: Hand me the phone. I'll get the pix since I can't reach her. Y'all need to get a couple of chairs. If you can't get her out, we'll have to call the air conditioning guy.

Annie: You are no help at all. Jo, Evvy, go grab a couple of chairs from the kitchen.

Slade: Mandy, are you okay?

Mandy: Mmm-hmm. I'm fine.

Slade: Can you back out?

Mandy: Nope. I'm stucked-ed.

Annie: Why are you in the air conditioning vent?

Slade: To be technical, it's the air return.

Annie: I don't care what it's called. How did you even get the cover off?

Mandy: I unscrewed it.

Annie: Why are you in there?

Mandy: We were playing hide and seek.

Slade: How did that work out for you?

Mandy: Not so good.

Annie: Right. Because now you're stuck.

Mandy: No, not because I'm stucked-ed. Because they found me.

Slade: Don't you think it's a good thing they found you? What if they hadn't found you and you were stuck in there and missed supper and had to spend the night there?

Mandy: That would make me the winner. Champion of all time at hide and seek.

Jo: Here's chairs.

Annie: You girls get up there and slide her out. Slowly, and be careful. I'll stand here and you hand her down to me. How did you get up there?

Mandy: I climbed-ed the bookshelf.

Annie: Are you ever going to do this again?

Mandy: No, ma'am.

Annie: Why not?

Mandy: Because what Papa always says.

Annie: What does Papa always say?

Mandy, Jo, and Evvy [*in unison*]: Next time you'll know better.

ARTICLES #3

"We do not comment on any active investigation."
~ Federal Bureau of Investigation

Dallas Morning News, Wednesday
Writer, spiritual adviser fatally shot

Slade Bennington, 58, was shot to death at his home an hour south of Dallas Tuesday night, along with a security guard working at the Bennington compound.

No suspects have been identified. The security guard has not been identified pending notification of next of kin.

The Ellis County Sheriff's Department has not released any details and would not confirm if any suspect was at large. Sheriff Reid Armey referred all questions to the Dallas office of the FBI, which is taking the lead on the investigation.

The FBI had no comment as it is an active investigation. Neither would they comment on why the FBI is involved in a local shooting.

Bennington was a double amputee and victim of severe burns from a car accident 29 years ago in Fort Worth. He turned that tragedy, in which his younger sister died, into his life story of overcoming trauma and physical barriers to live a fulfilling life.

Bennington's books, both nonfiction and fiction, made him one of the biggest-selling authors of the past quarter century. Five of his books have been made into movies, including his life story. Bennington also made a career as a spiritual adviser and counselor to the rich and famous.

Bennington married Schuyler Jones, the child star who played his sister in the film version of his life story. Jones, who left the movie industry and is now known as Annamarie Bennington, is an adjunct professor at Southwestern Baptist Theological Seminary in Fort Worth.

Mrs. Bennington could not be reached for comment before deadline.

The Benningtons have three daughters, ages 15, 13 and 6.

New York Post, Thursday

Slade Slay'd!

Shaman to the Stars Shot in Face Suspect Still Sought

Bennington Bodyguard Also Dead in Texas Shootout

Associated Press, Thursday

Security guard believed to be gunman in Bennington murder

The security guard who died in a hail of gunfire at Slade Bennington's residence outside Dallas is suspected to be the gunman who fatally shot author and motivational lecturer Slade Bennington, according to FBI sources.

Bremer Security, Inc., of Dallas, the contractor for security services at the Bennington compound, confirmed that the alleged gunman was Dave Marklin of Waxahachie, age unknown.

Marklin was working as a security guard at the Bennington compound. He had been employed by Bremer for three months and had been detailed to the Bennington location two days prior to Tuesday's shooting.

The FBI did not state why they suspect Marklin in the shooting and did not comment regarding the security guard's motivation.

***

Dallas Morning News, Sunday

Bennington murder details come into focus

The security guard suspected of fatally shooting Slade Bennington, area author and lecturer, has been positively identified as Mark Devlin, 52, stepfather of the late actress Nora Campo, according to an FBI press conference Friday night.

According to the FBI, Devlin approached the Benningtons' front door about 10 p.m. When Bennington opened the door, Devlin opened fire.

The FBI did not release details regarding Devlin's death.

Devlin, a former Navy SEAL, took a job with Bremer Security three months ago under the assumed name Dave Marklin. He was assigned to the Bennington compound last week, two days before the double shooting.

Devlin applied for the position with forged identification documents and rented an apartment in nearby Waxahachie. When an opening came up on the Bennington compound, Devlin requested the assignment, stating that it was convenient because he lived nearby.

Campo died nine years ago after having her legs surgically amputated in the Philippines, an action she claimed to take following spiritual advice from Bennington.

The Devlins filed a $250 million lawsuit against Bennington for the wrongful death of their daughter, which was settled in an out-of-court deal for an undisclosed amount.

***

New York Times, Monday
FBI: Bennington's wife kills guard in self-defense

Dr. Annamarie Bennington, wife of the late Slade Bennington, shot and killed security guard Mark Devlin in self-defense immediately after Mr. Devlin had shot Mr. Bennington, according to an FBI press release.

Dr. Bennington, a former child star and Academy-award winning actress who went by the stage name Schuyler Jones, is a theology professor with a doctorate in religious studies from the American University of Rome.

The FBI reports that Dr. Bennington was in her bedroom when she heard shots fired in the living room, where Mr. Bennington was reading. She retrieved a handgun from her side table and ran down the hallway toward the sound of repeated gunfire.

Mr. Devlin was standing over Mr. Bennington's body on the floor and still shooting when Dr. Bennington fired six rounds, striking Mr. Devlin in the head, chest and stomach.

The Benningtons have three daughters, ages 15, 14 and 6. All were in bed asleep when the shooting erupted. One of the Bennington daughters called 911. Ellis County Sheriff and local paramedics responded.

Mr. Devlin was reported dead at the scene from his injuries.

Mr. Bennington was still conscious and transported by helicopter to the Rees-Jones Trauma Center at Parkland Hospital in Dallas. Hospital officials report that Mr. Bennington died en route. A single gunshot wound to the head was listed as the cause of death. Mr. Bennington also suffered gunshot wounds to the arm and shoulder.

Dr. Bennington did not return calls for comment.

INTERVIEW #40

"Nothing to add to Slade's life. He lived it all up."
~ Matt Bennington

"There'll never be another Slade, that's for sure."
~ Chelsea Mandrake

Interviewer: I understand there's some happier news from you two during this time of grief. Care to share?

Matt: Chelsea is finally going to make an honest man of me. We're getting married after twenty-seven years of unwedded bliss.

Interviewer: I have to ask: After all this time, why now?

Chelsea: It's Slade's fault. He kept pushing us. We never really saw the point in it, but he'd tell us it meant something. It was that formal commitment for life that he thought was so important. I guess he finally convinced us both of that. And my mom passed away last year, so I don't have anywhere to run home to when Matt pisses me off. Might as well stay here and fight it out.

Matt: It also makes me eligible for Chelsea's Social Security in a few years. She just turned sixty, and I turn sixty in a few months.

Chelsea: He always has to point out that he's six months younger than me, like I was robbing the cradle or something.

Matt: We'd planned on telling Slade this week. I guess he knows now. Just like Slade to spoil a surprise.

Chelsea: And we got more news too.

Matt: Wait, what? You're pregnant?

Chelsea: Asshole. Of course not. At my age? I'd throw myself off a bridge somewhere. *[Chelsea playfully punches Matt on the shoulder]*

Matt: Oh, you mean the song thing. Yeah.

Chelsea: Yeah. After Slade died, I did a song tribute for him. I videoed myself doing three covers for his girls: "Jolene," "Evangeline," and "Amanda." Waylon Jennings wrote that last one, and it's a great song for little Mandy. Slade always called her the light of his life. I sang them at the funeral too.

Matt: Tell him how that went.

Chelsea: I'll get there if you stop interrupting.

Well, my cover of "Jolene" went viral. A lot of people saw it and linked to it because it was dedicated to Slade, to his sister and daughter, and then it just took off. So many people saw it that YouTube started sticking ads on it.

Interviewer: That's fantastic.

Matt: That's not even the news. She's working her way up to that. Hurry up before I tell him myself.

Chelsea: Don't rush me. I'm a storyteller. Anyways, it was several hundred thousand views, heading toward a million, and some Nashville producer caught wind of it. He was impressed with my version, I guess, enough to click around on my channel for a bit. And he liked two of my original songs.

Matt: So this producer contacted Chelsea and wants to shop her songs to some top country artists.

Chelsea: You just had to step on my story, didn't you?

Interviewer: Could this lead to a recording contract for you?

Chelsea: At my age? Nah. I'm more likely to get pregnant than get a record deal. But if even one song I've written gets recorded by some big name, and maybe even hits the charts, that would be a dream. An absolute dream.

Interviewer: With the events of last month, my publisher gave me some extra time to add anything to the story I'm telling about Slade. Any last-minute thoughts you want to make sure I know about? About Slade, his life, his death, his legacy?

Matt: Nothing to add to Slade's life. He lived it all up.

Chelsea: There'll never be another Slade, that's for sure. My heart breaks for Annie and the girls. Those girls are his legacy.

Matt: Yeah, the world ain't going to know what hit it.

INTERVIEW #41

**"Boats make me seasick, but I can't stand the
thought of Billy out there alone, no Slade."**
~ Bea Thomas

"Most men I've met aren't half the man Slade was."
~ Rev. Billy Thomas

Bea: I'm so sorry Billy couldn't join us today. He planned on it, but he's too distraught to talk yet. He spoke at Slade's funeral and barely made it through. I've never seen him that shook up, voice cracking, hands trembling, lips quivering. First time I ever thought he looked his age.

He's trying to go around and comfort and console everyone else, especially Annie and the girls, but who is there to comfort the pastor? I try to, but I don't have any words for him. I can hold his hand, and I want to say something, but no words will come.

Annie is so young to lose her husband. And in such a horrible way. I think it's worse when it's completely unexpected like that. Whether a shooting, a car accident, a heart attack. If he'd gotten the cancer or some disease, you at least have time to prepare yourself, to spend some time together, to say goodbye. You always hope you get a long life with your husband.

Then again, with something like this, you don't have a lot of long, drawn-out suffering. Maybe it's better like this. I don't know. I just don't know.

I just want to hug those girls all day every day. Annie too.

She's being so strong for her girls that I worry she's going to completely fall apart once she stops to take a breath.

Slade was Billy's best friend in the world besides me, and I'd never go fishing with him.

I might need to go with him now. I can't handle the rocking of the boat, makes me seasick. But I can't stand the thought of my Billy being out there all alone, no Slade around.

Billy said to tell you – hang on a sec, I wrote it down. Here it is. Billy said to tell you, "Most men I've met in this world aren't half the man that Slade was."

INTERVIEW #42

"They are all the same dead."
~ Rosaria Ocampo-Devlin

Interviewer: When was the last time you saw your husband?

Rosaria: It's been almost a year now. Not since before I moved back to Pili. I knew something wasn't right, but I had no idea he'd do something like this. He emailed a few months ago to tell me he'd quit his job as a defense contractor, said he was moving to Texas for work and he'd let me know his address as soon as he was settled. That was the last time I ever heard from him. And he had gotten a great job as a contractor after he retired from the Navy, so I don't know why he quit. He seemed very unhappy. He had never been happy since Nora died.

Interviewer: What were your first thoughts when you heard Slade Bennington was murdered?

Rosaria: When I heard about Mr. Bennington, I thought that was just horrible. Despite everything, I would never wish that on him or anyone. Him dying doesn't bring back my Nora. And I never thought it was all his fault for what happened to Nora. I don't think he did anything intentionally bad to Nora, but he didn't help. He just took advantage, and she was too weak to stand up to him.

We were hurting, and Mark especially was lashing out. I wanted to cry all day, but Mark wanted to do something. I think his job in the Navy made him want to do something, fix the problem. But there was no fixing Nora.

I talked to Mr. Bennington once after Nora died, and we cried together on the phone. Then Mark forbid me from talking to him anymore. He went and hired lawyers and he wanted to crush Slade. Financially, I mean. To punish him more than to get money from him.

Interviewer: Did you have any idea Mark was thinking of doing something like this? That he was capable of doing this?

Rosaria: Oh no, no, not at all. When I first heard, I thought, oh, I need to get in touch with Mark to let him know. I thought he would hear the news and get some feeling of closure or at least let go of his anger and hatred. It never occurred to me Mark might be involved. None of the news stories said anything like that at first. I never imagined that Mark would be a security guard. How did he get that job? And get assigned to Mr. Bennington's house? I don't understand.

Interviewer: How did you find out Mark was involved? And that Mark had died?

Rosaria: An FBI agent called and told me. I thought someone was playing a mean joke on me. I couldn't believe it. My head wouldn't accept it. Mark, a murderer? Mark, dead? I went all numb everywhere. I couldn't believe it. Even now, it doesn't seem true. Like Mark is going to call any minute and say it was someone else and they just thought it was him but it was all a mistake. Every time my phone rings, I have this thought that it's going to be Mark and all this is going away.

My first husband died, and he deserved it, and I hated him for what he did. My second husband died, and he deserved it. But I still love him. My daughter died, but she didn't deserve it.

Slade died. I can't say if he deserved it or not.

But they are all the same dead.

INTERVIEW #43

"Coincidence is God's way of remaining anonymous."
~ Albert Einstein

Shelby (movie studio executive): Awful stuff. What's this world coming to?

Danielle (psychologist): Mr. Devlin's mind had obviously gone to a dark place. Sometimes when faced with grief, people dive in so deep they can't find their way to the surface again.

Vicki (motivational speaker): Karma can be a bitch, and so can I.

Frank (airline pilot, retired military): That Slade dude played with fire, and eventually it burned him.

INTERVIEW #44

"All those guns. That's the thing that worries me
most about moving to Texas."
~ Dr. Richard Jones

"It's not like there aren't a lot of guns here in Chicago."
~ Celeste Jones, aka Celeste Rousseau

Interviewer: How is Annie holding up? How are you two holding up?

Celeste: Annie is strong, but she's devastated.

Richard: As are we.

Celeste: We both flew down immediately, of course. Just came back to Chicago to start packing. We're moving to Texas to be closer. We planned on that already, but I'm going to head back down next week.

Richard: I gave my immediate notice to the university. We'll be renting an apartment in Dallas while we look for a condo.

Celeste: Or maybe stay with Annie for a bit. Those girls need us. Annie needs us. She needs a break from being strong. She's taking care of the girls, so focused on them she hasn't stopped to grieve for herself.

Richard: Those two were so dependent on each other. Both so independent at the same time. She'll be fine, but she needs time.

Celeste: She needs us. I just can't believe all this. Who would do such a thing?

Richard: Who would shoot a man in his home, at point-blank range?

Celeste: A man in a wheelchair.

Richard: Over something that happened nearly ten years ago and wasn't even Slade's fault.

Celeste: I do feel awful for Mrs. Devlin. Her daughter dies so tragically. Mental illness and all, and all so publicly. Then her husband leaves her, murders someone, and then he dies too, and this is so publicized as well. This all has to be hard for her to live with.

Richard: There are way too many guns out there. That's the thing that scares me most about moving to Texas.

Celeste: Well, it's a good thing Annie was armed. Who knows if that man would have killed Annie and the girls too? And it's not like Chicago doesn't have a gun problem.

Richard: I really worry about Annie. I mean, she had to kill a man. She had to do it to protect her family, but that's got to be difficult to live with no matter what. I can't even imagine being in that position. Having to shoot a gun at another human being. To take someone's life.

Celeste: She did the right thing, what she had to do.

Richard: Yes, but it's going to be hard for her to deal with that trauma.

Celeste: And those poor girls. They saw their father lying on the floor in a pool of blood, heard all the gunshots. Annie's got them in counseling already, of course. Those children will be scarred for life. Those precious, precious babies.

INTERVIEW #45

"I'll deal with me later. I have more important responsibilities right now."
~ Dr. Annamarie Bennington, PhD, aka Schuyler Jones

Annie: You've got all the media reports and the police reports, the FBI information. I'm not sure if there's anything else I can tell you about that night. I've told the story so many times now, I really don't want to repeat it again.

Interviewer: I completely understand, and I won't ask you to. And yes, I've read all the documents and reports, all the news stories. Is there anything in all that you'd like to correct? Something they got wrong?
Annie: There are lots of details the media gets wrong, or things I might think are important that they leave out. But nothing critical. Nothing worth bothering them over. There was a press conference with twenty reporters, twenty stories were written, and you'd think they were writing about twenty different cases. They all contradicted each other. It's never anything big though, so it doesn't matter.

Interviewer: You haven't spoken to the press or given any kind of statement.
Annie: No, other than our attorney telling everyone to please leave us alone, family grieving, children need privacy, etc. Reporters from all over the world showed up, you know. The famous Schuyler Jones, child star, all that stuff from my previous life came roaring back.
I've been through all that and it's all behind me. I won't give a single one of them the time of day.

Interviewer: Is that more difficult living out here in the country, kind of secluded?
Annie: Just the opposite. We've got deputies, off-duty officers, and FBI all around the place. No one gets past the gate, and that's two hundred yards from the house. With all the trees, the paparazzi can't get a photo from out there.

One TV station was flying a helicopter over the property. The FBI told them they'd be considered a threat and would get shot out of the sky, so they stopped. Or at least moved a little farther out.

Interviewer: How are the girls?

Annie: About how you might imagine. Jo is crying all the time. Cries in her sleep. Mandy is having trouble processing it, understanding that her daddy isn't coming back from the hospital. She knows, but her young mind isn't accepting it yet. But at least she is sleeping through the night. No night terrors.

I worry about Evvy the most. It was her birthday. Her father was murdered on her fourteenth birthday.

She's being my rock. She's comforting Jo and Mandy. She's comforting me. But she's in shock. She saw the whole thing. She's the only one who saw. And she's not letting herself grieve. She tries to take care of everyone else. She's cleaning house, cooking, taking care of Mandy. She's staying busy all the time. Restless. I'm afraid that if she stops for a few minutes, it will all crash down on her. Thirteen years old – fourteen now, sorry – and an overnight adult.

Interviewer: Slade said she was always that way. A lot like you.

Annie: Yes, but this is too much to put on her. I think she's following my lead. Staying busy. Taking care of others. That's how I need to get through this, and she's doing the same. But she needs to grieve. To let me and others comfort her. She's too young for this.

Jo is old enough that, as hard as this is going to be for her, she is maturing into an adult and she will figure it out. Mandy is young enough that she has her whole childhood ahead of her, and the memories will fade. She'll accept it.

Evvy is exactly the wrong age, and the wrong personality type, to handle this right now. I try to keep a close eye on her. I hate that she will have this annual reminder on what should be her day to celebrate.

Interviewer: What about you?

Annie: I'll deal with me later. I have more important responsibilities to tend to right now.

Interviewer: Do you think you'll stay here? Or is it going to be hard to stay in this house without Slade?

Annie: This is our home. Yes, everything will be a reminder of Slade. But that's not a bad thing. I don't want to uproot the girls and take away their home as well as their father.

Interviewer: You feel safe here?

Annie: As safe as anywhere. When there's someone out there determined to kill you, it really doesn't matter where you live.

Interviewer: What about your teaching, writing?

Annie: I'm taking a semester off. Then I'll go back to it. Back to life. Life goes on, you know. You can't stay home and grieve the rest of your life. The girls will need our regular routine back. Of course, nothing will be the old routine without Slade underfoot.

Interviewer: You and Slade seemed to have had a very unusual relationship. You're a strong, independent woman, yet you chose to be a mostly stay-at-home mother and wife. You each had separate lives, and yet seem inseparable at the same time. This is going to be a major adjustment.

Annie: 'Til death do us part. We have parted, for now. We always knew it would be this way at some point in our lives. Slade had health issues, so I never anticipated that he might live to be eighty or ninety. And with our age difference, I always knew I'd have some years without him unless something unexpected happened to me first. No one is guaranteed tomorrow.

I never viewed our relationship as unusual though. Yes, it was traditional, old-school, in many ways. And yet Slade was so incredibly supportive of everything I wanted to do, everything I wanted to accomplish in life. I couldn't have done it without him. To have him here by my side was the biggest gift one could ask for.

One of Slade's favorite lines was, "We have a traditional home with the perfect balance. I am the head of the household, but Annie wears the pants in the family."

People always mention that I'm a stay-at-home mom, but they never mention that Slade was a stay-at-home dad. The past few years, I've traveled or been gone from home more than Slade. He'd become quite the homebody. Those occasional fishing trips with Billy were about the only times I could get him out of the house. He cooked more meals than I did. I usually taught the girls their lessons, then Slade would take over and do homework with them. That would turn into late-night discussions about whatever they were interested in, or Slade would read to them.

I'd have to intervene to make the girls go to bed. Especially Amanda, since she was the youngest. I'd have to make sure she went to bed, or she'd fall asleep sitting in the chair with Slade.

But now and then, Slade and Evangeline would stay up, the rest of us in bed asleep. I'd wake up in the morning, usually around five, and they'd still be sitting up talking.

I'd ask Slade later what they were talking about all night long, and he'd say, "Life, man. We're just talking about life."

He had always been working on something. He'd had so many projects – books, movies, lectures, on and on, all going on at once. Meetings with this group of people or that group. Literary agent and book publishers in New York. Studio executives in LA Sometimes in the same week.

But the past three years, he'd really cut back and settled into being a full-time dad. Maybe especially to little Mandy. You always love your kids equally, but you love them differently. Slade understood that better than anyone. And Mandy was his pet, no doubt about it.

When the other two were young, he was always working, traveling. With Mandy, he semiretired. Those two were best buddies.

His relationship with each of the girls was so completely different. That man never had a father, so I'm not sure how he learned it. He loved them so much, and he saw each one for the unique individuals they are. He's much better at that than I am. I was always amazed, and always trying to learn from him, but that doesn't come naturally to me.

Interviewer: I read that Slade was still conscious and talking after the shooting. Was he coherent? Did he realize what had happened?

Annie: Yes, he was fully aware. A lot of blood, but he was still conscious somehow. I got on the helicopter with him to the hospital. Billy and Bea took the girls. I held Slade's hand and we talked on the flight for a few minutes.

Interviewer: Do you feel like sharing what he said?

Annie: His first words after the shooting were, "Not again." He was cracking a joke to keep the tension down, but I think he realized at that moment he wasn't going to survive.

Jo called 911 while I held a towel on the bleeding. Evvy stood in the corner shaking, and I sent Jo and Mandy to be with her. I didn't want them to watch their father die, to see all that blood. But Slade kept motioning for them to come to him. He wanted to see them, talk to them.

We all sat down on the floor with him. Everyone held towels against different wounds. I kept pressure on the one on his head. I knew it wasn't going to do any good, but it was more to hide it from the girls. The couple of holes in his arms and shoulder didn't look so bad, and holding towels on them kept the girls busy.

Slade told them he loved them. He didn't say that to the group. He told each one, individually.

"Jo, you are my bright and shining star. Embrace it. Walk in the light to combat the darkness. I love you.

"Mandy, you're the light of my life. Never lose your joy. I love you.

"Evvy, you did the right thing. Always know that. You won't always do the right thing, and you must forgive yourself when you don't. But there is no need to forgive yourself for doing the right thing. I love you."

Interviewer: And on the med-evac flight?

Annie: We talked for a few minutes, but it was getting difficult for him. It was hard to hear over the engine noise, and his voice was weak.

But we both said we loved each other. I told him he made me complete.

He said, "You were always complete, and you always will be."

He said something else, but I didn't catch it. Then he said he loved me and to look after his girls, to hold onto that contentment and our memories for them.

Then he closed his eyes and lost consciousness. I moved aside while the paramedics worked on him until we landed. But the lead, I think her name was Serenity or Felicity or something like that, I wish I could remember. She reached over and grabbed my hand and looked me in the eyes. She didn't have to say a word.

He was gone.

INTERVIEW #46

"That little Rainbow Sig saved a lot of lives."
~ Roland DeVries, FBI agent-in-charge

Interviewer: Anything new from the investigation or anything important that hasn't been reported that you can share?

DeVries: We've confirmed now that Devlin was the source of the death threats three years ago. He'd used his government computer and his military training as a Navy SEAL to route phone calls through multiple switches so they were difficult to trace. He had computer software to mask his voice. Even remoted into the security cameras at the dance studio and knew how to pop a combination lock. Never left a single fingerprint or piece of DNA.

Interviewer: But he'd stopped the threats after a few months.

DeVries: Yes, and that's always a concern. Sometimes people stop the threats because they got it out of their system, or they're afraid of getting caught if they think we're closing in on them. Or something happens to them.

But sometimes it's because they've come up with a different plan, made the decision to follow through on their threats.

Interviewer: But a three-year gap?

DeVries: Yes, about two and a half or so. He used meticulous planning and misdirection to make the threats. Then he went underground and meticulously planned the execution of his threats.

Quit his job, created a whole new identity, including a job history, Social Security number, driver's license. Even a forged DD-214 to show an honorable discharge from the military. He moved to Texas, not far from the Benningtons' place. Then he applied for a job at the security firm that provided gate guards to the Benningtons. He applied three times over several months before he got hired.

Then he did several different assignments for them until he had the opportunity to get detailed to the Benningtons.

From there, he took two days before he marched up to the door and killed Slade Bennington.

Bennington probably didn't think anything about the guard coming to the door to check on them or bring them a package. UPS and FedEx always dropped packages with the gate guard.

Interviewer: Didn't Slade recognize Mark Devlin? I mean, they knew each other.

DeVries: No. Apparently, they'd never met face-to-face. Talked on the phone many years ago. Bennington had met Mrs. Devlin in person, but never Mr. Devlin.

Interviewer: Do you think Devlin would have killed the whole family if Annie hadn't shot him?

DeVries: It's quite likely. Looks like he was planning to. He had a Glock that holds sixteen rounds and three extra magazines on him. Sixty-four rounds isn't necessary to kill one person.

Interviewer: Good thing Annie was armed and trained.

DeVries: Yeah, that little Rainbow Sig probably saved a lot of lives.

INTERVIEW #47

"Sometimes in life, sir, there are questions best left unasked."
~ Dr. Annamarie Bennington, PhD, aka Schuyler Jones

Interviewer: I was looking through all the FBI reports again, and I hope you don't mind clearing something up for me. I hate to keep asking you to relive that night, but I want to make sure I get the details accurate. Newspapers can run a correction tomorrow. Correcting and reprinting a book is a lot more difficult.

Annie: Never a problem. We have the same goal here.

Interviewer: The reports say the first shot to Devlin hit him on the left side of the head, and that was instantly fatal. Then five more shots to the torso after he was on the ground.

Annie: Yes, I'm sure that's probably right. In a situation like that, you keep squeezing the trigger. I don't really remember the details. I just did it. Like a dream or something. I remember, but it's all fuzzy. I think it all took about three seconds. Seemed like hours. Seems like it never happened, like it wasn't real.

Interviewer: Slade was in the living room, right?

Annie: Yes.

Interviewer: What was he doing?

Annie: Talking to Evvy. He was staying up to spend some one-on-one time with her on her birthday. One of their late-night discussions, although it wasn't too late yet. That's how Evvy saw the whole thing, why she is so traumatized. I never told that to the FBI. I didn't want her further traumatized by being questioned about what she saw. I told them Slade was alone and the girls were all in bed asleep.

Interviewer: You had gone to bed?

Annie: Yes. I was still awake, reading.

Interviewer: Your bedroom is down the hall to the right of the front door.
　　Annie: Yes.

Interviewer: What was Devlin doing when you saw him?
　　Annie: Slade had fallen out of his chair. Devlin was standing over him, still pulling the trigger.

Interviewer: So you were on Devlin's right side. How did you shoot him in the left side of the head?
　　Annie: Who knows? It all happened so fast. It's a blur.

Interviewer: Had you already given Evvy that Rainbow Sig for her birthday?
　　Annie: Sometimes in life, sir, there are questions best left unasked.

INTERVIEW #48

"The world is a darker place without Slade in it."
~ Randall Kleifisch

Interviewer: Where were you when you heard about Slade's murder? How did you hear?

Randall: Ethan and I had finished a late dinner, cleaned up the kitchen, and sat down on the patio for an aperitif. Ethan was checking his phone, as he does constantly, and said there was a shooting in Texas. That didn't surprise me. I mean, it's Texas. That's hardly even news. But we wondered if it was another mass shooting at a mall or church or something. All that was being reported at that time were two dead and the shooter was still on the loose.

The next morning, I'm back out on the patio having coffee, and my phone rings about the same time Ethan screams. He's yelling, just incoherent, I'm trying to get him to shut up so I can answer my phone. It was Duncan, my admin from the studio, and he never calls without texting first, so I knew it was urgent.

Then I've got Duncan yelling in one ear and Ethan yelling in the other that Slade was murdered.

I was horrified. We were all crying and screaming, Ethan is hugging me, and then it dawned on me. The story from the night before said two were killed. *Oh my God! They killed Schuyler too* was the first thing that crossed my mind. And I must have said it out loud because both Ethan and Duncan are screaming even louder, "No, no, not Schuyler!"

Oh my God, it was horrible. I didn't know who to call or what to do. I threw clothes on and went to the studio. Duncan came in and was scouring the internet for every news story he could find, and he'd give me an update with a new detail every few minutes.

I was so relieved when I found out Schuyler was alive. I think it was about four or five hours I assumed she was dead. I called Ethan to let him know and we cried on the phone. Happy that Schuyler was okay and mortified that Slade was gone.

Slade was gone. It doesn't seem possible, does it? He'd survived so much, it felt like he was invincible. Immortal. How does it just end like that? Horrible, just horrible.

Interviewer: Have you talked to Annie, Schuyler?

Randall: I didn't want to intrude on her time right now with family. I had Duncan send flowers and a nice note, let her know she was in our thoughts and prayers, and that if there was anything I could do, to please let me know.

I haven't heard from her, but I know she's got her hands full. There was the funeral service, which was small and family only in their little town. Those take a lot of planning in a short amount of time. And she's got all those children to tend to. I think it best if I wait until things settle down for her before I reach out.

I'm devastated, I tell you. Gutted.

Interviewer: What did you think about Nora's father, stepfather, being the one who murdered Slade?

Randall: Horrible, horrible things in this world. The evil that will get into someone's mind and take them down such terrible roads. I just don't understand it.

Interviewer: Any final thoughts about Slade that you'd like to make sure I include?

Randall: What a brilliant man, such a kind spirit. He brought so much light to this world. The world is a darker place without him in it.

Interviewer: Thank you for your time, Mr. Kleifisch.

Randall: Any time. And call me Randall.

Say, is there a chance I could get an early copy of your book when you're done? Perhaps there could be a film rights deal for it. I mean, with all that is going on with this in the news, the timing would be perfect.

I spoke with Tom Fallon last week and he was up for the idea of reprising his role as Slade. When she's ready to talk, I'd love to see if I can convince Schuyler to return to acting for one more movie – to portray herself. Siena said she'd play Nora again.

Put your agent in touch with me. I can see the Oscar statues lined up for this one.

I'm telling you, this could be a blockbuster.

A LETTER FROM SLADE

"I caught my limit in life."
~ Slade Bennington

Dearest Robb:

Thanks for the advance review copy. Looking forward to seeing this come out in print. I will miss our discussions and your visits.

We'll have you over for barbecue goat if I'm able to convince the girls that it is indeed dinner, and not a pet. When they named it Merlin, I knew there would be trouble afoot. The fool thing follows Mandy around like a puppy. This isn't how our first attempt at raising meat was supposed to go.

Great to hear about your retirement and your pending move to the lake where you can write and fish full-time. Yes, get that boat in the water and I'll be up to visit. We'll feed some fish. But I'll have to fib to Rev Billy and tell him we caught our limit.

I believe I have caught my limit in life. It is probably illegal to have any more blessings than I do. Especially since I earned and deserved none of them.

Annie and the kids send their best. Stay in touch.
Your friend,
S

The End

...But please keep reading for some bonus material, including an **Interview with the Author** and two Special Sneak Previews, featuring excerpts of Robb Grindstaff's first two novels: *Hannah's Voice* and *Carry Me Away*.

INTERVIEW WITH THE AUTHOR

Q. Where did this story come from? What inspired it?
A. I never know the answer to this question.

I'm one of those lucky ones who can fall asleep within moments of lying down. I don't even have to be sleepy. If I lie down, I fall asleep. But one night I tossed and turned until about three a.m. because this character invaded my head and wouldn't shut up.

Q. What about the unusual structure of the story? It's not written in standard fiction narrative.
A. When Slade invaded my head, I didn't know the story and I didn't know much about the character. I crawled out of bed at three a.m. and started jotting some notes down, since he wasn't going to let me sleep anyway. I decided to use an old technique to get to know the character and his background: interview the character. I've used this on occasion and I recommend this to other writers, my editing clients, and in courses that I teach. I just asked questions and let Slade answer while I took dictation. When he'd mention some other character, I would interview that person.

I didn't set out intending to write a novel as a series of interviews. The interviews kept growing, the characters revealing the story one layer at a time. I had every intention of taking what I learned from the interviews to craft a normal story, a narrative with characters, setting, plot, dialogue, description—all the usual elements of writing a novel.

But as the interviews progressed, it occurred to me that it might actually work as a collection of interviews. That required a few additional interviews, creating some background material such as newspaper articles and journals, and organizing it all into the right order.

When I was done, I wasn't sure if I had a novel or just 60,000 words of raw material that I needed to completely rewrite to turn it into a novel. I passed it around to a few trusted readers—ones I knew would be brutally honest and tell me this was a pile of crap.

But they liked it. They had great and helpful feedback to make it better, but they liked the nonstandard storytelling structure.

So, I went with it.

Q. The story never fully answers the question: Was Slade a wonderful human being or a manipulative con man? How do you see him? You invented him, after all.

A. I don't know the answer to that question. That will be up to each reader to decide. It could be some of both. With very few exceptions, people aren't fully great or fully evil. We are all a mix. Even when we have the best of intentions, sometimes we fail. We have flaws and imperfections. We can care about others and still be selfish and self-centered.

No matter what someone does, some people will view them as a good person, admire them, even love them. Others will view them exactly the opposite.

The other characters' views of Slade depended on their perspectives and their interactions with him. Readers can also be of two different opinions, depending on which characters they felt had the most accurate perception of Slade.

The question also arises: Was Slade manipulative or was he manipulated by others?

Q. I'll make that my next question then. How would Slade have been manipulated, and by whom?

A. This sounds like I'm interviewing myself, sort of like when I wrote the book.

However, I think I'll decline to answer that. Some readers might pick up on this, some might not. I don't want to direct a reader's attention to something specific. In fiction as in real life, sometimes things aren't what they might appear to be on the surface. Other times, what you see is what you get.

Q. I found the various interpretations of faith and religion between the different characters interesting. Was this the major theme of the story?

A. Maybe it turned out that way. I didn't start with a theme in mind. The characters just told me their stories. I didn't intend to write a religious or faith-based book, and it's certainly not in the Christian fiction genre. But the characters, like people in real life, all have different perspectives and differing beliefs, from a traditional faith to a more general spiritual belief to nonbelief.

Q. How much of Slade's outlook on life and faith are yours?
A. I'm closer to Annie than Slade. But Annie and Slade have been debating in my head for half a century now.

Q. You like to surprise, or even shock readers, don't you?
A. That's the greatest joy of reading, isn't it? Being surprised. A twist, an unexpected moment—whether emotional, terrifying, shocking, satisfying, whatever. If you always know what's coming, what fun is it?

That gut-punch moment is always one of my favorites to read or to write. John Irving (*World According to Garp, A Prayer for Owen Meany,* among many other novels) is a master of this. I tried to learn from him. When you can be laughing out loud at some scene, then turn the page and realize something awful happened while you were laughing—a gut punch. And you feel guilty for laughing.

When I'm writing, if something surprises or shocks me, I'll know readers are likely to be surprised and shocked as well.

Q. Moving away from this particular work, what is your usual creative process? What's a day like in the head of Robb Grindstaff?
A. You don't want to know. It's scary in there.

I don't have a usual process. It seems every book or story I've written comes to me in a different way, and it gets written in a different way. I've taken years to write a novel. I wrote the first draft of Slade in three weeks. I have gone months without writing a word, and I've had weeks on end when I will write for eight or ten hours every day.

But always—or almost always—it's the character who shows up first. Then I have to get the character talking to me, capture his or her voice, and let the character tell me the story.

Once the character starts talking, I start writing. Sometimes I'll have a sketch of an outline, sometimes a more detailed outline, but often I have no idea what comes next.

When writing, I'll start each morning by rereading what I wrote yesterday, making edits and changes along the way before I start on the next chapter or scene. Sometimes I might reread the previous three or four scenes, or even the whole book up to that point. By the time I've finished a first draft, I've probably read it several dozen times, constantly revising and editing on each pass.

Once I have a completed first draft, I will set it aside and work on something else for a month or two before I come back to it with fresh eyes. I will reread it, edit it, tweak it, add or delete scenes, over and over. Dozens more, if not hundreds of times.

Then I'll enlist the help of a few trusted test readers (bless their hearts). With their input, I'll make more revisions.

Then my publisher assigns it to an editor, and the real work begins.

My writing routine, when I'm writing routinely, generally starts at six or seven in the morning for two or three hours, then again later that evening, after supper, for another two or three hours. That way I still have the bulk of the day to do other stuff, like fishing or grilling some hamburgers or taking a nap.

I also edit and mentor other writers, teach the occasional course on the craft of writing fiction, so all that keeps me involved in writing even when I'm not writing something of my own.

Q. You mentioned using an outline, but you also said you let the characters talk while you take dictation. Do you consider yourself a plotter or a pantser?
A. Both. Depends on the book, and often a combination of the two.

Most of the time, I get to know the character and let the character tell me the story. Pure pantser, at least to start. I don't know the story, so I have nothing to outline. But as the story comes into focus, I'll sketch out an outline.

For one book, *Hannah's Voice*, the entire story and character came to me in an instant. A flash while I was driving. I drove straight home and wrote down the quick synopsis and outline. Then it took me five years to write it and three more years to get it published.

When I have an outline, however, it's just a general guideline. If the story veers off in a different direction, I let it go. Let the character run with it and see. Then I have to decide whether to change the outline or change what I've written to get it back on track.

I try to use the outline as a map with a route that leads from Point A to Point Z. But if the story detours, maybe we just take a different or more scenic route and still wind up at Point Z. Or maybe we go somewhere completely unexpected.

Typically, I can't get rolling with the writing until I have the first sentence and the last sentence: Points A and Z. Then I only have to write the 10,000 sentences that go between the two. Easy.

Q. Your background is in newspaper journalism. How is that different from writing fiction?
A. I'll quote Slade on this one because he said it better than I could: "Fiction contains more truth than nonfiction. Or at least it's easier to digest."

But the experience in journalism is crucial to my fiction writing. Write tight, my journalism professor said, and I heard that repeatedly from editors throughout my career. Be spare with words. Write directly. Simply. Plainly. Understandably. The fewer the words, the better.

Q. How did you get into editing fiction and mentoring other fiction writers?
A. In addition to a forty-year career in the newspaper business, I've written fiction most of my life as well. I started getting serious about fiction more than twenty years ago. I soon discovered that combining my experience as a newspaper editor and a fiction writer made a good partnership that allowed me to help other writers. While it was a sideline to my day job in newspapers, fiction has been my passion for decades.

In college, I planned to major in English but decided to double major with journalism. I'd need an actual job until I wrote the Great American Novel and became rich and famous.

That was one of the best decisions I ever made as a teenager. Journalism and the newspaper/news media world was a wonderful career, and it gave my family and me the opportunity to live abroad for many years and see a large chunk of the world.

I retired from the newspaper business a couple of years ago and now devote all my time to writing, editing, fishing, and being a grandpa.

Q. What's next for Robb Grindstaff?
A. I have finally—years in the works—completed the first draft of *Turning Trixie*. Trixie, a single mom and the small town's only prostitute, knows the winning lottery ticket in her purse is about to change her life. Trouble starts when she decides the rest of the town needs changing too.

I have three other novels in various stages of outlines, sketches, notes, and partial manuscripts that are competing for my attention, along with a dozen more ideas. We'll see which character talks the loudest.

Q. Last question. Your stripper name is the color of your shirt and the last thing you had for lunch. What's yours?
A. My shirt is gray. I had tacos for lunch. I don't think I should play this game.

ACKNOWLEDGEMENTS

A tremendous thank you to Evolved Publishing for taking a chance on me a few years ago, and for publisher Lane Diamond for his willingness to take an even bigger chance on this weird book.

To my guinea pig crew — test readers who suffered through rough first drafts: You all provided such wonderful (and sometimes painfully honest) feedback that helped me improve the story and writing, and encouragement to keep going at just the right times. My test readers included some exceptional writers and some nonwriters who are avid readers: Jonas Saul, EC Stilson, Ryan R. Campbell, Tamra Reynolds, Jillana Sweet, David Schwartz, and Greg Peck.

A huge thank you to Dr. Resa Willis, PhD and Lizard Queen, for her guidance and advice on social media marketing. If you purchased this book because you saw a social media post of mine, you can thank (or blame) Dr. Resa, AKA Dre SA.

My greatest kudos, and deepest sympathies, to my phenomenal editor, Jessica West. The hardest customer any editor can have is another editor. She could be tough as nails and make me think it was my idea. This story is much better because of her. Any errors you may find in this book are mine and mine alone. Probably something Jess told me I should change but I refused. *Laissez les bon temps rouler.*

ABOUT THE AUTHOR

In addition to a career as a newspaper editor, publisher, and manager, Robb Grindstaff has written fiction most of his life. The newspaper biz has taken him and his family from Phoenix, Arizona, to small towns in North Carolina, Texas, and Wisconsin, from seven years in Washington, D.C., to five years in Asia. Born and raised a small-town kid, he's as comfortable in Tokyo or Tuna, Texas.

The variety of places he's lived and visited serve as settings for the characters who invade his head.

His novels are probably best classified as contemporary southern lit, and he's had more than a dozen short stories published in a wide array of genres. His articles on the craft of fiction writing have appeared in various writer magazines and websites, and one of his seminars was presented at the Sydney (Australia) Writers Festival. He also has taught writing courses for the Romance Writers of America, Romance Writers of Australia, and Savvy Authors.

Robb retired from the newspaper business in the summer of 2020 to write and edit fiction full time.

For more, please visit Robb online at **www.RobbGrindstaff.com**.

WHAT'S NEXT?

Robb Grindstaff is at work on his fourth novel, *Turning Trixie*, which we hope to release in the fall of 2022. To stay up to date on this and all important news from Evolved Publishing, please subscribe to our newsletter at the link below.

~~~

www.EvolvedPub.com/Newsletter

HANNAH'S VOICE

PROLOGUE

"Pancakes."

With that one word, I broke my silence of a dozen years.

"I said I want the goddamn pancakes."

Finally, I got what I really wanted. Not the pancakes, but some silence. Everyone else shut up. Finally.

I hadn't decided to stop talking forever, or even for twelve years. I'd just chosen not to speak at a moment in time.

Sometimes decisions have a way of forging your future, setting a path before you that you must travel, even if you're only six years old when you make the choice.

CHAPTER 1

TWELVE YEARS EARLIER....

"Hannah, did you clean your room?"

Yes. I'd already answered Momma twice. I always answered the same question more than once, and always told the truth, so there was no need to keep asking, checking to see if I'd trip up and change my answer. Some kids are born with lies in their mouths, but I didn't know how. Why make up a different answer other than the one I knew in my head or could see with my eyes? I remembered cleaning my room.

She could have looked rather than asking me three or four or twenty times. She always did that, whether about cleaning my room or brushing my teeth or studying my Sunday School lesson on Saturday night. She had to ask the same questions over and over.

"Hannah, I asked if you cleaned your room. Answer me. Don't just stand there like you're deaf and dumb."

It wouldn't do any good to answer her. She'd just ask again in a few minutes. Answering her wouldn't make it any cleaner, but I wouldn't get supper until she knew it was spotless. Every day I cleaned my room. Every day I used the feather duster and the can of furniture polish and the vacuum cleaner that was taller than me, even under the bed and behind the dresser.

Momma didn't want the devil hiding in the dust under the bed. That was what had taken Daddy. Since Daddy was a Christian man, the devil couldn't keep him, so Satan had put the dust in his lungs and made him go to sleep forever, leaving Momma and me alone. I kept the dust out of my room because I wanted to wake up in the morning. Mostly. Some nights I prayed to God to let me be with Daddy, but then I'd pray for forgiveness, because it wouldn't be right to leave Momma all alone.

"Hannah, has the devil got your tongue? I asked if you've cleaned your room."

I took her hand, led her down the hallway and pointed to my room.

"Oh my, what a lovely job you've done." She leaned down and gave me a kiss on the forehead, her glasses falling off her nose and hitting me on top of the head. "Why didn't you just say so?"

She hugged and kissed me and was very proud of the job I'd done.

"Such a good little girl deserves a special dinner. How about pancakes tonight?"

***

"Hannah, did you brush your teeth?"

"Yes, Momma."

"Good. Now come give me a kiss goodnight and let's say your prayers."

I crawled into her lap and leaned in to give her a peck on the lips. My nose would always bump against her reading glasses, the half-glasses that sat on the end of her nose with a chain holding them around her neck so she wouldn't lose them when they fell off.

"I'm too young for my eyesight to be getting so bad," she always said. "And if I don't have these around my neck, I can't ever remember where I put 'em."

Just as my lips were about to meet hers, she pulled back, disgusted.

"Hannah, did you brush your teeth? You're not kissing me goodnight with those nasty teeth and bad breath."

"I did already, Momma."

"Don't you lie to me, young lady. Now go brush those nasty little teeth before that lie sticks to them and they rot out of your head." She acted like she would throw her Sunday School lesson book at me, but she wouldn't.

I hopped off her lap and ran to the bathroom to brush my teeth again, and brushed the devil out of them this time.

I crawled back into her lap, curled my lips up to show her how white and shiny they were, and exhaled my minty fresh breath for her to smell.

Her blue eyes sparkled behind her glasses like the biggest jewels in a treasure chest. "Oh lovely, what lovely teeth you have. You have your father's teeth."

I didn't have my father's teeth. His were still in his mouth, his lips closed tight over them. I'd kissed him goodnight last year at the church. Momma said he was going to sleep and would wake up with Jesus and the angels.

I didn't even have all of my own teeth. The two top front ones were gone, along with one on the bottom, so brushing the few I had left didn't take long. But I scrubbed them three times a day to make sure they were shiny and clean when I kissed Momma goodnight.

"Okay, love, give me that kiss with your lovely teeth."

I kissed her goodnight, and my nose left a smudge on her glasses. She moved them to the top of her head, where they disappeared in the thick waves of black hair. I curled up on her lap for our bedtime prayers, to keep the devil away.

"Amen," Momma said.

Amen, I thought.

She didn't wake me up later that night, like she did some nights, to ask if I had remembered to brush my teeth.

Yes, Momma, I brushed them. I brushed them twice. I answered you before. I brushed them until I spit red streaks with the white foam. I keep my mouth so clean, no lie can ever grow.

CHAPTER 2

Momma kissed me goodbye on the front porch, and I waved to my snowman. Momma had helped me build him in three parts, taller than me. He still stood, a little shrunken, in the near-constant shade under the magnolia tree, next to the tire swing Daddy had made on my fourth birthday.

Snow still covered parts of the road in front of our house from last week's storm, even though today was warm enough to wear just a sweater on my three-block walk to school. Momma said small North Carolina towns like Spencer didn't waste money on snowplows that would seldom be used. We lived an hour from the beach, and saw more hurricanes than snowstorms.

I settled into my desk at school, in the back row next to the window. Elizabeth, three desks away, stared at me through her thick glasses that made her eyes look huge and frightened. The sun shone through the open blinds, and the reflection off her gold eyeglass frames cast two eerie curves of light across her forehead. Starting at the top of her nose, each light shined up and out like two glowing devil horns.

Outside, the sun glittered off the few remaining snow patches still sprinkled across the playground.

"Class, it's time for this week's spelling quiz. Did you all spend extra time studying your word list last night so someone else can win and we can have a new weekly champion?"

Mrs. Velasquez always gave out some trinket for the spelling quiz winner — maybe a pack of crayons, or a tiny stuffed animal, or a pencil with a clown for an eraser. *If you win the spelling quiz, why would you need an eraser?*

Every Friday, the same thing: in the morning, a spelling quiz; after recess, a champion named and honored, and given a prize to take home. Every Friday afternoon, on my way home, the prize would find its way into the dumpster at the 7-11 behind my house. Only then would the shame fade from my face.

"Elizabeth," Mrs. Velasquez singled out the horned, frightened demon for a challenge, "I know you studied your words extra hard this week. Your mother called and told me so. Maybe this is your week to take the championship away from Hannah."

Not even the pink ribbons in her pigtails made her look less evil. She kept staring at me, even when the teacher spoke to her, as if she might burst into tears, or scream and fly across the room to rip at my hair and peck at my eyes.

"Pencils ready, everyone."

Mrs. Velasquez paced back and forth in front of her big metal desk, then behind it. She leaned up against the whiteboard, getting red marker dust on the padded shoulder of her navy blue dress. She called out each word and made up a sentence with the word in it.

"Mess."

M-E-S-S, I wrote.

"Michael's desk is a 'mess.'"

All the kids laughed. I didn't. I'd been to Michael's house with Momma to invite his family to church. I didn't think Michael could help being so messy. It was all he knew. As we left his home, Momma had taken deep gasps of air, like she'd held her breath the whole time we were inside. I liked the smell of the pipe his father smoked. Besides, it helped to cover up the stink of the dirty dishes piled in the sink.

"How can people stand to live like pigs?" Momma had asked herself out loud as we climbed back into the car to go visit the next family on the list.

"Dress."

D-R-E-S-S.

Mrs. Velasquez walked up and down the aisles between our desks, peeking over our shoulders, working her way to the back of the room. She stopped at Michael's desk, woke him up and helped him find a pencil. Next she stopped at Madison's desk.

"Madison's 'dress' is very pretty," she said. A flower print, with lace around the collar, like I would wear to Sunday School if I had one that pretty.

"Dirt."

D-I-R-T.

Mrs. Velasquez's high heels clicked up the aisle behind me, and pinpricks tingled the back of my neck as she looked down at my paper. I pretended to keep writing, not wanting her to see I had already finished the word before she used it in a sentence.

"Hannah has 'dirt' under her fingernails and needs to wash better."

Everyone laughed. Everyone but Michael. His head lay on the desk, eyes closed again. Elizabeth's cackle rose above all the others, but I refused to look at her, glancing at my fingernails instead.

"Shirt."

There would be ten words in all. Always ten—never nine, never eleven. I had to miss some words, or I'd have to stand at the front of the class to receive my prize while all the other kids giggled, or stared at me with envy and anger. Elizabeth might shriek and flex her bony, scaly wings and sail across the room in a flash, too quick for me to even dive under the teacher's desk before her claws dug into my flesh.

If Mrs. V gave harder words, it would be easier to miss some. Momma had me copying pages from the Bible by the time I was four, and I could spell Jehoshaphat and cubit and swaddling and revelation. I couldn't even figure out how to get "mess" wrong. Use only one "s" maybe? That would just be silly.

Elizabeth usually missed one, so I had to miss at least two. But what if she missed two this week? Maybe I should miss three, just to be safe. No, two would be enough. Was it lying to miss words on purpose?

"Pencils down. Everyone turn your paper in at my desk on your way to the gym for recess."

The whole class groaned in unison. Not the gym again.

"But it's warm out," Madison protested.

"It's still too muddy to play outside. Michael, wake up."

Boys threw basketballs toward hoops much too high for first-graders. Girls jumped rope. Elizabeth sat by herself on the bleachers and read a book—a second-grade book—hoping everyone would notice.

I walked past the girls with the jump rope, not stopping to play this time, but headed straight to the restroom to wash under my fingernails.

The loud thump brought everything to a stop. Everyone turned toward the hollow echo, a dull thud like when Daddy once dropped a watermelon on the back porch. Miss Emily, the teacher's aide, screamed and ran to the girls with the jump rope, only to slip and fall on the blood pooling beside Madison's head and onto her lace collar.

Will Maddy's momma be angry that she stained that nice dress?

It wasn't the first time someone fell on the gym floor, but it was the first time for blood. I always wore my sneakers, but girls like Maddy who wore their nicest shoes to school had to take them off to play on the gym floor in their sock feet. Sock feet and slick, varnished wood aren't good for jumping rope.

As a bloodstained Miss Emily led a bleeding, crying Maddy to the nurse's office, the other girls moved the jump rope a few feet to the left and started up again. I forgot about my fingernails, and walked over to the blood on the floor. I knelt down to look at the small puddle. My hand could cover most of it, except for the long skid mark from Miss Emily's slide. Shiny and dark, it was an odd color red, and it smelled like sweat, only stronger—pork chops, maybe.

"Hannah Cross! Come here."

Mrs. Velasquez's voice sliced through the chatter and laughter. Was I in trouble for looking at the blood? I hadn't touched it. I stood up to find half a dozen boys gathered around looking at it, too.

"Cool."

"I dare you to touch it."

"I dare you to taste it."

Michael dipped a finger in it as I turned and headed to the door where Mrs. V stood. Why wasn't she calling the boys, too? I only looked at it; they were touching it. Maybe more.

The teacher rested her hand on my shoulder and led me back to the classroom. She sat me in the chair next to her desk and pulled out my spelling quiz.

"Hannah, you want to tell me about this?"

"About what, ma'am?"

"Don't 'what ma'am' me. We've been taking these spelling quizzes every week for three months, and you've never missed a word. Today, you missed three."

"Three? I only missed two, Miz Velasquez, I promise."

Her eyes seemed darker and larger than usual, even though she squinted at me. Giant, thick eyebrows rose up to different heights. Caterpillars. Her eyebrows looked like caterpillars. I knew how to spell 'caterpillar,' too.

"And how do you know you missed two? Did you misspell words on purpose, Hannah? Tell me the truth."

"Yes ma'am."

"Why would you do that?"

"I wanted someone else to be champion. It's not fair for me to be champion all the time, and I don't like being champion."

"Being champion is good, Hannah. It means you're the best. You're the smartest, the best speller. Why wouldn't you want that?"

"Because I have to stand up front and everyone looks at me. And they laugh."

"They only laugh because they're jealous."

"I don't want them jealous at me."

"Well, if you're going to make something of your life, and be somebody, you have to be the best. Always *be* the best. Always *do* your best."

She set my test down in front of me as she read upside down.

"You know how to spell 'suit.' Why did you spell it this way?"

I looked at the paper. S-O-O-T.

"It sounds the same almost. And other words were mess and dirt."

"But you knew it was wrong. I said, 'The man wore a suit to work.' Do you know what 'soot' is?"

"Yes, ma'am, we have it in our fireplace at home." We never used the fireplace anymore. Making the fire and cleaning out the ashes had been Daddy's job. It sat there, cold and dark, full of charred remains from the last time it held the warm comfort, since the last spark had gone out.

"Then you know a man wouldn't wear soot to work. You got that wrong on purpose?"

"Yes ma'am." I pictured a man wearing soot to work and thought it made sense if he cleaned chimneys for a job.

"And 'pants?'"

P-A-N-C-E.

"Yes, ma'am, I know how to spell 'pants.'"

"I want you to stay after school today and take the test over. And I'm going to send a note home to your mother. She has to sign it, and you bring it back tomorrow."

"Yes, ma'am, but that was only two. What other word did I miss? I know all of them."

"I'll discuss that with your mother."

I glanced back down at the paper in front of me and spotted it instantly. I knew how to spell that word. How did I get that wrong? Was I in a hurry, or daydreaming, or nervous because Mrs. V was standing next to my desk or all the kids were laughing at my fingernails or Elizabeth was screeching and flying around the room waiting for the opportunity to rip the meat from my bones?

I stared at the paper.

"Shirt. Tommy is wearing a blue 'shirt.' Shirt."

S-H-I-T.

After looking at the word printed on the page in my own careful handwriting, an oily slickness coated my tongue again. My throat burned again. The fumes of dish soap ached deep inside my nose again.

***

Daddy sat in the living room—in his big green recliner with the scratchy fabric and the arm covers that always fell off—watching television and laughing at something funny. Whatever it was, it must have been hilarious, so I ran to the kitchen laughing, not knowing why it was funny other than it made Daddy laugh until tears came down his face.

"Momma, Momma, Momma." I tugged hard on her apron, jumping up and down to get her to see me. She stood at the sink full of suds with her bright yellow rubber gloves, the ones I liked to wear because they came up past my elbows and turned me into Cinderella.

"I'm busy, child. Stop pulling at me, or you'll make me drop this glass."

"But Momma, it was so funny."

"What was, baby?"

"That man on TV. He said, 'You can just go to hell.' Ain't that funny, Momma?"

***

The flavor of the soap had lingered for hours, days maybe. Now it returned in a flash, just looking at S-H-I-T on my quiz. And the teacher had written it all down in a letter—how I cheated to lose, how I wrote a dirty word on my paper, how I looked at Maddy's blood, how I imagined Elizabeth as a demon in pigtails. Momma would read it, wash my mouth out and send me to bed without supper.

"Mrs. Velasquez," Miss Emily shouted as she threw open the door to the classroom. Blood still streaked across her milky white thigh and onto her gray gym shorts. "I think Maddy's hurt worse than I thought. The nurse can't get the bleeding to stop and Maddy fainted."

The sirens from the ambulance and fire truck pulling into the school parking lot grew louder.

"Hannah, go back to the gym with the others. We'll finish this later." Mrs. V ran down the hallway with Miss Emily to meet the ambulance men at the main entrance and lead them to the nurse's office.

I stood in the doorway of the classroom and watched the men in blue coveralls walk the stretcher down the hall. Why didn't they hurry? They took their time and talked on their radios while Miss Emily and Mrs. Velasquez ran ahead, motioning for them to keep up, come this way, hurry.

They didn't hurry. Perhaps if they had hurried, it would have helped. Perhaps it wouldn't have mattered.

Perhaps Maddy was already dead.

CHAPTER 3

Mrs. Velasquez forgot all about the spelling test and the letter to my mother. We didn't even have school for two days.

Maddy's funeral was on Tuesday, and almost all the kids and their parents went. I'd been to funerals before so I knew what to do, what to expect. I don't think many of the other kids had ever been to one. Most were too scared to go down front and see Maddy in her coffin. Elizabeth sat stiff in the pew beside her mother, looking more frightened and terrible than ever.

Walking down front to say goodbye to Maddy didn't scare me. She was sleeping with Jesus and the angels. I'm sure she wished she could have worn her flower print dress with the lace collar, but the blood probably wouldn't wash out. Besides, she had another pretty dress to wear for her funeral, a blue one with little white and pink flowers.

I stood there holding Momma's hand, looking at Maddy's closed eyes, her mouth drawn tight around her teeth. I wondered if she'd gotten all ten of her spelling words right, if she would have been the champion and gotten the prize last Friday.

On Wednesday, we went back to school and counselors met with all us kids.

Our pastor, Brother Ronnie, was there. He came over and hugged me. "How are you doing, Hannah?"

"I'm fine, sir. How are you doing?"

"I mean, how are you feeling about losing your friend Madison? Is anything bothering you? Have you been crying a lot, or having bad dreams, or anything?"

"No, I'm fine. Thank you for asking."

Brother Ronnie held my hand in one of his and patted it with the other. He had bushy knuckles, but his fingernails were very clean. So were mine.

"You know she is in heaven with Jesus now, where there's no more pain."

"Yes, I know. My daddy's there, too."

"Yes, he is, Hannah. Your father was a very good man, an extraordinary man."

He looked out the window where all of last week's patches of snow had disappeared except under the trees, but it was still too muddy to go outside for recess.

"Brother Ronnie, I do have a question."

He turned from the window and looked me in the eyes. "Go ahead."

"If we had played outside, Maddy would have gotten mud in her hair when she fell, but it would have been soft and she wouldn't have gotten hurt. But we played inside, so when she fell she busted her head because the floor is so hard."

I stopped to look out the window where Brother Ronnie had been looking, and pictured Maddy, her dress and hair caked in mud, crying, running inside to clean up. I could see her shiny black shoes with the gold buckles covered with muck and grass, tracking through the hallway as she raced to the girls' room. I could see her slip on the linoleum floor, falling and cracking her skull.

"What's your question, Hannah?"

"Never mind. I guess when Jesus wants you, there's not much can be done about it."

"That's a very wise thing for a little girl to say."

Wise. W-I-S-E.

"Hannah, can you come up here, please?" Mrs. Velasquez called me away from my counseling session with Brother Ronnie, and he gave me another quick hug before I turned to leave. "Hannah, Mr. Terry wants to see you in his office."

The principal's office. Perhaps he wanted to talk some S-H-I-T with me. I didn't say anything to Mrs. V before heading out the door and down the hallway, over the long, slick linoleum floor past the girls' room where, as I'd imagined minutes earlier, Maddy died a second time. At the glass door, the secretary waved me on through to the waiting Mr. Terry.

"Have a seat, Hannah." He pointed to the adult size chair in front of his, with armrests too high and far apart for my arms to use. My feet didn't reach the floor. I felt tiny in front of the huge steel desk with Mr. Terry peering over the top of his glasses at me just like Momma does.

"Hannah, what can you tell me about what happened when Maddy fell down?"

I remembered my reflection in the pool of blood. I didn't know if I should tell him about the boys touching it, daring each other to taste it.

"I was in the gym for recess and I heard this loud boom. When I turned around, Maddy was on the floor and then Miss Emily fell down, too."

"That's all you saw?"

"Yes sir."

"Where were you when Maddy fell down?"

I thought about it for a bit, trying to remember. I had walked past Elizabeth and her book, past the boys trying to throw the basketball as high as the net, past the girls jumping rope. I started toward the girls' room to wash the dirt from under my fingernails.

"I was in the gym."

"Where in the gym, Hannah?"

I didn't recall exactly.

"One student tells me you pushed Maddy. Hannah, did you push Maddy?"

"Who said that?"

"It's not important who said it. I'm just trying to find out what happened."

"I didn't push her. She just fell down because she was jumping rope in her sock feet and she slipped."

"I thought you said you didn't see her fall."

"I didn't. I heard the noise and then I saw her on the floor."

"Then how do you know she was jumping rope and slipped if you didn't see it?"

"I don't know. I saw her jumping rope. Then later I heard her fall down. She was in her sock feet."

He took his glasses off and twirled them in one hand. "Hannah, it is very important for you to tell the truth. There's a policeman outside who wants to talk to you about this. We're trying to reach your mother to come down, because she has to be here for the police to talk to you. But if you will just tell me the truth now, it will be much easier for you, for everyone."

I had told him the truth. Twice. Why would he ask me again?

"You can talk to me, or you can talk to the policeman. I'll give you one more chance to tell the truth."

He stared at me so hard I had to look away, down at his desk. A piece of paper lay there, upside down. I couldn't read it all, but my name was on it, with Elizabeth's name printed in the top right corner, where Mrs. V always had us write our names.

The demon in pigtails had said I pushed Maddy down on purpose.

I raised my eyes to meet his. Blue eyes. Bright blue. Pretty blue eyes, but they were also red, like mine after I go swimming at the city pool. I started to speak, to ask why she would make up a story like this, why she hated me so. Was it because I always won the spelling championship? But I didn't say anything.

I'd told him the truth. Saying it again wouldn't make it any truer. If he didn't believe me the first time, or the second time, why would he suddenly believe me if I said it a third time?

We sat there staring in each other's eyes like a blinking contest. The second hand on the clock was as loud as someone knocking on the door.

He broke away first and straightened up some papers on his desk. "Fine. If you won't talk to me, you can talk to the police. As soon as your mother gets here."

I sat in a chair by the secretary and waited for Momma.

WE HOPE YOU ENJOYED THE PREVIEW

FOR MORE ON THIS GREAT BOOK, PLEASE VISIT
www.EvolvedPub.com/HV

A SPECIAL SNEAK PREVIEW

CARRY ME AWAY

PROLOGUE
Life Begins, Again

Washington, D.C., May 2004

Finally, they painted these walls a different color. Pale green wouldn't have been my first choice, but it beat hell out of the stark white from before, and it didn't hurt so much to open my eyes this time. My throat burned. Talking was out of the question, but I could swallow, so the doctor must have taken the tube out. That was a good sign.

Tubes filled with different color liquids ran from my arm to bags hanging overhead, like a roadmap, each highway leading to another city. Another led south, but I didn't look at that one. A quick memory check of the past ten years as the cobwebs cleared: were they all there, or did they slip away again?

Mika sat on the pillow beside my head. Nearly twenty-three years old and I still slept with my doll.

Life always begins as a crisis. Everything that came before diminishes in importance, fades from memory. For me, life began at the age of twelve. My life had been pretty full in the decade since, so if Death came for me this time, I could live with that.

Most of my first dozen years had faded away like a dream. They didn't feel like memories, more like looking at an ancient, dusty photo album. Was it the accident that left me with only a handful of snapshots? Or does everyone's childhood turn into a shoebox of black and white Polaroids just out of reach on top of a cluttered closet shelf?

The pictures remained clear in my mind, but that little girl could have been me or someone else—just flat, grainy pictures of people who looked vaguely familiar in foreign, exotic places. Did I really remember that white poodle, or only the photograph of her on my lap, my hair in pigtails, skinned knees peeking out from the blue sundress and my bare feet not quite reaching the floor? We gave her away because we weren't allowed to bring pets to Turkey.

I couldn't even remember Turkey, and we'd lived there three years.

Only three distinct childhood memories remained—moments, images, even smells as vivid as if they'd happened today. Those smells could still breach the levee and trigger the deluge. Three memories pretty well summed up my entire childhood, my entire existence until the accident. Maybe that was why these particular dreams didn't fade with sunrise.

BOOK ONE

**HOME IS NEVER WHERE YOU LEFT IT
VIRGINIA 1990-1994**

CHAPTER 1
Before the Deluge

Roses, Pasta and a Banshee, Virginia, July 1990

"Carrie, don't worry about your brother," Daddy said. "He's not your problem. Get in the car."

My parents were going to another family's home for dinner, someone from Daddy's work. Sammy didn't have to go, so why did I? We'd just moved from Turkey, which still made me furious about leaving my friends and starting over. The taste of anger lingered on my tongue.

"Why does he get to stay home?"

Daddy didn't give me a choice. We left Turkey for the suburbs in Virginia, on the outskirts of Washington, D.C., with his latest military assignment. Now I had to go to dinner and be a polite little lady. At nine, they wouldn't allow me to stay home alone, of course.

"Because he's old enough to stay by himself and you're not."

Sammy was thirteen, old enough to teach me to cuss and smoke and old enough to stay home by himself.

"Why can't he watch me?"

"He's not old enough to handle you yet."

He probably never would be.

Daddy marched me to the car, where I pouted in the back seat. They outnumbered and outsized me. They could force me to go, but they couldn't force me to smile or speak.

Mom put on a fake smile and used her little Japanese girl voice—a mistake, since it irritated the shit out of me.

"They have little girl about your age," she said in her not-quite-right English. "You going to same school, so you make friend tonight. That way when school start, you not alone."

I wouldn't speak to this girl all night. They would see my strength, how wrong they'd been to make me move, and how stupid they were to bring me to this stupid dinner with this stupid kid.

I would eat just enough to be polite, but little enough so the hostess would know I didn't like it, despite my protests. *Oh no, ma'am, it's delicious. I must not have a very big appetite this evening.*

The father met us at the door, shaking hands with Daddy at first, which morphed into shoulder grabs and backslaps, and eventually into giant man-hugs. If this guy was such a good friend, why had I never met him before, or ever heard of him? He wasn't even military—no Marine bearing, his belly stuck out a little, he had a moustache, and his light red hair flopped over his forehead. A civilian. He seemed small next to Daddy. Probably one those "danged bureaucrats" Daddy always bitched about.

The aroma of tomatoes and herbs teased me as we entered the house and, against my will, my mouth watered. Pasta for dinner. Not playing fair. This could be tough, but maybe it would taste worse than it smelled.

Another scent hid just under the spaghetti sauce. Flowers. Roses perhaps.

Daddy introduced us all to the little man. Mr. Light then called out to his wife, who came clicking to the front door in her apron and heels, drying her hands on a dishtowel and apologizing for looking all a mess. She looked like something from one of those old black and white sitcoms on Nickelodeon. An apron and high heels in the kitchen, for fuck's sake.

"For fuck's sake" was Sammy's expression of the month.

Introductions were repeated all around for Mrs. Light's benefit. Why didn't we just wait until everyone was there and do it once? Adults could be pretty stupid sometimes.

Mrs. L turned and opened a door behind her, near the front door. It looked like a closet, but opened to a stairway heading down.

"CinDee, your guest is here. Come upstairs."

They keep this kid in the cellar? Not a good sign.

A banshee cry from down below pierced the air. Well, I didn't really know what a banshee was or what one sounded like when it cried, but it let out an ear-splitting squeal mixed with a blood-curdling scream, so maybe that was how they cried.

A great thunder rumbled up the stairs, like six or eight feet pounding up the dungeon stairs. Mom had said they only had one kid.

"Quick, shut the door before they escape," I wanted to scream. But I froze in silence, small and timid, about to be overwhelmed and devoured by a pack of squealing banshees.

What emerged from the basement frightened me more than wild beasts set loose to feed on my flesh. She didn't look my age—a head taller, with hair so blonde it nearly hurt to look at her. She seemed to have more than four arms and legs, like trying to count the blades on the ceiling fan in my bedroom.

She looked about eleven or twelve, all gangly and awkward. She even wore a bra under her t-shirt, with little bumps where breasts tried to sprout, something I'd never even contemplated. That would never be a major issue, thanks to the Japanese curse from Mom's side.

She stared at me. I stared at her. She said something, but her words didn't get past all the thoughts in my head. She turned to her mother, keeping her eyes cut in my direction, and asked, "Does she speak English?"

I answered—in Turkish.

Daddy tightened his grip on my shoulder.

The blonde banshee stopped fidgeting and stood still. Her eyes grew rounder, bluer somehow.

"Carrie's feeling a little shy tonight, CinDee, but I'm sure she'll loosen up quickly." Daddy's grip didn't loosen up.

"Hi Carrie, I'm CinDee," she said a little too slowly and a little too loud, still not clear on the English thing.

Duh, heard that already. Martha Stewart called your name. My daddy just said it.

"Hi, I'm Carrie." *Double-duh.* I wanted to crawl away and hide, repeating my own name as if she hadn't just said it herself.

She didn't notice and became her ceiling fan self again. "Wanna come down to the rumpus room with me?"

I stared but didn't answer. *What's a rumpus room?* Didn't clear up any questions about my English skills.

"Follow me. I've got games and my own TV and stereo." The longer her sentences, the higher pitch her voice became, until it turned into a squeal again. Her arms and legs spun out of control as she ran down the stairs, waving for me to follow.

"Dinner will be ready in twenty minutes," Mrs. L called out a bit too cheerfully.

Daddy eased his grip on my shoulder and gave a gentle nudge.

I was only two steps down, she was about halfway, when she stopped, crouched and swung her arms back and forth. Then she flew so gracefully, I skipped a breath. CinDee landed on the floor, clearing at least six stairs without missing a beat, not even a stumble. She looked like an Olympic gymnast nailing a perfect landing as she raised her hands in victory and hissed the sound effects of a cheering crowd.

She looked up at me and lectured, "Don't you try that. You're too little and you're not properly trained. You'll break your neck."

I walked down halfway, gingerly, as if the stairs might collapse under me, and looked at the floor below. She was right. Down a few more steps until it looked survivable, a quick glance to see she wasn't looking, and I jumped. My landing wasn't as graceful as hers, and half the distance.

She heard me land and turned to see me standing there. She didn't know how far I'd jumped, and I didn't tell her.

"Wow. Did you...? Are you...? How high up were...? Oh wow." She was so impressed, she couldn't finish a sentence. "Shhhh," she hushed herself. "We're not supposed to do that. My dad yells at me for stair-jumping."

Whew. At least she won't ask me to do it again.

Now we shared a secret. We'd violated a house rule together. We both could jump from halfway up the stairs, or at least she thought so. We bonded. Sisters.

Turned out she was only nine years old—just three months older than me, but much more advanced physically. Her athleticism, like her bosom, was just beginning to bloom.

By the end of the evening, we'd become inseparable. Best friends for life. We promised that night never to say goodbye, only "see you later."

I had three helpings of pasta.

***

Cologne, Silence and a Lesson, Virginia, June 1991

"Mom said it's okay for me to ride the bus home with you today." My first lie of the day.

I followed close behind CinDee as we stepped up so the driver wouldn't notice a guest passenger with no permission slip. He never looked up from his magazine.

"Mom will bake us brownies if you want," Cin promised, "and we can dance in the rumpus room again." She needed sugar like I needed a bra.

Soon after arriving in Virginia, we'd moved from our temporary apartment on the military base to a house three blocks from CinDee.

Daddy allowed me to walk to her house in the daylight. We went to school together, in the same fourth grade class, but because of how the routes were scheduled, we rode separate buses. I asked several times to ride home with CinDee after school, but Mom always said no. I had to come home, do my homework and chores, and eat dinner when Daddy came home from work. Then I could go play at Cin's some days. We had a lot of rules at our house, Daddy being a Marine and all.

But after a year, temptation overwhelmed me. I turned ten the week before, and in another week school would end for the summer. Daddy was out of town, as he often was, off killing bad people or blowing up some shit. Mom would be at one her volunteer groups, and Sammy probably wouldn't be home. He wouldn't care anyway. He never came home right after school. I could ride home with CinDee, have a snack, dance and talk for a while, and still make it home before anyone else. No one would know.

"I have to be home by five, so don't let me forget." Each lie slid off my tongue with less resistance.

Two brownies, one glass of milk, and six songs later, "Shit, it's after five. I've got to go."

I grabbed my backpack, ran out the door and down the street while rehearsing my story in case Mom got home before me. Good thing, too. There she stood, waiting for me at the door with her hands on her hips.

"Where you been?" It wasn't her little Japanese girl voice, but the stern Asian mother voice, a little worried, on the verge of anger, with a not too subtle dose of disappointment.

"At school. I stayed late to work on a project and missed the bus. You can't come get me, so I had to walk." Mom never learned to drive in America, or anywhere except Japan, for that matter, so she always carpooled or took the bus to work.

A pleasant, faint trace of spices or a nice candle scented the air, familiar, but it made me uneasy somehow.

"Is that right? Can I call your teacher to check?"

"Go ahead if you don't believe me." My hands were on my hips, too. "I'm sure she's already gone though."

"We already called." Daddy's stern Marine officer voice joined the discussion as he appeared in the kitchen doorway. "We also talked to Mrs. Light."

Cologne. It was his cologne, the one he always wore. The fragrance usually soothed me, warmed me, made me feel at home. This time, the unexpected scent burned my face.

A long silence followed. If they allowed me to ride home with CinDee once in awhile, we wouldn't be in this situation. *It's their own fault.*

"Do you have anything to say?"

I remained mute. What was he doing here anyway? If he hadn't been here, Mom and I would've had it out like always and it would've been over. He'd make a federal case of it.

"Fine. Stay silent. You lied to my wife."

My wife? Not "your mother"? He emphasized "my wife" like I'd crossed some sacred boundary and they'd removed me from the tribe. They'd change their secret handshake to exclude me.

"When you lie to my wife, you lose my trust. Go ahead and remain silent. I can't believe anything you say anyway. You will not speak in this house for three days. Then we'll see if you're ready to speak the truth."

Not speak for three days? *Fine.* I wouldn't speak for four days, maybe five. This wasn't punishment. It would be a relief, a pleasure, not to have to speak to these sorry excuses for parents.

Anger made day one easy.

"Hey sis, how was your day at school?" Sammy looked across the kitchen table at me between bites. He laughed, knowing I couldn't answer him, and a partially chewed green bean fell out of his mouth onto his lap.

"Doan talk with your mouth full. You choke."

"I told you she's not allowed to speak," Daddy reminded him. "Quit asking her questions."

Sammy didn't need reminding. He grinned and popped the AWOL bean back into his mouth.

After dinner, Sammy waved me upstairs to his room. "You can talk in here." He opened the window and lit an incense stick. "What did you do to piss Dad off so much?"

I flopped down in the black beanbag chair beside his futon.

He leaned on the windowsill and faced out, his back to me as he lit a cigarette and blew the smoke through the screen. He glanced over his shoulder at me and raised one eyebrow, waiting for an answer.

I wouldn't give him the satisfaction.

"Fine. Be that way, bitch."

I slid off the beanbag and leaned on the windowsill beside him. He took another long drag of smoke and handed the ciggie to me. I took a quick puff and gave it back.

"Here." He slid the pack over to me.

Last thing I needed was to get caught smoking on top of the shit I was already in.

"What's the matter? Don't be a pussy."

I grabbed one from the pack and lit it.

We sat in silence and finished our smokes. When he pulled half a joint out of his sock drawer, I went to the bathroom to wash the cigarette smell off my hands and face and brush my teeth, then holed up in my room the rest of the night.

Day two, my anger faded into determination. Sammy asked me a few more questions and got irritated when I ignored him.

Day three—silence became natural. Words no longer mattered. Sammy stopped asking me anything.

When I got home from school on day four, Daddy waited on the couch for me. He called me into the living room and pointed to the cushion beside him, and launched into one of those Daddy lectures about family, trust, respect, and honor.

I'd heard it all before. *Save it for your troops, assbite.*

His eyes grew moist. This giant of a man with silver temples and gunmetal eyes choked up.

"You must apologize to your mother." At least she was my mother again, not just his wife. "Never lie to her again. To regain my trust, first you must regain hers. The next words you speak must be to tell her you're sorry and ask for her forgiveness. And it must be the truth. If you don't mean it, then stay silent until you do."

I went to my room in silence. And shame.

That pretty much took away the effect of a self-imposing extra day of silence. Now it would look like I wasn't sorry for lying, for making Daddy cry. Mom never cried. She'd get quiet and cold, her jaw would clench, and cabinet doors would slam.

No one called me for dinner. I stayed in my room and cried myself to sleep—silent, bitter tears. Lt. Col. Sam Destin, U.S. Marine Corps, had cried because I lied to his wife.

The next morning, unable to contain the shame any longer, I buried myself in my mother's arms. Gasping, heaving sobs convulsed my body, but no intelligible words made it through.

That afternoon after school, Sammy waited for me in his room, blowing little blue clouds out the window that floated above the backyard before they disappeared. As I lit up and puffed out the window beside him, he elbowed me in the ribs. Hard.

"Stop it. That hurt."

"Too bad you're talking again, bitch. I kind of liked the peace and quiet."

We smoked a while longer. He stubbed out his butt on the window ledge and wrapped it in a wet tissue to flush down the toilet later, then he stared at me. Taller than Mom or me, catching up to Daddy quickly, he'd reached six feet before he got out of eighth grade. He parted his silky thin black hair in the middle and tucked it behind his ears. We shared the same eyes. His eyelids turned down at the corners, giving shape to his big round eyes. But Sammy's eyes had a blue tinge to the deep brown, his skin a shade lighter than mine. A light sprinkling of black freckles dotted his nose. He looked *Hapa* — half Japanese.

Most people thought I was fresh off the boat.

He stared at me with those eyes that perfectly blended Mom's and Daddy's until he irritated me out of silence.

"What are you looking at, dickface?"

"I hope you learned your lesson, young lady." His imitation of Daddy had gotten better since his voice quit cracking and settled into a lower register.

"Yeah, don't ride home with Cin anymore after school."

"You dipshit. You completely missed the whole fucking point." His impersonation of Daddy faded back to his own voice. "Do I have to explain everything to you?"

"And don't lie to Mom."

"God, why do I bother? You're so fucking dense. Your brain's smaller than your tits."

"What then? Explain it to me, shithead."

He lit another ciggie.

My head still floated just above my neck from the first one.

"Here's the deal. Three rules to live by. With Dad, most important, trust is everything. Second, when you must disobey, and sometimes you must, don't get caught." He stopped to drag and send a stream of smoke through the window screen.

"Yeah, I got that all that. What's the third rule?"

"When you do get caught" — he paused for another slow inhale and exhale — "and sometimes you will get caught, just admit you fucked up, because trust is everything."

***

Rain, Pot and a Band-Aid, Virginia, May 1994

Sammy barely gave Mom and Daddy time to round the corner before he headed out the door. "I'll be right back."

"You're supposed to take me to Cin's, anus-breath."

Every Friday, Cin and I spent the night together, one week at her house, the next at mine. I'd walk unless it was raining and Daddy drove me. At Cin's house, the gentle scent of fresh cut flowers always welcomed me. Never overpowering, but Mrs. Light always had a bouquet on the table or potpourri warming on the stove. And the food... always the food. She seemed to be cooking something all the time—cookies or pie or pot roast. Breakfast at my house was cereal and milk. At the Lights', it was chocolate chip pancakes or macadamia nut waffles or biscuits and gravy with hash brown casserole.

Sammy had turned sixteen and gotten his license, so he could take me unless he was grounded, which was most of the time. "I said I'd be right back."

"Where are you going?"

"That would be your fucking business because?"

"You don't have permission to drive around, remember?"

"I said I'd be right back. Fuck off." He flipped me the finger as he headed out the door. He knew I'd never tell. Not telling wasn't the same as lying.

In seventh grade, staying home alone for a few minutes wasn't a big deal, but rain threatened, so walking to Cin's was out of the question. I shoved my doll, Mika, into the backpack on top of my pajamas, toothbrush, and the Chili Peppers CD that Sammy hadn't found. Mika always slept with me. She hated to sleep under the covers, but she'd have to put up with staying in the backpack a few minutes to keep out of the rain.

Mom and Daddy had an "engagement," some banquet or something. They'd left first, with instructions to Sammy to take me to CinDee's, and then he could go straight to his friend's house for the night but he'd better not be driving around or he'd get grounded.

And don't forget to lock the door when we leave.

The rain picked up and thunder rolled in the distance. So I waited, fuming. He'd get a piece of my mind. What if he didn't come back? Maybe he ran away, leaving me home alone in this storm with no way to get to CinDee's.

CinDee's parents would come get me. Let him go away. It would be a relief.

It took an eternity for him to return, probably ten minutes or more. The engine rumbled out front and he banged on the horn every few seconds.

I grabbed my backpack and ran to the car. The rain pelted me with large, thumping drops. With each crack of thunder, the lightning searched the ground for a target.

"You didn't lock the door, Scarrie."

"It'll be fine. Just go."

"Go lock it, you twat."

I ran and locked the door and ran back, sensing a bolt racing toward the back of my head.

Sammy had locked the car door and sat inside laughing his ass off.

I wanted to hit him.

He flicked the lock up.

"Asshole." My wet clothes stuck to the vinyl seats. I slammed the door and locked it to keep the lightning out.

"Aw, you must be cold." He pretended sympathy and handed me a cigarette.

The full body shiver made it hard to hold still enough to light it.

Sammy leaned over and thumped one of my nipples, which stood straight out through my soaked t-shirt. "You need a Band-Aid for that mosquito bite."

Daddy had taught me how to kill him with my bare hands. I could do it.

Then the aroma hit me.

"Daddy'll kill you if he catches you smoking up again."

"Don't worry about it, shit-for-brains."

"I'm not worried, fucktard."

We rode off in silence. I shivered uncontrollably and my nipple hurt like hell.

CHAPTER 2
Demons in the Mist

Virginia, May 1994

"Where are you going, you nutsack?"

CinDee lived a whole minute away by car, but Sammy always took the opportunity to drive around the block to squeeze in an extra forty-seven seconds of unsupervised driving time.

"I'm taking you to Cin's, so shut the fuck up."

But he didn't go around the block. He went straight three blocks to the end of the street and turned right.

"Then why are you going this way? I was supposed to be at Cin's like half an hour ago."

We'd driven this way many times, over the hill where more trees lined the streets, where brick mailboxes guarded long blacktop driveways that led to houses bigger than ours. The road narrowed into a country lane in the middle of the city, barely wide enough for two cars to pass, bordered by deep ditches gargling with rain runoff. Ahead of us, the road squeezed together for a one-lane bridge over a tiny creek, followed by a long, sweeping curve to the right, before taking a sharp bend to the left and heading down the hill again. After that, we would turn right at the intersection, back toward Cin's.

Sammy didn't answer me except to wave his middle finger in my direction.

I grabbed the black eight-ball knob off the stick shift, held on only by sun-dried electrical tape. The chrome, curved stick jutted its threaded tip up beside his thigh.

"Put that back on, goddammit."

"I'll give it back when you get me to Cin's. When you gonna fix this piece of shit anyway?" I shoved my cigarette through the barely open window into the rain, rolled it up the rest of the way, and tossed the heavy eight-ball from one hand to another.

"If I cut myself on this, I'll wipe the blood in your hair and laugh when you faint." Sammy grabbed the stick by the shaft to change gears.

I turned my back to him as far as the seatbelt allowed. The rain cut tiny horizontal rivers across my window as we climbed the hill. A long expanse of green lawn led up to a big white house with pillars across the front porch. The house had a small, round corner room upstairs with a cone-shaped roof. I loved that house. I wanted that room.

As the road narrowed, the trees formed a canopy over the road, combining with the dark clouds and rain to bring nightfall in an instant. Sammy flicked on the headlights, clicked the wipers up a notch, and cranked the radio a little louder.

I refused to look at him. The raindrops shoved each other across my window. I shivered and discreetly massaged my still stinging nipple.

We slowed for the bridge. The raindrops raced on the other side of the glass. Heavy, dark trees and brick mailboxes lined the road. The drops mesmerized and the thumping wipers hypnotized. My eyelids wanted to shut.

The trees spun to my left until the bridge we'd just crossed swiveled in front of me. The raindrops on my window stopped racing past me and stood still, jiggled and danced in place. Everything seemed odd, out of place for a moment until the view shifted back to where it belonged. The trees grew so close to the road here, the brick pillars holding mailboxes beside them at the edge of the street. So close.

"What was that?"

"We just fuckin' hydroplaned. Cool, huh?" Sammy slowed and brought the car back under control, leaning forward over the steering wheel to see the edges of the road better.

The side view mirror flew off with a quick crunch. It bounced and flipped into the ditch, triangles of mirror flying like glitter confetti. Reflected shards of brick mailbox pillar and wet grass and black tree trunks floated into the ditch.

"You idiot. Daddy's going to kill you. You better go back and get the mirror."

"What mirror?" Sammy laughed. "I didn't see anything. Someone must've hit the car when it was parked."

I twisted sideways to face him, leaning against the door and propping one foot on the dashboard, tapping the windshield with the toe of my tennis shoe.

He glanced at me and grinned, then leaned farther into the steering wheel, peering carefully through the rain and shadows to see the road.

Like a hamster wheel, the road bent upwards ahead of me, up, up and back over the top of my head.

"Sammy?" My stomach flipped. Something slammed against my door like a sledgehammer, punching me in the back and the ribs. The air emptied from my lungs with a grunt. The glass exploded against the side of my face and into my hair, stinging like a swarm of bees. Two headlight beams searched for squirrels in the trees, then dropped again to light the tall grass and rocks in the ditch as we burst through the guardrail as easily as a runner breaking the winner's tape. A deafening crack of thunder rocked the roof of the car.

The car slammed to a stop, and the seatbelt locked me into place, but not before the dashboard slammed against my hip and side.

A moment passed, perhaps two seconds, perhaps two minutes. An eerie white-green glow floated around me. Screaming pierced the air as the echo of the thunder faded.

"Sammy, are you okay? Are you hurt? What's wrong?" He just sat there grinning, staring through the windshield. I turned the radio off and the scream ended with a click.

"You might have gotten away with just the mirror, but now you are fucked big time."

Sammy laughed until he coughed and rested his chin on the dash. His long, straight hair stood on end, straight up.

I started laughing, too. "You should see your hair."

The tips of his hair pressed against the roof. I tried to reach up to see if mine did the same, but the still-locked seatbelt tangled around my arm and tied me into place, sideways, leaned against the door, pinned between the seat and the glove box.

"I can't get out of this thing. Give me a hand, dickweed."

Sammy giggled and coughed but didn't say anything. He didn't take his eyes off the road even though we weren't on it anymore.

"You ass. You better get straight before the cops get here. They'll know you're high. Oh, you are so fucked. Daddy's going to ground you for the rest of your life."

Daddy had always told him to keep it between the ditches, but Sammy never listened.

When I tried to turn in the seat to undo my seatbelt, an ancient samurai warrior drove his sword through my back and twisted. Hot rain poured onto my face, choking and hiding my scream.

The glow from the dashboard lit up the white rubber sole of my tennis shoe. *How the fuck can I see the bottom of my foot?*

I fumbled for the button until the buckle clicked. My head crunched against the roof.

"Goddammit, Sammy, I can't get out. I have to get out."

With both hands, I pushed against the roof to take the weight off my head and neck, but only managed to shift to the side of my face. Bits of glass dug into my cheek.

The bottom of my shoe taunted me, peering up at me, or down at me. I clawed with one hand to find the door handle, but it wasn't where it should have been. Crawling out the window didn't work. The opening was too small to get my head through.

My weight shifted again and my body ripped in two. The samurai sword sliced through my back and my side, piercing me with an ice cold flame. I opened my mouth but couldn't draw in enough breath to scream it out again.

***

"Come on out here and help me, child. Don't be afraid of the bees." Mama Carissa, my grandmother, worked in her flower beds.

I stepped down from the porch and floated across the yard to where she sat in the grass at the edge of the flowers. When a honeybee buzzed by my ear, I ran as fast as my legs could carry me back to the house, but the porch moved farther away. The bee stung my cheek. Then another. Bees surrounded me, swarming around my head, stinging my face and my neck and the top of my head. When I swatted them away, they stung the palms of my hands. My legs sank into mud, each step harder to follow with another.

***

"Sammy," I whispered. "You've got to help me. Get the bees off me."

He was busy trying to see through the broken windshield into the dark, trying to get it into gear, trying to keep it between the ditches.

The white-green glow faded. Sammy leaned so far over the dash that the steering wheel disappeared into his chest.

I felt around for the gear knob, through bits of broken glass and the warm, sticky rain that poured across my face. When my fingers touched the slick eight-ball, it rolled against my forehead.

I tried to put it back into place, but couldn't see where to slide it onto the shifter.

Sammy's car door groaned and swung open.

"Where are you going? Come get me out of here."

His footsteps squished in the mud as he came around to my side of the car. He leaned over outside my window and reached a hand through, calmly picking the bees from my hair, brushing them from my cheek.

"I can't get out. I have to get out." My legs wouldn't move at all, wouldn't run from the bees. The sword twisted with every breath.

"Relax. We'll have you out in a minute." He reached both arms through and wrapped them around me. He didn't try to pull me out, just held on until I quit squirming.

"Here." I handed the gear knob to him. "Here, take it."

Sammy didn't reach for it. He let go of me and slid away from the window.

"Where are you going? Get back here." His footsteps moved away, splashing in the water running through the ditch. "Don't leave me, Sammy."

I reached for the gear shifter again, forcing my eyes open to see where to place the eight-ball.

Sammy still sat in the driver's seat, leaned against the dash, face pressed against the broken windshield, eyes open wide to see the road. His hair stood on end, his butt a good six inches off the seat. The stick shift twisted at an odd angle, and disappeared into an unspeakable place.

***

Mama Carissa fried bacon, or pork chops maybe, in the kitchen. Sizzling, popping. The smell of grease and meat. The steam. A red mist floated up from the stove.

***

A red mist floated up and surrounded Sammy until he disappeared behind it. The red flickered blue, then red again. A baby cried in the distance. The screaming started again, but the stereo controls were out of reach.

Demons hid in the mist. Demon hands reached through the red fog, grabbing for me, grabbing my hair, my face, my arm, holding me in place with cold, clammy hands, screaming at me, stabbing me in the back and the side with swords and spears, beating my leg and ribs with their medieval clubs. Ripping my body in half. The bottom of my foot stared at me, useless, unmoving.

Demons rose through the red mist and grabbed for me.

"Don't try to move," the demons warned. "We'll have you out in a minute."

CHAPTER 3
A Tumble Down the Stairs

Virginia, May 1994

"Carrie, are you awake?" Daddy's voice echoed from far away.

The white walls glared brighter than CinDee's hair. I couldn't stop shivering. My eyes refused to stay open. Too bright. Too sleepy. And the pain. Sharp, throbbing on the outside. Burning on the inside.

Sleep would make it hurt less, but the pain wouldn't let me slip away to finish my dream. Mama Carissa worked in her flower beds, honeybees flitting from bloom to bloom. Another woman sat on the ground next to her. In my dream, I knew this tall blonde with bright blue eyes and a smile from a toothpaste commercial. But her name faded with the dream.

"Carrie, can you hear me?" One of Daddy's big hands brushed the hair out of my face and my eyes opened to a squint.

He sat on the edge of the bed beside me, his voice far away. The more sight and hearing came into focus, the hotter the fire burned inside me. Something dug into my back, a shovel biting into my flesh, twisting and burrowing into me.

Next to Daddy, a gray-haired nurse slipped a needle into a tiny bottle of clear liquid.

I'd fainted during all my vaccinations or flu shots or blood tests as a kid. Every time we moved and nurses gave me 158 shots to protect against some unknown disease in a godforsaken third-world country, I'd faint 158 times.

But this time, bring it on. Give me two. She could stick them in my eyes if it would make the fire go out. It hurt too much to speak, to move, or even cry.

Daddy waved off the nurse. "Can I have a minute first?" he asked her.

I couldn't take this for another minute. Someone grabbed my guts and stretched them as far as they would go, then twisted them into a knot.

Mom sat in a chair by the wall, and Paul, a close friend of our family, stood next to her with his hand on her shoulder. Why was he here? He lived in Texas, not Virginia. He looked like shit. Pale. He hadn't shaved and looked like he'd slept in those clothes for a week.

Paul grew up down the road from Mama Carissa, in the same small east Texas town where Daddy was raised, although Daddy was fourteen when Paul was born, and crawling through Vietnamese jungles by the time Paul started school. They became friends years later.

Mom looked awful, too, and ten years older. How long had I been in the hospital? Daddy looked the same, except his eyes were red and glassy like he'd smoked pot.

Had I fallen down the stairs at CinDee's? I was up to five stairs, and CinDee could jump from eight. Maybe I'd finally broken my neck as promised.

Daddy would launch into his lecture. *We told you and told you and told you not to jump the stairs or you'd break your neck now look what you've gone and done.*

"Carrie, can you hear me?"

I tried to answer, but nothing came out. Nothing moved.

"Do you remember what happened?"

I managed to croak, "Stairs." Someone had rubbed a cheese grater over my throat.

He looked at the nurse kind of funny, but she just shrugged and tapped more air bubbles out of the syringe.

"Carrie, I need to talk to you before the nurse gives you some medicine to help you sleep."

I wanted to sleep. *Lecture me later, jarhead.*

"Carrie, you've been hurt."

You don't say?

"You're going to be okay, but you're going to be in the hospital for a while. We're all praying for you, and the doctor says you'll get better. I know you're in a lot of pain right now. Don't give up, okay?"

Give up? Give up what? What is he talking about?

"Carrie, Carrie." He spoke to me like I was three years old again. Slow and easy, clearly enunciating his words, repeating himself. Like he was unsure of my English skills.

"Nod or blink if you can hear me."

Nodding hurt too much, so I tried blinking. My eyes closed easily enough, but it took a concentrated effort to pry them open again. He got the message.

"You and Sammy were in a car accident on your way to CinDee's. You've been injured. You've had surgery, and you're going to need some more."

That prick got stoned, didn't he? Yeah, he smelled like pot and he locked me out of the car.

A bee stung the back of my hand and I slipped back to Mama Carissa's flower garden.

I'm going to choke the living shit out of that asshole.

WE HOPE YOU ENJOYED THE PREVIEW

FOR MORE ON THIS GREAT BOOK, PLEASE VISIT
www.EvolvedPub.com/CMA

MORE FROM EVOLVED PUBLISHING

We offer great books across multiple genres, featuring high-quality editing (which we believe is second-to-none) and fantastic covers.

As a hybrid small press, your support as loyal readers is so important to us, and we have strived, with tireless dedication and sheer determination, to deliver on the promise of our motto:
QUALITY IS PRIORITY #1!

Please check out all of our great books,
which you can find at this link:
www.EvolvedPub.com/Catalog

Thank you!